P9-AZX-261

The Fairest Kind of Love

Crystal Cestari

HYPERION

LOS ANGELES   NEW YORK

Text copyright © 2019 by Crystal Cestari

All rights reserved. Published by Hyperion, an imprint of Disney Book Group.
No part of this book may be reproduced or transmitted in any form or by any means,
electronic or mechanical, including photocopying, recording, or by any information
storage and retrieval system, without written permission from the publisher.
For information address Hyperion, 125 West End Avenue, New York, New York 10023.

First Edition, March 2019
10 9 8 7 6 5 4 3 2 1
FAC-020093-19018
Printed in the United States of America

This book is set in 11.5-point Bembo/Monotype
Designed by Jamie Alloy

Library of Congress Cataloging-in-Publication Data

Names: Cestari, Crystal, author.
Title: The fairest kind of love / by Crystal Cestari.
Description: First edition. • Los Angeles ; New York : Hyperion, 2019. •
    Summary: Before setting out for college, magical matchmaker Amber hopes to
    learn if Charlie is her true match, but consulting a fellow member of the
    magical community stirs up trouble.
Identifiers: LCCN 2018041823 • ISBN 9781368038843 (hardcover)
Subjects: • CYAC: Magic—Fiction. • Love—Fiction. • Best friends—Fiction. •
    Friendship—Fiction. • Fairies—Fiction. • Chicago (Ill.)—Fiction.
Classification: LCC PZ7.1.C465 Fai 2019 • DDC [Fic]—dc23
LC record available at https://lccn.loc.gov/2018041823

Reinforced binding

Visit www.hyperionteens.com

SUSTAINABLE FORESTRY INITIATIVE Certified Sourcing
www.sfiprogram.org
SFI-00993

THIS LABEL APPLIES TO TEXT STOCK

R0454522862

To Todd
for showing me love in the afterlife

One

LOVE IS KIND OF THE WORST.

No, for real, hear me out for a second. Think of all the insane consequences that get kicked up due to matters of the heart: people fight for love, literally battle over it, and, even worse, write horribly sappy songs that live on for eternity on adult contemporary radio stations. It's a killer, honestly—a menace to society. We long for it, dream of it, even though our logical minds know the chances of everything ending up happily ever after are slim to none. And yet, any tiny glimmer of romantic possibility gets our weak hearts working overtime, forcing us to put it all on the line time and time again. Do we ever learn?

Of course not. We're all a bunch of dummies, myself included. Which is exactly why I'm pacing back and forth in a place I never thought I'd step foot inside: a black magic shop. Or, as it's officially referred to on its website, an "Alternative Alchemy and Enchantment Establishment." I nervously gnaw at my nails, chomping them short so I don't accidentally scratch out my eyeballs upon seeing the horrors around me. Sometimes you have to go to greater lengths to get what you need. Trust me when I say that coming here is a last resort.

"Amber, I swear to the Gods, you're going to give us both a panic attack if you don't just sit. Down." My best friend—the light of my life—Amani Sharma, gives me the kind of disapproving look I thought was only reserved for Wiccan mothers. Long, dark lashes blink in objection while she nervously tugs at the edge of her blush-pink skirt. She doesn't want to be here—*I* barely want to be here—but because she's ride-or-die, she's tagged along anyway. She sits on a backless, low-to-the-ground stool, upholstered with a fabric that seems more about style than function. Just like me, she's doing her best not to gawk at our surroundings, because they're almost too ridiculous to be true.

Windy City Magic is not the only shop in the city that caters to magical clientele; we're just the most visible—and reputable. There are other underground shops and merchants that wheel and deal in products and services Mom would never allow in our store. Things that don't take skill or talent to make dangerous. Things that put power in the wrong hands.

You'd expect a place like this to be dark and seedy, but this exposed-brick loft is bright and cozy, sunlight streaming in on all the darkness below. It's almost like stepping into an indoor farmers' market where everything is organic, gluten-free, and, oh yeah, illegal. The entire space defies dark magic stereotypes, bringing its blacklisted inventory aboveground and housing it in a clean, contemporary showroom that could easily inspire a "farmhouse Goth" Pinterest board. Row after row of glass cases perched atop repurposed shipping crates present true horrors like they're cool flea-market finds, showing off disjointedly scary items like a barely beating heart, seeds for a poisonous carnivorous flytrap, and something called "Black Night," which coats the glass in a color and texture that is straight out of my nightmares. The juxtaposition of "scary" and "trendy" is so off-putting, I can barely function.

"I'm sorry! I can't help it," I whisper-screech, nearly spitting out a pinkie nail. "On top of hating this place with every fiber of my being, I am both completely terrified and unbelievably psyched that maybe I'll get some answers today."

Amani pinches her lips, sealing up whatever discouraging thing lives inside her brain, which is kind, considering what I've put her through these past couple months. Ever since I looked into my boyfriend Charlie Blitzman's eyes and saw only static, I have been dragging my supernatural bestie all over Chicago trying to understand why. We've read every single one of my mom's grimoires, crashed countless coven meetings of Dawning Day, and went to an event called WizardCon, which turned out to be a total bust (false advertising, if you ask me). I've done meditation and yoga, swallowed a lifetime supply of healing herbs, and laid crystals over my entire body to no avail. Amani has been there every step of the way, and done her precog best to try to see my future, but since she can't force her visions, nothing has materialized, and probably won't at this point, since we pissed off the Fates pretty badly one desperate afternoon when we conjured them up in her bedroom. I bet they worked overtime to tie up any and all loopholes now, just to keep me guessing. I really hate those guys.

Why have I been so insane about this? Well, if Charlie's bad reception was an isolated event, maybe I could let it go (but let's be honest, probably not). Since winter, my matchmaking sessions have been on a slow, strange decline. I started seeing really messed-up stuff: not the matches themselves, but the way they were presented. Sometimes I'll look into a client's eyes and see two alternate realities playing out side by side; other times my visions flicker, randomly showing me flashes of two, or even three, potential happily-ever-afters.

As you can imagine, this is extremely upsetting. At first, I thought the Fates were just messing with me by manipulating Charlie's match; you'd think they'd be busy, oh, I don't know, watching over the trials and tribulations of the entire world instead. But as the futures of total strangers began taking equally confusing turns, I realized the problem was not with Charlie but me. I wasn't seeing clearly anymore, and it was making me crazy. During my regular matchmaking shifts at Windy City Magic, I probably looked like a robot short-circuiting, desperately trying to hold on to my programming while my motherboard slowly burned to a crisp. I scared Bob on more than one occasion as I cursed over my fragmented visions. It got so bad, I begged my mom to let me temporarily close down my matchmaking table until I figured out what's going on. Matters of the heart are sensitive enough as it is. I can't, in good conscience, give out bad information. But I've been searching for months, and now, at the threshold of summer, I've yet to see a clear match.

Am I broken? What is happening to me? For over a decade, every minute of every day has been a constant reminder that love is real, happy endings flooding my view in perfect clarity. Why would I go from firing on all cylinders to sputtering to a halt? What changed? What did I do? Did I pull an Ivy Chamberlain and somehow use up all my magic before I'm even legal? Match-making has always been such an inconsequential talent in the magical community, I didn't think anyone would bother to keep tabs on me, which is probably why no one can find me answers either.

Two months ago, I found out about this shop—Roscoe's Runes—through one of our regular gemstone suppliers. He gave me a very "wink wink, nudge nudge" suggestion that I could possibly find answers in the über-trendy West Loop neighborhood, a place where old warehouses have been converted into glam yoga studios and wine bars—places for those who are too cool for school to take selfies that tout their VIP status. It's a part of the city I rarely venture to, mostly because I could care less about being cool and don't have time to keep up with the hipster trend of the moment. To help achieve the level of exclusivity that's so painfully desired in this area, Roscoe and his runes are available through appointment only, and the earliest consultation I could schedule was today. Graduation day. Inconvenient? Yes, but perhaps also serendipitous, as maybe I'll be able to leave both high school and my magical drama in the past in one glorious swoop.

"If he doesn't come out soon, we'll have to bail to make it to the ceremony on time," Amani says, kicking the duffel bag that holds our caps and gowns, which sits on the floor near her feet. "I suffered through four long years at that school, and I'm not going to miss the chance to tell all the people I hate good-bye forever."

"I know, I know." I nod my head, still pacing. I want to give one final side-eye to all my enemies, but I also can't wait another two months for a new appointment with Roscoe. I would like to alleviate this inner turmoil so I can enjoy my summer in peace. The acoustic covers of '90s hip-hop playing on a loop are bringing more irk than Zen, and I'm curious as to what could possibly be preventing a warlock from keeping appointments on time. It's not like he's performing brain surgery. I've now memorized the annoyingly cool sans serif font that spells out OFFICE and PRIVATE

COLLECTION on the two doors before us. "Hey, what do you think is in the private collection?" I ask Amani, who can't stop checking the time on her cell.

She looks up. "Well, for a place that keeps exotic snakes out in the open, it has to be something truly weird." She taps her nails and rose-gold flats in the same anxious rhythm. *C'mon, dude, come out here before my best friend snaps.*

Finally, the office door opens, and a woman with ferociously amber, practically orange, eyes calls my name. I try not to flinch at her catlike aesthetic, bored yet commanding in her effortlessly casual "I woke up like this" topknot and relaxed button-down, a calico-colored tail wagging behind her. She hardly takes notice of us, but I feel like she could instantly destroy us with a flick of her razor-sharp claws. She must be a shape-shifter who holds on to shadows of her feline identity even while in human form.

"Can I offer you some kombucha? LaCroix?" she purrs with disinterest, guiding us into a small, windowless room illuminated by candlelight. Her bare feet quietly tiptoe through the space, and I feel she could easily hop onto the armoire in the corner, curl up, and take a nap. I shake my head, blinking rapidly to adjust to the near darkness. There are no chairs, but piles and piles of oriental rugs and floor pillows, and some seriously stinky incense burning. "Roscoe will be with you shortly, then."

Once Catwoman leaves, Amani shoots a death look at the door. "What is with this place and uncomfortable seating?" she huffs. "I cannot sit on the floor in this skirt." She's decked out in her graduation dress, a short, summery shift that shows off her long legs. I'm also wearing a skirt, though against my will, because apparently wearing semiformal attire is required at graduation, even though we'll all be covered in gowns, so whoever came up with this rule is truly evil. Amani's outfit is happy and bright, while I think I last wore this black skirt to a funeral.

"I don't know, dude. Just do that weird cheerleader sit pose. Here, I'll do it too." I sit down, awkwardly tucking my heels behind me. "Go, team!" She gives a small laugh, placing a massive pillow over her lap as she plops down beside me.

"I hope this works out," she says, candlelight dancing on her face.

"Gods, me too." Just then, the man of the moment enters. Roscoe, wearing a large-brimmed fedora, V-neck tee under a satin vest, and jeans with strategically placed holes and rips that make them look like he's worn them for years but in reality they're probably brand-new. Patchy facial hair creeps up his jawline, like he was trying to grow a beard but failed, and mystically bent tattoos cover his fingers and forearms. He's simultaneously exactly yet nothing like what I'd expect for a warlock in this part of the city.

"Welcome, ladies. I'm Roscoe," he says, pressing his hands together in prayer position and giving a small bow. "I apologize for the wait. I had a shipment of dragon eggs come in just as you arrived, and they require extra care during delivery."

I do a wildly erratic double take typically reserved for

cartoon characters. "I'm sorry, did you say *dragon* eggs?"

Roscoe smiles devilishly, revealing a gold tooth on the right side of his mouth. "Yes. Two of them, to be exact. They are extremely rare, as I'm sure you can imagine. To find a pair was quite a stroke of luck."

For a second, I forget all about my matchmaking woes, thinking about how cute Charlie's face will look when I tell him this news. "But, I mean, dragons are real? Like, for real?" Not my most eloquent thoughts, but . . . dragons!

"They are nearly extinct and have become nocturnal creatures out of survival, only hunting and flying at night."

"And they breathe fire and all that?" I can't hide my excitement. Gods, Charlie is going to lose his damn mind!

Roscoe, confused by my wonder, says, "Yes, but I'm sure your mother has told you all this? Though she has been out of the exotic trade for quite some time."

"Wait, you know my mom?" I guess I shouldn't be surprised. Mom knows all the black market merchants, though I'm not particularly interested in the reasons why. I'll file this acquaintance under "mistakes of Mom's youth" and try to never think about their association again.

"We used to collaborate, yes," he confirms with a grin I want to immediately wipe from my memory. Amani gives an equally disgusted reaction to his reminiscing, frowning at his delight. "Though I'm guessing you must be in quite a spot to come to me instead of her for help."

I was already nervous enough being here—at the end of my magical rope—but now that I know this aging hipster has Sand-family history, my insides are coated with an extra layer of grime. Mom has done her best to help me too, but every potion and spell she's tried has come up short. It's too late now; I told myself I'd stop at nothing to get the answers I need. "Yeah, well, I'm a matchmaker, and my magic seems to be on the fritz."

He leans forward, tatted fingers touching his lips. "Interesting. How so?"

"When I look into people's eyes, sometimes their matches are clear, but sometimes they're . . . off. I don't understand why, and I want to know what's wrong with me." Amani reaches over, squeezing my hand for support.

"Can you see my match?" he asks curiously.

I lock eyes with the warlock, and while the vision I receive is clear and unpixelated, the images are upside down, making it hard to discern the features of his future lady love. They sit together eating spaghetti, completely normal save for the fact their feet and the table are all topsy-turvy. So unless Roscoe and his love are able to walk on ceilings, this is another example of my malfunction.

"Not exactly," I groan.

"Hmm." As he considers this, Roscoe swirls his two pointer fingers around each other, creating a cyclone of pale blue waves and sparkles around his hands. I can't figure out what the symbols on his hands mean, and I wonder if he's doing this little performance to razzle-dazzle us, but honestly I've seen way too much crazy stuff to be awed by something as basic as this. I'll only be impressed if he can actually help me. "Well, Amber, truth be told, in all my travels I've never met a matchmaker before. And I don't mean to offend, but I'm sure you understand that your particular kind of magic is rather . . . trivial. While most wouldn't bother to work with you, I like a challenge. I'm going to need to do some additional research, but I would like to take on your predicament."

This is the complete opposite of what I wanted to hear. I've already been dealing with this for months, and I was hoping he'd have a quick solution. The idea of sitting on my hands while he does his *research* feels like pure torture. Deflated, I ask, "So, you can't help me today?"

"Unfortunately no, but I see great potential here, especially considering that Lucille is your mother."

Uh-oh. "What does that—"

"I take payment in many different ways, Miss Sand," Roscoe continues. "Money is nice, though it's quite common, don't you think? I'm more interested in uncovering the one-of-a-kind jewels of our community."

I don't like where this is going, especially since there's no way I can compete with dragon eggs. What does he want, for me to pull a unicorn out of my butt? (I mean, that would be pretty epic.)

He makes his way over to the armoire, shuffling what sounds

like paper. "For me to help you, I'll need you, or perhaps your mother, to return the favor with a supernatural item or service." He pulls out a legit scroll, unfurling the parchment to reveal lines and lines of magical legalese in the most magnificently curly calligraphy I've ever seen. I can barely read it, let alone understand what it says, yet he hands me a quill, waiting for me to sign on the bottom line.

"But, um . . . I don't have anything to offer." My voice quivers, hope slipping away. "What happens if I can't come through on my end?"

Darkness collects on Roscoe's face. "I wouldn't recommend that route, but let's just say there are always those who need human bones for their witchcraft." Oh good, glad I asked.

"Amber," Amani whispers in a warning tone, big brown eyes wide in alarm. "You don't have to do this."

"Don't I?" I've exhausted every option, explored every avenue. I can't go off to college and start the next stage of my life when this part is broken. What else can I do? It's not like I didn't know this place would be shady: any guy who sells pulsating animal organs in an Instagrammable display case is total bad news.

"If you're somehow unconvinced of my magical prowess," Roscoe adds, sensing my hesitation, "let me give you a taste of what I can do." He leaves the office, returning with a small, fuzzy caterpillar in his palm. He presents the brownish-green bug, hovering his other hand above like a claw. After a few seconds, the caterpillar begins squirming, quickly twisting itself into a color-changing cocoon. It's happening so fast, like watching a time-lapse video in real life, and seconds later, a gypsy moth breaks free, flapping its white-and-brown-speckled wings wide. A complete metamorphosis in a minute flat.

"Holy—!" I shout, but it doesn't stop there. After enjoying a few moments of flight, the moth returns to Roscoe's palm, curling its wings around its body and somehow returning to a cocoon(?!?!), then breaking free as the original caterpillar. It's one of the most incredible and messed-up things I've ever seen, and these eyes have encountered a lot.

"With the right spell or talisman, I can unlock the magic of any creature," Roscoe sneers, setting the little bugger free to crawl around the floor. "I'm sure I can pull the matchmaking magic out of you too, Miss Sand."

My heart is pummeling my stomach like a mortar and pestle, grinding my insides into paste. Maybe I could find a worthy magical trade without involving Mom; maybe Roscoe just gets off by upping the intimidation factor. I've watched so many people put their hearts on the line for what they want: to get the big reward, you have to take big risks. Yes. I have to do this.

Holding back the urge to vomit, I reach forward to sign the scroll, hand shaking as I contemplate finalizing a deal with a devil. But thinking about how he held that moth's life in his hand makes me wonder what he could do to me, and just before I tie myself to a dark warlock I barely know, I drop the quill.

I want my magic fixed so badly, but there have to be other options; something better than a backroom deal with an evil stranger. I guess I'm not as gutsy as I thought.

"I'm sorry." I sigh, shaking my head in frustration with myself. "I just . . . can't."

"Suit yourself." He shrugs, rolling up the scroll. "If you ever change your mind, you know who to call."

Let's hope I never have to.

Two

AMANI AND I AWKWARDLY WRESTLE INTO OUR CAPS AND GOWNS in the cab on our way north to school.

"I can't believe you did that," she says, purposely looking into her compact mirror to avoid my eye.

"You mean, totally chicken out?" I ask, zipping up my silky emerald-green gown.

"No, I don't blame you. That guy was a creepfest."

"A creepfest who could find me answers."

"I love you, but that was a horrible idea. He could kill you and not even think twice. And if your mom finds out, she may just kill you anyway." She's right, of course, but my stomach continues to churn with doubt. I'm still right back where I was: broken without answers. But it's too late now, and I want to focus on something else besides my swirling intestinal dread. "I'm so relieved you didn't sign."

"Speaking of horrible ideas, who decided wearing a square on your head should be a symbol of knowledge?" I flash her a cheesy smile, batting my cap's tassel out of my vision like a cat playing with string. Fitting the ridiculously shaped hat over my black, green, and blue strands helps my drama fade away, and watching Amani slide on hers brings home the weight of this once-in-a-lifetime moment.

"We're graduating," I say, stating the obvious, but it had to be said. Amani examines herself in her tiny mirror, smoothing her dark brown hair under the elastic cap. Even though I haven't checked my appearance, I can guarantee she's pulling this goofy look off way better than I am. "There were times I didn't think this day would come."

"Like when we had to do country line dancing in P.E.?" Amani smiles.

"Or dissect owl pellets in Biology?"

"Or breathe the same air as our mortal enemies day in and day out?" She laughs, but I'm suddenly overcome by an uncharacteristic swell of sentimentality, so I unbuckle my seat belt to properly turn to my partner in crime and say, "You know I never would've made it through without you, right? Like I'd still be stuck doing the grapevine in the gym if you weren't there to guide me through."

She smushes my cheeks with her palms. "Don't make me

cry! I just put on mascara, which is near impossible in a cab!"

"It's true! You are my everything . . . near, far, wherever you are . . ."

"I believe that the heart does go ooooooooon," Amani starts singing in a weird, warbly voice.

"You're here, there's NOTHING I fear!" I belt out in an equally awful tone.

Arms flung wide like we're the kings of the world, we sing about our hearts going on and never letting go, hugging and laughing as our cabdriver eyes us from the rearview mirror, but there are tears behind my smiles. Everything's about to change. And though I've been praying for this day to come since forever, I still can't believe it's here. High school is over. The pain, the suffering, the pointless papers about wars and scientific debates: up to this point, so much of my time has been spent doing things I had to do. Subjects I had to study, sports I had to play. None of it was my choice, and even my magical life was dictated by the rules and constraints set forth by the Fates and every other mystical creature more powerful than me (read: all of them). But that's all about to open up, doors flung wide with possibility. And that's what I want: I've been waiting too long for this freedom to have anything holding me back. I want to drop this anchor of matchmaking uncertainty and run free into the future. Clear eyes, full heart, can't lose. Chicago Culinary Institute, here I come!

We're about a block away from Manchester Prep, and Amani does one last makeup check, reapplying her sparkly lip gloss for the third time. I rustle through the duffel bag we packed, stuffing the anti-tear handkerchief I yanked from home into my billowing gown pocket, just in case. (It's enchanted to keep you composed if you don't want to be blubbering in public, and since I still don't want to show any signs of weakness in front of my horrible classmates—even though, Gods willing, I will never have to see them again—I want to keep this charm handy.) As we pull up to school, the electronic announcements sign flashes, CONGRATULATIONS, GRADUATES! GOOD LUCK!

The football field is set with a stage, hundreds of white folding chairs, and green balloons. I can honestly say I never attended a single sporting event, but I can't imagine it ever looked anything like this. Almost instantly, I'm spotted by my beautiful boyfriend, Charlie, who bounds across the grass and wraps me in a hug. He somehow manages not to look like a giant dork in his graduation costume, accessorizing with a tie printed with foxes (our school mascot) and plug earrings. The gowns bring out the forest green in his eyes, and I just want to smother him with kisses.

"Amber Sand, are you ready to leave this teenage wasteland behind?" he asks, still holding me close.

"Yup, I'm gonna leave this place in a blaze of glory."

His eyes light up behind his glasses. "You mean . . . you finally wrangled up a dragon from one of your black-market-magic friends for me?"

OMG, this adorable boy. Little does he know! "I meant a

metaphorical blaze, but I do have some news for you." I pause for dramatic effect.

He stares at me expectantly. "And?"

"Well, you know how I had that appointment this morning?" I look into those eyes I've spent all year obsessing over. While most couples wax poetic about each other's eyes, it's been a complicated situation for me. The static remains, but for once, Charlie is in the loop on what I see; he knows all about the fuzzy, pixelated images that never unscramble, and how his girlfriend may have even less magic than ever. I've decided that keeping secrets from him only leads to drama, and being able to talk to him about my worries has brought us closer. So much of our relationship has been steered by outside forces; for once, I'm taking the wheel.

"With the scary dark-arts man?" he asks.

"Yup. The matchmaking cure is TBD, but you will never guess what he has in his shop."

Charlie grips me tighter. "Don't toy with me. I am emotionally fragile right now."

I lean in, lips brushing his ear. "Dragon eggs," I tease, and instantly he shoves me backward, fireworks in his brain causing all his limbs to flail in amazement.

"ARE YOU SERIOUS?!" he yells, arms swinging around, revealing the flaming dragon sleeve that reflects his sweet, nerdy heart. "What are we even still doing here?! Let's go see them! Right now!"

"Hold on, hold on," I laugh, placing my palms on his chest. I feel his fanboy heart fluttering with joy. "We should probably graduate first, don't you think? Perform this vital rite of passage?"

He looks at me like I'm insane. "Who cares about a stupid ceremony when dragons are REAL?!"

"Listen, I will make this happen for you." I ball up his gown in my fists, since he's basically a flight risk at the moment. "I swear on my nonstick commercial-grade baking pans that we will find a way for you to see the dragons. But let's listen to speeches about how the future is ours first, okay?"

His fingers find their way to my jawline, thumbs brushing over my cheeks. "God, I love you." We kiss, his excitement over mythical creatures transferring to me, lips warm and wanting, not caring about the crowds around us or that our silly pointy hats keep crashing into each other. Despite the static and confusion surrounding my status, Charlie and I have never been closer, and kissing him has never been better.

I pull back, though I'd rather stay in his embrace. "I love you too. Dork."

We're greeted by the rest of our merry band of misfits. Kim Li, also pulling off the grad look with a collection of rainbow-colored accessories, skips over with glee, telling each of us how much she loves us. She and Amani ooh and aah over each other's dresses and hair as I spot another familiar, albeit surprising, face coming our way: Ivy Chamberlain.

"Guys! Hey!" I snap my fingers to get the group's attention.

"It's Ivy!" Confused eyes search the crowd for the declawed siren, whom nobody's seen in over two months. Losing her sister and her powers in one fell swoop was not easy for my former archnemesis, though with all of her awful magic used up, she became slightly more tolerable to be around. Her brazen "I own you and the entire universe" attitude dimmed, and since none of her "friends" could be compelled to cower at her feet anymore, she started hanging around us. But her personality was not the only thing that shifted; as the weeks went on, her beauty faded, transforming her from a high-fashion perfume ad to a plain, forgettable face. Not that plain is bad—I am as plain as they come—but she's always been the epitome of polish, so the change was extreme.

Then she started missing school. The occasional day stretched into longer absences, and when she did show up to class, she was barely present, sunken eyes and lethargic movements erasing the former swagger and sass she used to commanding effect. When we asked Ivy what was wrong, she'd snap and say, "Nothing," refusing to show weakness despite it being written all over her body. After she missed two straight weeks, Amani and I went by her house to check on her, but the Chamberlains' butler informed us the entire family was out of town, dealing with an urgent "family matter." The siren who terrorized me for years completely disappeared without word or warning. After everything we all went through during our mermaid adventure, I thought maybe we'd upgraded our relationship from "venomous" to "it's complicated," but apparently that's a nut I'll never crack.

"I didn't think she'd be coming," Amani says to me as a ghostly version of Ivy nears our circle. "Can she even graduate after missing so much school?"

"Who knows." I shrug. "I mean, her parents are still sirens; worst case, I guess they can finagle her a diploma."

"She does not look great." Kim cringes in concern. "What do you think is wrong?"

But there's no time to speculate; the four of us turn Ivy's way as she nods in recognition. "Hey" is all she says, as if she hasn't just materialized out of thin air. *Hey?* That's it? What the hell?! Part of me is annoyed: you don't just disappear off the face of the earth without letting someone know, especially if that someone risked life and limb to help you. I've been worried about her—a chunk of my heart torn up over her well-being—and now she shows up like it's no big deal? What is that? But Ivy looks even worse than I remember, her glossy blond locks traded in for dull strands of straw, sun-kissed skin turned sallow, so my resentment takes a back seat to genuine concern.

"Ivy, where have you been?" I ask, skipping the small talk I have no patience for. "We've tried calling, we went by your house—"

"You didn't have to do any of that." She glares, eyes free of shimmer.

Ugh. Still with this tough act. "Are you for real? We didn't know what happened to you!"

"Yeah, Ivy, we're your friends," Kim says sweetly. Ivy tries to shoot her a cutting look, but that fire is gone, replaced with appreciation for our concern. She turns, shielding her frighteningly pale face with her graduation cap. I think I hear her sniffle, but she wipes away any signs of emotion before replying.

"We can . . . talk about it later, if you want," she submits, tossing her limp hair over her shoulder. "You all look horrible, by the way," she adds, trying to lighten the mood. "I didn't miss any of you while I was gone. Especially since you're all so hideous."

Well, well. I guess not all of her siren ways have been erased. Tension easing, I say, "Aww, Ivy, you always know how to make special moments feel all warm and snuggly," to which she rolls her eyes.

"She's not wrong, though," Charlie jokes. "These gowns are an insult to society." He spreads out the emerald fabric like wings.

"We need to take a group picture, no matter how ugly we look!" Kim chimes.

"Yes, we wouldn't want to forget this precious memory," Amani deadpans, tilting her cap to an even weirder angle. We beam at each other, so much so that it makes Ivy shift uncomfortably in her heels.

"So what now? Do you losers group-hug or something?" she asks.

Amani and I lock eyes, smiling mischievously. "Well, now that you mention it . . ." The four of us lunge forward, capturing Ivy in a green tornado of affection, listening to her squeal in resistance as we cram together tighter. I never thought I'd be one to participate in mass cuddling, but here I am, right at home in the embrace of all these magical weirdos. I'm woman enough to admit that I like it, having multiple pals nestled into my heart, which used to be a sparse, barren space.

As we each cross the stage, collecting our hard-earned pieces of paper and symbolically shifting tassels to represent the transition to the next part of our lives, I cheer for my strange group of friends and wonder what I would ever do without them.

Three

SUMMER IN CHICAGO IS A MARVELOUS THING. WE PRAY FOR warmth all winter long, and when we finally feel sunshine on our skin, we don't take it for granted. People bust into flip-flops the moment it's above freezing, and every weekend is bursting with some sort of outdoor craft fair, farmers' market, or music festival. Navy Pier in particular packs in as many events as possible, so when people get bored at Taste of Chicago or Lollapalooza, they can mosey on over to ride the Ferris wheel, take in a show, and shop, shop, shop. This summer, they have planned a ginormous Beat the Heat! promotion, with daily water balloon fights, snow cones, and live appearances by random local celebrities on the air-conditioned main stage. Normally this nonsense would make me crazy, but summer is my favorite season, the warmth melting some of my frosty edges. And while Navy Pier isn't exactly a Zen garden, at least I can walk along Lake Michigan covered in light.

My matchmaking gig may be on hiatus, but I'm still working at Windy City Magic. Mom let me sleep in and miss the morning shift, and even though I spent a lazy couple of hours eating donuts and watching *Gilmore Girls*, I somehow got to the pier thirty minutes early. I could go in and help Bob organize the essential oils shipment, or I could grab an iced coffee and not be helpful at all. Decision made!

I make my way to the water's edge, walking all the way down to the easternmost point of the pier, where most tourists are too tired to venture. I flop onto a bench facing away from the pier and toward the lake, doing my best to soak in the serenity before I plunge into inventory duty back at the shop. Sunlight sparkles on the gentle waves as a daily cruise ship rounds the bend, riders laughing at the tour guide's corny jokes.

I have big plans for this summer, in that I have zero. While I absolutely cannot wait to start at the Chicago Culinary Institute and begin my ascent into dessert heaven, I want to enjoy these next few months by doing as little as possible, spending time with my friends before we're scattered to our respective schools. Much to Vincent's and Ella's dismay, I'm taking way fewer hours at both the Black Phoenix and MarshmElla's, and Windy City Magic too. You're only on the brink of adulthood once, and I want to be lazy whenever I can. Amani and I are hoping to marathon all seven seasons of *Bristol Bay*, some terrible soapy drama she swears I will love (or love to make fun of), and Charlie and I have vowed to take turns planning "fancy date nights" for each other, where we surprise the other with mystery outings. I'm up first, and I bought us discounted tickets for a chocolate walking tour around the city. It's going to be great.

I smile at the thought, making my way down the rest of the pier, but I stop dead in my tracks when I spot a line of people winding outside Windy City Magic. What in the world? What is going on in there? We're usually busier in the summer since the pier as a whole is more jam-packed, but I've never seen a queue of people waiting to get inside, not even when Mom ran her special "buy one, get one" aura-cleansing promotion.

"Who are all these people?" I say to no one, gesturing wildly to the line before me. *Where did you all come from? What do you want?*

Before I can dream up wild scenarios, Kim comes vaulting out the shop's door, practically vibrating with some sort of information. We took her on as a part-time clerk to help with the summer rush, and she's been bursting with happiness ever since we told her she was hired.

"OMG, Amber! You'll never guess what's going on!" she squeals.

I raise my eyebrows in suspense as she bounces on her heels with glee.

"Please don't make me guess," I say.

"Well!" Kim chirps. "A Navy Pier employee just came by with a media announcement. There's going to be a live recording in the IMAX theater this afternoon." Vendors always get notified when something out of the ordinary will be happening on the premises, allowing us to plan ahead and bring in extra staff for big events. We already received the finalized Beat the Heat! calendar, though, so this must be a last-minute addition. "When I first heard, I was totally shocked! I mean, I feel like the Fates must have brought this together!" Her neon bracelets jangle happily around her wrists as she describes the whole interaction, drawing out a story that could have been summed up in one sentence. "And then I was thinking—"

"Spit it out already, friend. What is the taping?"

"Matchmaking Magic!" Kim cheers, with some extremely unnecessary jazz hands. "Madame L'Amour, live and in person!"

I stare at her blankly. "Um, am I supposed to know who or what that is?"

Kim's jaw drops. She examines my face, looking for signs that I'm kidding. "Wait, are you serious? You don't know about *Matchmaking Magic!*?"

"I know that *I'm* a matchmaker who is magic . . . ?" I grimace. "Is there something else?"

"OMG! I thought you knew! Are you living under a rock?"

"No, but that does sound cozy."

"Ugh!" Kim grabs my wrist, dragging me past the line of waiting customers to the counter, where she pulls up YouTube on the shop's computer. As she types into the search bar, I notice my matchmaking table has been set up for the first time in forever, complete with its FIND TRUE LOVE! CONSULT A MATCHMAKER! sign.

"Um, Kim? Why is my table out here?" I ask, eyeing it suspiciously.

"Shh!" she scolds, cueing up a video. "Watch this."

On the screen, the words "Matchmaking Magic!" appear, twinkling with a cheesy animation effect. As they fade, an older brunette with waves piled messily on her head and lavender bejeweled spectacles on the tip of her nose smiles at the camera as "Madame L'Amour" flashes in the chyron below. She swirls around a blindingly fluorescent-pink set, dress embroidered with hundreds of little hearts with arrows darting through, an eccentric, grandmotherly style that would put Miss Frizzle to shame.

"Wait, this person is a matchmaker? Like, for real?" I ask, clearly struggling to understand the concept of something called "matchmaking magic" outside of my own self. I've honestly never been presented with a real-life example of a matchmaker besides the peacock-haired girl living in my mirror, and my only pop culture reflections residing in *Fiddler on the Roof* and *Mulan*, neither of which have anything to do with my personal experiences. For years, I begged my mom to help me find another matchmaker to learn from, but it was like looking for a four-leaf clover; our magic is so mutated and rare, you'd be lucky to find it. Could it be I'm not alone in this strange, never-ending rom-com? A flutter of hope I'd silenced long ago awakens in my chest.

I squint at the screen, searching for similarities in this potential Cupid Sister. Her wacky aesthetic is a 180 from my plain-as-can-be wardrobe, and even just the act of publicizing her sessions means we are not exactly in sync, philosophy-wise. Still, consider me intrigued.

"But her name's not really Madame L'Amour, is it? That seriously cannot be her name," I say, watching my digital counterpart twirl across the screen.

"Just keep watching," Kim scolds.

From what I can tell, *Matchmaking Magic!* combines the upbeat insanity of an early morning talk show with the dread and discomfort of a dating app, all rolled into one roller coaster of heightened emotions. I usually aim to make my matchmaking customers feel calm and comfortable, but this show throws that out the window, looking for the biggest reactions possible. In a clearly fake French accent, Madame L'Amour (I will never get over that name) starts describing her first guest, weaving a weepy tale about a man whose parents deserted him when he was sixteen, causing him to push away love and affection from everyone in his life. In an attempt to make his match reveal all the more heartwarming, this backstory is purposely pulling out the most depressing aspects of the man's life.

"That is super sad, though," Kim interjects.

I give her some major side-eye. "It's a little emotionally manipulative, don't you think?"

"I guess so?"

"I would never share anyone's personal details like that." I frown, crossing my arms in superiority. I don't want to hate on perhaps the only other matchmaker I'll ever encounter, but something about this performance is ringing false. Love is a sensitive subject, and broadcasting the intimate details feels a little opportunistic. Although I guess a billion seasons of *The Bachelor* prove I'm alone on that point.

The man comes onstage and takes a seat next to Madame in a fuzzy fuchsia armchair. The two exchange some small talk, and then it's time to get to business: the matchmaking. I feel nervous as she takes his hands. I've never in my life seen another matchmaker at work, and my curiosity takes over. Will it be totally different? Clearly her approach is much cornier than mine, but will the general flow be the same? Have I been doing it right all these years, or have I missed steps along the way?

Madame coos about being in a safe space and how the process is painless. "Now, look into my eyes," she instructs as the camera zooms in on both their faces. After some truly theatrical eyebrow work, she launches into describing the physical and personality details of his match. "I can already feeeeeel a connection to your future bride," she adds to his delight.

On a screen hanging behind them, a computer-generated image of his match begins to appear like a police sketch rendering, not unlike what Bob does for me. As a swell of triumphant strings play, the man turns around to see the image, tears streaming down as he gazes upon his romantic future. The live studio audience cheers as he thanks Madame L'Amour for finally giving him hope. She blows a kiss to the camera, the corners of her eyes wrinkling with joy, as a theme song plays her out.

"Finding love is magic! Open your heart and see!"

Well. It's sappy and schmaltzy and dorky as hell, but the channel has nearly half a million subscribers, so what do I know? Being sugary sweet has never really been my brand, but I guess people like that kind of thing. I have to wonder if Madame is the real deal, though. Who knows what's happening behind the scenes of this streaming show?

"How can it be so popular without me knowing about it?" I wonder.

Kim wipes a tear from her eye, cementing her place in the target audience. "It's so hopeful! And so sweet," she sniffs. "The world is full of so much sadness that sometimes it's nice to be reminded of things that are good. Why do you think all those people are lined up outside? They want to meet with a matchmaker and find some hope!"

I don't want to burst her love bubble, but I have to ask, "How do we know it's real?"

"What do you mean?" Kim whimpers, visibly offended by my accusation.

"It's great that she's spreading love and rainbows and all that, but is she actually matchmaking?" I ask. "There's no real way to verify if this woman can see true love; she could be showing any image on the screen and no one would be the wiser."

Kim bites her lip. "Um, not to be rude, Amber, but isn't that true of you also?"

"What?" I snap, feeling betrayed by a member of my inner circle (not that I have multiple circles). "I mean, maybe. Technically! But you know I'm not faking. Amani and Vincent are the proof! And besides, this is real life. Pretty much nothing online is true."

"But it's so lovely, who cares if it's fake?" Kim asks.

"I do!" I raise my hand. "Because first of all, this zany woman is putting matchmaking on the map for maybe the first time ever, and if she's faking it, she could obliterate any shred of reputation I've managed to maintain. And second, if she *does* have the goods, maybe she can help me figure out why mine are broken!" I didn't even realize I was thinking it until I said it, but as soon as the words leave my mouth, I know I have to pursue this avenue. If I could get some face time with this cheeseball love guru, maybe I could pick her brain about her magic, her life, and if she's ever, oh, I don't know, short-circuited while envisioning a match. It was hard to tell with the lighting and costumes, but Madame appears older than me, and if she's still kickin' and thrivin', maybe she knows the secret to matchmaking longevity. Madame and her amazing Technicolor fashion sense may be the answer I've been looking for, Roscoe be damned! That is, if she's actually magical.

"Amber, I never even thought of that!" Kim claps her hands, black hair swinging happily. "This taping today truly is meant to be! And—OMG!" Her whole face lights up as she grabs my shoulders. "When it's all said and done, maybe she could even tell you *your* match!"

Whoa, now *that's* interesting. I was only thinking about my botched-up abilities, but hey, if Madame L'Amour could definitively tell me whether or not Charlie is my match, well, that'd be icing on the cake. Okay, decision made: time to put on my fangirl pants and stalk an Internet-famous matchmaker.

Four

I'VE BATTLED MURDEROUS WITCHES AND CHASED DOWN PACKS OF goblins, but nothing has prepared me for this. I've never met someone like me, though I dreamed about it a lot when I was little. Working through my matchmaking abilities on my own was no easy feat, and seeing Mom with her coven made me wish I had a support system of my own. I've longed for someone I could relate to, someone who would completely understand what it's like to be flooded with visions of love, day in, day out. While Amani has been a sympathetic ear, she doesn't live and breathe my issues, and the thought of sharing my troubles with a person exactly like me has my heart tangled up in cautious optimism. If Madame L'Amour truly is a matchmaker, all my worries could be over.

I walk into the massive IMAX theater, and the amount of glitter per square foot is absolutely astounding. Everything is drenched in pink and sparkly fabric, and on the stage there's a replica of the *Matchmaking Magic!* set, complete with fuzzy wing-backed chairs. The sixty-foot-high screen is all ready to display the forthcoming match revelations, with a banner reading OPEN YOUR HEART AND SEE! dangling across the top. The room is humming with hopeful voices dreaming of falling in love, set to the soundtrack of generic pop beats. There have to be, what, three hundred people in here, some of whom I recognize from past Windy City Magic sessions. I try not to be bitter that my matchmaking performance alone did not satiate their need for love.

The shop was given a set of complimentary tickets, which is lucky, since the place is so packed. Charlie, Amani, Kim, and I file into aisle seats not too far from the stage; I told my bestie and boy to get to the pier ASAP so they could witness this potentially life-changing meeting. The first step, though, is to determine whether or not Madame is legit, and my crack team of superfriends have come up with an A-plus scheme.

"Man, they really laid down the red carpet for this thing I never knew existed until this morning," I mutter, staring at a giant cardboard dove hanging directly overhead.

"What a weird and strangely specific phenomenon," Charlie says, scanning the crowd before turning to me to tease, "Why don't you get this kind of treatment, babe?"

I scrunch my nose and eyebrows together. "I will cut you, Blitzman."

He grins, wrapping his arms around my waist before quickly kissing my collarbone. For a split second, the insanity of our surroundings melts away, and I disappear into him: his sunny laugh, his adorkable face. The boy really does have a knack for distracting me.

I lean over his lap, poking Amani in the shoulder. She bats her eyelashes, fanning herself with the little heart-shaped fans we were given at the door. "Yes?"

"Are you ready for the plan?" I say with more force than necessary.

"Hmm, what now?" She feigns ignorance.

"Kim, you too!" I yell.

She smiles at me, giving an enthusiastic thumbs-up. "Yup!"

The lights dim, and the crowd erupts into ecstatic cheers as the *Matchmaking Magic!* theme song blares. *"Finding love is magic! Open your heart and see!"* After watching that first video, I binged the entire series at the shop while waiting for this taping to start; I've now heard this song so many times, I'm worried the tune is tattooed on my subconscious. I'm getting nervous, so I reach for the bottom of my seat just to have something to claw at, but Charlie intercepts, locking his fingers between mine. "Breathe, babe," he instructs, and I do, trying my best to keep my brain from melting out my ears.

A man prances out onstage, a spotlight following his wild

waving. Gleaming a megawatt smile, he raises both hands to quiet the rabid fans. I don't recognize him from any episodes. It's not like there's a supporting cast of characters. He's decked out in a pink polo shirt and white pants. Whenever someone manages to wear white on their bottom half without it immediately getting destroyed, I have to assume dark magic is at play.

"Hello, Chicago!" he cheers, causing an additional round of hollers. "Who is ready to fall in love?" More screaming, more thunderous applause. He smiles even wider somehow, pretending to be blown back by the crowd's enthusiasm. I catch Ivy out the corner of my eye. She looks like she's going to vomit.

"My name is Paul, and I'm a producer for *Matchmaking Magic!* I'm so happy to be here with you all today. Did you know we film every episode right here in Illinois?" What, what, what? I did not know this has been brewing right under my nose. Another matchmaker, in my own state! Charlie, sensing my extra pinch of tension, squeezes my hand harder. "That's right! And because you've shown us so much support, we wanted to return the love. Today, Madame L'Amour will be conducting three live matches from our audience, right here at Navy Pier!"

"Yes!" I find myself cheering along, despite the fact that live matches have been happening here literally every day for the past five years or so, courtesy of ME. Whatever—shake it off, Amber. I need to focus on our plan. Before I go spilling my heart out to a stranger, I made Amani and Kim promise they'd volunteer to go onstage given the chance; that way, when their matches are revealed, I'll be able to tell if Madame is real or a fraud. Preferably Amani, because even though I've become more familiar with visions of Kim's new match, I can't totally trust that pairing, seeing as how he only started coming into view when I started falling apart. I feel most confident with Amani, since her real-life love story with Vincent has unfolded right before my eyes. Both girls are wearing good-luck talismans from my mom's private collection, plus they are both so adorable, who wouldn't want to put them on camera?

"Any volunteers?" Paul asks, covering his heart with mock surprise when the crowd goes nuts yet again. "All right! I'm releasing three cupids into the audience—if you're chosen, they'll lead you backstage, and then the fun will begin! Good luck!"

"Finding Love Is Magic" plays throughout the room as a trio of poor unfortunate souls sporting wings and slings of arrows appear onstage. You could not pay me enough to wear those tacky costumes. They leap into the audience, running through the aisles as people scream and reach for them. Occasionally they stop and point an arrow into a section, causing a total frenzy, before dashing off again. I purposely sat us next to the aisle to be more visible, and my heart jumps into my throat as a blond cupid makes her way to our area. She waves her arrow around before firing at her final target: Amani. I leap into Charlie's arms in excitement as the cupid takes my best friend's hand. Amani quickly signs a *You're welcome* before disappearing into the disappointed crowd.

"Wow, your plan is actually working!" Kim says, working hard to share a smile. I think she likes *Matchmaking Magic!* more than she's let on, and I'm sure she would've loved the thrill of being chosen.

"Thank you for helping me with this," I tell her. "All of you. Now we can sit back and see if love is real."

Because the Fates hate me, Amani goes last. We sit through two other hopefuls, watching their future lovers come to life on-screen. One contestant cries, holding on to Madame L'Amour so tight that Paul has to come out and pull her away. The crowd is eating it up, though, waving their heart fans in the air like they're witnessing the Second Coming. I'm so anxious, I'm practically vibrating.

Finally the second participant leaves the stage, and it's time. Madame turns to the crowd, a tiara of diamond hearts crowning her long, frizzy hair. I can't imagine where someone would acquire such a tacky accessory, and honestly I don't want to know.

"When I met with our third guest backstage, I was instantly enchanted," Madame begins in her French accent. She's framed by a single spotlight, and I have to admit she commands the stage. No one is shuffling in their seats; no one can take their eyes off her. Even when I was at the top of my matchmaking game, I could never stand in front of spectators like this, hungry hearts waiting for answers. It's one thing to do a job well; it's quite another to do it in front of an audience. "A recent high school graduate, my final contestant feels confident she may have already found her true love, but today, we'll find out for sure. Please help me welcome . . . Amani!"

My best friend walks onstage, human perfection in a light blue sundress. There's a slight shake in her step, but she smiles bravely as she takes a seat on her fuzzy throne. I am going to bake her so many treats after this.

"Welcome, my dear," Madame coos. "You are so lovely."

"Thank you." Amani blushes, tucking a stray hair behind her ear.

"Tell us about yourself, won't you?"

Amani swallows hard, looking into the blinding stage lights. "Well, um, I met someone last year. At first, I couldn't stand him. Everything about him seemed too cheesy, too fake. And even though I could tell he liked me, the feeling was not mutual."

"Mmm." Madame nods. "How many of us have been in that situation before?" The audience applauds in agreement.

"But then," Amani continues, "something changed. I don't know how. The more I got to know him, the more I learned his come-ons were an act; he was nervous around me." A smile spreads across her whole face. "Which was actually kind of cute. And now we're inseparable. I can't imagine life without him." The crowd sighs.

Madame wipes a tear from her eye. "Then what brings you here, dear? Is there a lingering question in your heart?"

"Ugh, that's so manipulative!" I mutter. "I would never—"

Charlie presses a finger to my lips. "Shhh, we're almost there."

"Well, I feel lucky, I suppose, to have already met my soul mate." Amani directs her gaze to exactly where we're sitting. She's up there for me, of course, so we came up with a believable line. "I guess I just want to know if all this"—she gestures around the stage—"is real." Nailed it.

"Of course, sweet child. Let's take a look." Madame reaches for her and takes a deep breath. "Now let's gaze into your happily-ever-after."

Here we go. The screen behind them lights up, and an image begins to form, almost as if someone is sketching it live behind the scenes. With every stroke, my heartbeat quickens; I could very well go into cardiac arrest before this is done. Faster and faster, a face takes shape, and I don't even realize I'm clutching Charlie's leg until he lets out a small yelp of pain.

"Sorry," I whisper, releasing my death grip, but keeping my eyes on the screen. Any minute now, I'll know for sure if Madame L'Amour is friend or foe: someone who can guide me on my bumpy matchmaking journey, or just a game show host who's enjoying fifteen minutes of fraudulent fame.

Madame lets go of Amani, whose hands go straight to her face when she gazes at the screen. And it looks like we're all winners today, because smiling down at us is Vincent.

Five

ANOTHER MATCHMAKER. ANOTHER ME. ANOTHER PERSON TO *understand the craziness in my head.*

The truth creeps into me slowly, like food coloring seeping into water, spreading its shade to full saturation. I wanted Madame to be real—I hoped for this outcome—yet the cynical core of my crusty heart had prepared me for disappointment. I sit, stunned, as Amani confirms the man on the screen is her boyfriend, to the thunderous approval of the audience. Fans wave, feet stomp, and Madame beams, wrapping her guest in an enormous hug, before thanking everyone for joining in the romantic fun.

"Be sure to visit the Finding Gifts of Love Is Magic gift shop on your way out!" she coos, gesturing to the exit. "Use the hashtag 'open your eyes and see' for a chance to be featured on our next season of webisodes!"

The applause goes on and on, even as the spectators exit the theater, until only a few people remain, including Kim, Charlie, and myself. I cannot move, I cannot breathe.

Eventually my eyes come back into focus to see Kim's face hovering in front of mine. "She looks really pale," she says to Charlie.

His concerned expression comes into view as well. "Yeah, let's see if we can go find Amani backstage."

They guide my nearly petrified body through the theater. I hear passing comments of "Best show ever" and "Did you see her face? So heartwarming" as we weave toward a door offstage. Charlie drops the Blitzman family name with the security guard (which is basically a skeleton key to the city thanks to his dad, John, being the mayor) and we're in, witnessing the behind-the-scenes actual magic of *Matchmaking Magic!*

It's not a lot, actually. A few people mill about with clipboards and headsets, while contestants one and two eat heart-shaped cookies at a sparsely stocked snack table. I'm in such an altered state that I don't even reach for a treat; you know I'm far gone when my brain bypasses sugar.

"Kim and I will go look for Amani, okay?" Charlie says, stroking my upper arm. "Don't go crazy. Just stand right here." I don't move. "Perfect, just like that." They walk away, and I'm drawn toward a bright light on my left; a single dressing table glowing with white lights and fake jewels. And there, sitting on a director's chair, is Madame, genuine matchmaker and potential salvation, working to untangle her tiara from her hair.

"Excuse me, Madame?" I croak, my voice wavering like a fangirl meeting her boy-band crush.

"Hmm?" Her gaze doesn't leave the mirror, as a particular wave of her hair seems determined to live in the tiara forever.

"I wanted to congratulate you on your success, and . . . maybe see if we could share some tips, because, uh . . ." Well, there's no real way to dance around it. ". . . I'm a matchmaker too."

She stops detangling to give me a once-over, confusion clouding her eyes. "You're what?" she says in a midwestern accent so thick it almost knocks me over. She then clears her throat and repeats her question, this time in her familiar French. "You're what?"

Okay, that was weird. "Yeah, I live here in Chicago. I only found out about your show this morning, but I feel like we were destined to meet." I cringe at my own phrasing. "Sorry if that sounds corny."

"Well, that's . . . wonderful." But her tone doesn't convey wonder, more like bewilderment. There are piles and piles of rags on her dressing table, caked with makeup she's wiped off her shockingly young face. On the screen and even onstage a little while ago, I thought she was in her late fifties, but sitting here now, she looks only a few years older than me. And, am I crazy, or is that a fake nose peeking out from under the rags?

"I've never met another matchmaker before," I say, my earlier doubt starting to creep back in. "I thought maybe we could meet up sometime, exchange some stories." Her eyes dart around the room, like she's looking for an escape. This fidgety creature before me is the opposite of the confident, whimsical woman who just wowed hundreds of people. "What do you think?"

Madame gets right in my face, revealing that the crinkles by her eyes were definitely drawn on. "Now, you listen to me," she threatens, *le français* gone for good. "I don't know who you are, but stay away from her, okay? She's been through enough already, and I'm only trying to help." A pointer finger dangles in my face, threatening to scratch my nose.

What? My brain on tape delay, I can barely get out a response to that nonsense. "Who are you . . . What are . . . Huh?"

"Did my aunt and uncle send you? Ask you to play a *'match-maker'*"—she puts the word in air quotes—"to try to butter me up? Gods, they are unbelievable." She leans back in her chair, arms crossed. "I told them that everything would be fine, and I'd bring her back in one piece, but no, they can never break out of their tiny worldviews!"

My using the m-word was apparently a trigger for some kind of strange family drama, but I don't want to give up when I'm so close to gaining an ally. "I didn't mean to upset you, I just need—"

"I don't care what *you* need," Madame snaps, cutting me off, flames in her eyes. "I only care about her. Now, get out of here before I have Paul call security." She turns back to her mirror in a huff.

This is what I get for trying to connect with one of my own: a total crackpot. The light at the end of my tunnel goes dim as I resign myself to never understanding what is wrong with me. "Listen, I don't know what you're talking about, and I certainly will stay away from *her*, whoever that is, since I definitely don't want anything to do with you." I turn on my heel, scolding myself for putting faith in something as stupid as a streaming show, when Amani sweeps in from the abyss and drags me away.

"Everything is hopeless!" I'm whining as she pulls me in a corner. "For half a second, I believed we'd found an answer, but—"

"Amber, shut up for a second," Amani instructs. "You're right: Madame's not who you need. But there's someone you have to meet before you go dig yourself a grave."

"But—"

"Nope. Zip it."

I close my mouth, but only because when it comes to my best friend, she usually knows what she's doing. She guides me to a back office about the size of Windy City Magic's supply closet. Inside sits a tiny wisp of a girl, hair sea-foam green, with a constellation of freckles dotting the bridge of her nose. Cautiously, she approaches, like a little woodland creature venturing outside her nest, looking up at me like she's hoping I'll give her a lollipop.

"Is this your friend, the matchmaker?" she asks Amani, voice like a baby bird. She barely clears four feet, and can't be more than eight years old. What is this kid doing back here?

"Yes, this is my best friend, Amber Sand." Amani gestures to me like I'm a game show prize. "Amber, meet Jane Wisteria."

Jane's soft brown eyes crinkle with a smile. "It's . . . nice to meet you," she says, bashfully bowing her head as she grabs at the hem of her floral tee.

"Sure, uh, you too." I sign a subtle *WTF* to Amani, because while I'm sure this little sprite is quite darling, I'm pretty much over this whole scene and would like to go eat my body weight in ice cream.

"So, when they took me backstage, I figured I'd be doing a quick meet and greet with Madame to get the whole backstory banter thing going," Amani starts, "but actually, I didn't get any face time with her until we were onstage. After I signed some sort of nondisclosure thing, that Paul guy took me to meet Jane. Turns out, she's the actual magic behind *Matchmaking Magic!*" I look back at Jane, who gives a small, friendly wave. "She's a real-life, honest-to-goodness matchmaker. *She's* the one who saw my match with Vincent; she's legit."

This is one reveal too many. My head is spinning, so all that comes out of my very eloquent mouth is "Wha?"

Amani ignores my bewilderment. "When Jane started describing Vincent in perfect detail, I freaked out." Jane's eyebrows knit in worry over this comment, so Amani quickly adds,

"In a good way! It was amazing. I mean, Amber, it was almost like talking to you, minus the years of hardened bitterness."

"My vision was so clear too," Jane confirms, just above a whisper. She seems incredibly nervous to be talking to us, as if someone nefarious is listening to our conversation. "I could see you both all snuggled up in each other's arms." She shakes her head like she's said something wrong, yet adds, "It was so beautiful."

Amani keeps going, despite the uneasy energy emanating from our tiny new friend. "Amber was the one who helped me find him!" my bestie brags. "She met him in real life, and after envisioning him for so many years, she led me straight to him."

"That's wonderful." Jane manages her first real smile, revealing a mouth full of baby teeth. "I've only seen one of my visions actually come to life, and it was really cool for me." Her eyelashes dance with a dreamy flutter as she and Amani both look at me with emoji-heart eyes.

"Okay, um, can we pause for a second?" I ask, breaking the lovefest. "I'm sorry, but I don't understand what's going on. You're a matchmaker, and yet that woman out there is, what, channeling you? Why?"

"It's . . . complicated." Jane plays with a stack of woven bracelets around her wrist, eyes on the floor. I'm beginning to worry about why she's so skittish talking about her talent. If she weren't standing there like a shaking baby deer, I'd be all over her with my questions, but something tells me if I press too hard too fast, she'll just melt into a puddle of her own anxiety. "I promise you that all the show's matches have been real, though. If I were you, I bet I'd want to know about that."

"Did that woman come up with the super-corny theme?" I ask.

Her face drops. "You don't like it?"

Seeing this innocent critter fade instantly makes me feel like a monster, so I try to save face. "We just have different styles, I guess. Unique matchmaking techniques."

Cheeks red, she nods in agreement. "I'd love to learn all about yours. Um, I don't want to sound like a weirdo, but I've never met anyone like me before, and Amani thought we could be friends." She stops for a second, light chocolate eyes probing mine. I know that look; I know what she's doing. Only I've never had anyone look at me like that before, like she's staring into the deepest parts of my existence, digging up truths unknown to even myself. It's intense, intimate, and I suddenly feel very exposed. Is this how my customers feel when I'm working with them? No wonder they get so squirrely. I blink away so Jane can't continue, but I know it's too late.

"Do you want to know?" she whispers.

My response catches in my throat. Do I want to know my match? It's something I've craved since the second I learned it was a possibility. My thoughts tornado to Charlie: How long have I anguished over this uncertainty? How much turmoil has seeing every other happily-ever-after but my own caused? Jane could tell me, right here, right now, and it would all be over, yet suddenly I'm scared, the complete opposite reaction I ever expected. What is wrong with me? What's with the hesitation? I've dreamed of this, prayed for this, even conjured the Fates for this, yet it feels too fast, too easy, and maybe my blood sugar is low or something, but it's all just too much.

"Would you want to know?" I ask, dodging the question.

She shakes her head, mint-green hair cascading over her shoulders. "Definitely not. I want falling in love to be a surprise. That is, if boys ever stop being gross."

I laugh to myself; I don't want to spoil her about most boys being eternally disgusting. In fact, I got pretty lucky to find a diamond in the rough, a guy who loves me for me and stands by my side, no matter what random stuff I throw his way. I was never one to imagine a "dream guy," a mental amalgamation of all the unobtainable features of the male species, but if I did, mine would be Charlie, 100 percent.

"Okay, tell me," I suddenly decide, bracing myself as if I'm about to be dunked in a tank of cold water, waiting for the rush of her reveal. No matter what she says, there's no turning back, so I'll just have to be my totally chill, easygoing self and accept whatever the Fates have decided (because that's always been my MO, right?).

Jane instantly brightens, gently taking my hands like a tender patron of love. Her fingers feel so small in my own, and I wonder how long she's been matchmaking. A year, tops? My talent emerged when I was seven, but I was a raging blabber-mouth for years, unable to deliver matches with any sense of style or sympathy. I didn't start working my Windy City Magic table until I was around thirteen, since my habit up until then was to just blurt out whatever I saw as soon as I saw it. This girl is light-years ahead of me, a charming little doe pleasantly weaving hearts together like it's the most natural thing in the world. At her age, I was stacking up enemies left and right, but she has thousands of fans. Kids today!

She looks up at me, sweet as sugar. "Your match is—" But the most important sentence of my life is cut off by shouting and sounds of a struggle behind us. Like a frightened bunny, Jane scurries and cowers behind me, grabbing on to the back of my leg. Selfishly I want to shake her free, along with the last word of her sentence, but based on the terror on her face, she knows exactly what that yelling is all about.

"Jane!" Madame shouts, running toward us from offstage. Gone is all her stage makeup, and the wavy brunette wig; instead, she wears a lavender fauxhawk, with multiple face and ear piercings. Quite a reversal from her wholesome grandma image. In close pursuit is an older couple, stomping forward in a furious rage. Jane squeals behind me as Madame joins our cluster, though Amani and I have no idea what's going on.

Madame stands firm as the aggressors approach, unclasping the cloaks around their necks. Suddenly, two pairs of wings spread wide above us, our jaws dropping as they flutter to attention.

Good Gods . . . fairies! This just got way weirder!

I've never seen fairy wings so close up—the few fairies I've met always keep them hidden—and I'm astounded at how intricately detailed they are. Similar to dragonfly wings (which I've studied on slow days at the shop), hundreds of swirling membranes create a waving, fluttering pattern, illustrating a summer breeze. Each prismatic section bends light like the edge of a bubble casting rainbows, and I'm so hypnotized it takes me longer than it should to realize that, beside me, Jane has been holding her breath for longer than should be humanly possible.

A gentleman with ice-blue hair, a potbelly, and a slight hunch steps forward, brilliantly blue wings expanding to reach full span as he walks, giving him an extra air of authority.

"Jane," he says, poker-faced, dark gaze focused solely on her. "We've missed you."

She exhales sharply, eyes instantly glassy. "I'm sorry, Papa," she cries. *Papa?* Her hand grips my thigh so tightly she very well may draw blood.

A plump fairy woman stands behind him with cotton-candy-pink hair, clutching a handkerchief to her lips. "We are so glad you're okay!" she blubbers.

"I'm sorry, Mama," Jane echoes, rising to stand by my side. Her head hangs low, minty strands covering her freckled face. The three share the same paler-than-pale skin and pastel-colored tresses, yet Jane seems to be lacking her parents' appendages. I quickly check her back to see if I somehow missed this very distinctive feature, but there's no telltale outline underneath her clothes. Interesting.

Though the fairies express concern, this is not a happy reunion. Their faces turn hard as they address Madame. "How could you do this? She is an innocent girl!"

"She's not a victim! I was trying to help her," Madame spits back. "You are suffocating her with your antiquated ways!"

"Our ways have kept our family safe, Rose, or have you forgotten since you left?" Papa scowls, bushy eyebrows full of resentment. *Rose? Is Madame's real name Rose?* I'm trying to keep up, but we're definitely only getting a tiny sliver of this Wisteria family drama.

Madame/Rose crosses her arms, offended. "I didn't abandon anyone, least of all Jane. I love her. I would never do anything to hurt her." She pauses, swallowing down a sob. "She needs support, encouragement—"

"She needs her family, not some opportunistic cousin to fill her head with lies and muck up her morals," Papa retorts as Mama nods silently behind him. "She is coming home with us, right now." He points to the empty space beside him, willing his daughter to step forward.

Jane slumps in defeat, but Rose has not given up her fight. "You don't understand what she's going through," Rose pleads, reaching for her little cousin. Jane looks back at her, biting her lip like she knows there's no point in speaking up. "I was only trying to show her that there's a world outside—"

"ENOUGH!" Papa bellows. In one swift movement, he flies over to Jane, scooping her up in his arms and rejoining his wife. She reaches into her purse and pulls out a fistful of golden sparkles, blowing the glittering dust over herself and her family. Before I can even process what's happening, the Wisteria parents mutter something under their breath and vanish right before our eyes. It's so fast, so unexpected, the disappearance takes my breath away.

As quickly as she came, the matchmaker is gone.

And I know I need to find her.

Six

ROSE IS ON THE FLOOR, SOBBING INTO HER HANDS. AS SHE HUNCHES
over, the back of her shirt creeps up to reveal the tips of shiny
purple wings, which I did not notice until just now. Whoa. Not
only is Madame not a matchmaker at all, she's a fairy.

Amani crouches down beside her, carefully setting a hand
on her shaking shoulders. "Are you okay?"

Rose wipes her face, truly taking us in for the first time.
"Why were you two talking to Jane?" Suspicious, puffy eyes
examine me. "Wait, you're that other matchmaker."

Yup, that's right, the girl you told to get lost. "Yeah. I'm Amber,
and I don't want to intrude or anything, but I feel like we're
pretty involved now. . . . What just happened? Did Jane just get
kidnapped by her own parents?"

"What do you care?" Rose asks with more venom than necessary. It's clear she's going through a lot right now, but she doesn't have to bite off our heads. "You don't even know her."

"You're right. I don't. But I've also never known another matchmaker, and she hasn't either. We could help each other."

Rose considers this, wiping away smeared mascara. "That would be . . . nice, actually." She sighs, head hanging heavy from the troubles she's been carrying around for Gods know how long. "Thank you."

"Let's go someplace that's not here," Amani suggests, turning up her nose as a stagehand carries a giant cardboard cupid by. "Like MarshmElla's?"

"I love the way you think," I say. "Let me go find the others."

As Amani continues to console the former Madame L'Amour, I hunt down Charlie and Kim, who were busy sitting in the fuzzy armchairs pretending to interview each other. Kim has her eyes closed, wiggling her fingers in midair. "Your match . . . she's coming into focus. . . ."

"Wait, I see her now!" Charlie leaps out of the chair, picks me up, and swings me around the stage. "You're here! It's a miracle!"

"Put me down, put me down!" I laugh, kicking my legs. He does but not before making me pay a kiss as a toll.

"Did you meet the matchmaker?" he asks.

"Um, did you guys not overhear the giant argument happening only a few feet away?"

They look at each other blankly. "No?"

"Good Gods." I shake my head. "Come on, my innocent little gems. There's drama waiting in the wings."

Before we all head off to MarshmElla's, I sneak Charlie away from the group, curling my hands around his suspenders and pulling him in for a kiss. Maybe all the talk of happily-ever-after is catching up with me, or maybe my heart is still pounding over almost discovering my match, but I have a sudden and intense need to feel close to him, not just emotionally, but physically. It starts soft and sweet, but after mere seconds, a fire burns bright and I can't get enough. I want him, all of him, wrapped around me so tight that I'll never lose him, no matter what we're destined for.

When we come up for air, he looks down at me, dark green eyes questioning behind his frames. My head is filled with his static, the ambiguity of my magic. I shake it away as he asks, "What was that for?"

"Just . . . I love you." I cup his face with my hands, running my thumbs over his cheeks. How can someone be this cute, this good? "Plus you're pretty kissable."

He smiles, leaning into my palm. "You're not so bad yourself." I rest against his chest, head swirling with questions. What is the deal with Jane? Why did those fairies whisk her away?

Even if we find her, will a kid be able to help me? Did she see Charlie in my eyes? I have to know.

MarshmElla's greets us with a warm, sweet-scented hug. I always feel so proud bringing new people here, like, "I just changed your life. You're welcome." I shepherd everyone to a booth like an unofficial hostess and run into the back room to find Ella, the goddess herself, with flecks of lemon rind clinging to her blond bangs. She's been on a real citrus kick this summer—orange marmalade cupcakes, key lime pie, grapefruit tartlets with a honey crust—and is currently whipping up an impressive batch of lemon-lime thumbprint cookies. Seemingly hundreds of little shortbread circles dot the countertop, each with a healthy dollop of fruit filling and white icing curved in a whimsical daisy design. Even though we just walked in from the June heat, it smells even more like summer in here. Sometimes I think this woman dreams in desserts, which is exactly why I love her so.

"How is the summer of citrus going?" I ask, using all my willpower not to grab a handful of cookies and shove them all in my mouth.

Ella's head pops up, startled. "Amber!" she yelps, squeezing a stream of frosting into the air. "You scared me!"

"Sorry! I should've warned you somehow. I know how in the zone you get with your piping bag."

She wipes her hands on her apron, taking a deep breath. "It's good to see you, though. Congrats on graduation!"

"Thanks." My fingers inch closer to the cookies, and Ella laughs.

"Oh, just take one already. I know you're probably dying from temptation." I'm already chewing before the words finish leaving her lips, the tart but sweet flavors mixing on my tongue.

"Soooo good," I sigh. She smiles with pride. "Hey, I brought you some customers and guess what—one of them is a fairy!"

Ella's brow furrows. "Are you for real?"

"Have I ever lied to you?"

Ella looks off dreamily. "Wow, I don't believe I've met a fairy yet."

"And," I continue, chomping on another treat, "her little cousin is another me!"

"Huh?"

"A matchmaker! It's, like, a whole crazy thing; I don't know what's going on. Feel free to eavesdrop!"

She picks up the piping bag, chuckling. "I'll be out in a second."

I head back into the dining area, where my friends are all oohing and aahing over Rose like she's a mythological creature. And to be honest, I'm probably making the same face. Not really about Rose—I've interacted with fairies plenty at the shop—but thinking about Jane. I'm hypnotized by the reality that I've met another matchmaker. Has she experienced a similar journey as me? She's so young, and even though she's channeled her energy into a successful platform, there's no way she has the full grasp of her magic yet. Having this fake Madame L'Amour character as the face of her show leads me to believe there's been at least some drama along the way. . . . Is she beloved by those around her? Reviled? How have the people she's actually matched in real life taken her news? Good Gods, there is so much I want to ask her, but we'll have to find her first.

"Amber, hurry up and get over here!" Amani demands, waving me down. "Rose is waiting to spill all her secrets."

"Sorry, sorry, I was just alerting Ella to bring out the good stuff, sheesh."

"You smell like lemons. And vanilla. And sunshine," Charlie says as I scoot in next to him. "Have you already been eating treats?"

"Shh. You know nothing, Charlie Blitzman."

Kim is gushing, spilling out the kind of girl talk I could never pull off. "Rose, let me just say, I am a big fan of *Matchmaking Magic!* and I love, love, love that you're a"—she lowers her squeal—"fairy! How completely amazing!"

"Seriously, that's so cool!" Charlie exclaims. He can always be counted on to go full fanboy for anything magical. "Can we see your wings?"

I give him a small punch on the arm. "Charlie, oh my Gods, you can't just ask someone to show you her wings!"

"Sorry, I didn't know." He grimaces. "It just seems so badass."

"Oh, well, thanks." Rose brushes off the compliments, a permanent scowl on her pierced lips. She sits hunched in the booth, constantly pulling at the back of her unseasonably warm leather jacket. I have never been one to obsess about my appearance too much (my neuroses lie elsewhere), so I can't imagine what it must feel like to be pressured to disguise part of your body under fabric. As I watch her wince in discomfort, I think about what it'd be like to keep my arms strapped down under my shirt and how terrible that would be.

"So tell us more about yourself, new friend," I say, hoping a conversation will help take her mind off her wing troubles. "Like, why are you playing a matchmaker online?"

Rose chews at the inside of her mouth. "Well, I don't know how matchmaking has been for you, Amber, but it hasn't been easy for Jane."

Amani jumps in before I can. "Oh, Amber's life has kind of been a nightmare. Bullying, shunned by the magical community, little to no respect for her talents—did I miss anything?"

"Gee, pal, I think you covered it all," I deadpan to her laughter.

But Rose looks up with a solemn expression. "I'm sorry to hear that, though selfishly I will admit it's comforting. My family has never understood what Jane does. Most of the time, they look at her like she's a mistake." Chipped, black-polished nails run over the shaven sides of her head. "Even though everyone in my family is a fairy," she continues, "Jane was born without wings. So she's . . . not. And that's made life hard for her. Our hometown is small—smaller than small—consisting only of other fairies who work on our farm. Without wings, Jane can't contribute to our way of life, and her magic is very confusing for everyone else. After she tried breaking up some pretty prominent couples in the community because they weren't matches, her parents made her shut it down completely, forbidding her to use her talent."

The four of us sit back, unsure of how to respond. I know that experience; I've walked in Jane's shoes. Trying to break up couples because I thought it was the right thing to do, only to be greeted with scorn. Never being able to explain how people would be happier if they just followed what I saw in my head. My heart is breaking as Ella brings over a heaping tray of dark chocolate–orange brownies with citrus sprinkles. I can't even bring myself to take one due to a sinking feeling in my stomach.

We're mistakes—magical mistakes. I thought it was just me, that my being a matchmaker was some kind of supernatural consolation prize for not measuring up to the Sands before me. Like, *Oh, we couldn't bring together the traits of your family tree, so here, now YOU can spend the rest of your life bringing people together! Fun, right?* It's either poetic or a sick joke. But I had no idea this was a trend, that the common denominator of undesirable magical mutations was matchmaking. With all the supernatural hookups that have occurred through generations, you'd think there'd be millions of matchmakers walking around, all cursed/blessed by the visions that trail us every single day, and yet this is the first time one has crossed my path. Thinking about Jane's sweet little face, it's like a sad upside-down mirror; two little freaks trying to find their way in this cruel world. Maybe I do need a brownie after all.

"I didn't mean to kill the vibe." Rose forces a nervous laugh. "Please, you guys, eat the treats. They smell amazing." No one moves, not even me, so she grabs the brownie on top, shoving a giant piece into her mouth. Her eyes almost roll back in her head as she mumbles, "Oh my Gods."

We follow suit, and she's not lying: Ella has outdone herself once again. I try to think of something helpful to say as I chew the chocolaty goodness, but all I can think of is "Sorry Jane's destiny sucks as hard as mine." And that doesn't exactly seem comforting.

"Anyway, it's not like she could stop matchmaking," Rose says between bites. "Parent approval or not, it's a part of her; it makes her happier than anything else. She wanted to share it, but she didn't want to bring any more embarrassment to our family. So she came to me for help. I'm already the black sheep since I left home to go to art school instead of staying in the family business, so there wasn't much to lose.

"We came up with the idea for the matchmaker show. It started really small; we'd film episodes on my phone, matching her stuffed animals and stuff. But Jane wanted to actually use her magic, so we started bringing on my friends as guests." Rose shakes her head, smiling for the first time. "I had no idea it'd become such a thing. The more views we got, the more Jane's confidence grew. It was awesome. Her parents had a trip coming up, so I offered to watch Jane, thinking it'd be a great time to show her another part of the world. I didn't think they'd lose their minds over it."

"So . . . *you're* the kidnapper?" I gargle through brownie, stray crumbs escaping my mouth.

"Technically, I guess. But whatever, it was worth it." She scowls once more. "Showing her around the city, seeing all these people show up for the taping . . . for the first time, she was truly flying. And I know that having a matchmaker friend in her life would be a turning point," Rose says to me. "Someone to share stories with, someone to make her feel less alone. I've done what I can, but, Amber, if you'd be willing—"

"Of course!" I jump in. "I would love to be Jane's pseudo Big Sister!" And I mean it, not just because Jane holds the secret to my own match and could possibly help me understand why I'm short-circuiting. Having a mentor was all I ever wanted growing up, and while I may not be the world's best role model, I'm betting I'm light-years ahead of anyone at her farm.

"That's great." Rose leans back, finally relaxing and ignoring her wings for the first time. "I'm sure Jane's back home by now, and you wouldn't have to go there or anything, just the occasional phone call or—"

She's cut off by Ivy, who comes in out of nowhere and just

makes herself comfortable at our booth. "Who's this?" she asks, nodding to Rose.

"Well, hello to you too," I say, suppressing an eye roll, but only because Ivy looks rough, even worse than the other day. With it being summer, you'd think a beauty queen blonde like Ivy would be taking advantage of all the extra sunlight, getting that coveted tan and those sun-kissed strands. But Ivy somehow looks even paler, taking a cue from Vincent's playbook. Wait, she couldn't have gone vamp, right? No (*Duh, me*), or else she couldn't have just strolled in here on a sunny afternoon. Still, she definitely needs more vitamin D. "You okay there, killer?"

"Fine, I guess." She shrugs. "Another day in paradise."

"I'm Rose, by the way," the fairy says, extending a hand, which Ivy leaves hanging.

"And I'm in need of banana pudding." She goes over to the counter, and Rose squirms in her seat, giving me a look like "You know this unfortunate person?"

I get jumpy around Ivy too, but this has to be a record for her inflicting discomfort upon others. "Well, that pleasant creature is Ivy Chamberlain. She's our friend, kind of. Honestly, not sure where we stand on that."

"She seems . . . lovely."

I nod. "She *was* the worst person on earth, until she gave up her siren powers to save her sister from a wicked witch. Now she's just kind of . . . adrift."

Rose scrunches up her pierced nose, frowning. "An ex-siren? Is that even possible?"

"Well, Ivy is one in a million."

The fairy takes another bite of brownie, dark purple brows pinching in thought. "Actually, now that I think about it, I seem to remember someone coming by our farm once, looking for a way to get siren powers back."

And of course, since my life is nothing but a series of unfortunately timed events, that's the exact moment Ivy sits back down with her treat. "I'm sorry," she says with a creepfest smile. "Did you say something about getting siren powers back?"

Everything feels like it's moving in hyperspeed to an ending I didn't even know was a possibility, yet I'm suspended in molasses, unable to stop whatever's coming.

Rose has no idea what she's stepping into as she says, "I mean, yeah. Fairy dust will cure anything."

Anything? I exchange a hopeful look with Amani.

Even broken matchmakers?

Seven

"COME ON," IVY SCOWLS, WAVING AWAY ROSE'S REVELATION. "FAIRY dust isn't real. It's just some childish, storybook MacGuffin."

Rose crosses her arms, tossing back equal sass. "You want to tell a fairy that fairy dust isn't real?"

Ivy cackles. "You're a fairy?" She gives Rose a judgmental once-over. "Yeah, sure."

"She's not lying," I shoot back, feeling defensive for my new friend. Ivy rolls her eyes, shaking her head. "Besides, fairy dust is real."

"Really?" Kim's eyes glow with wonder, as do Charlie's.

"Yeah, but it's dangerous, or it must be, since my mom won't stock it anymore," I say.

Rose nods. "It's true. It's been known to—" But before

she can finish, her phone starts going nuts, lighting up with a furious feed of messages. She excuses herself to take a quick call in a separate corner of the store, then returns in a huff to grab her bag. "Sorry to be dramatic, but I have to run. Apparently Jane's parents talked to mine, and everything is blowing up at the farm." She heaves the heavy sigh of someone who has dealt with unnecessary drama for years. "It was nice meeting you all. Amber, we'll talk soon?"

Ivy swings around, eyes blazing. "Wait, you can't just drop that information and leave!"

I wave Rose away. "It's fine. I'll handle this mess; you handle yours."

The fairy dashes for the door as Ivy looks at me like I've just committed one of the seven deadly sins. "How could you let her go?"

"Calm down, it's fine. She's not dropping off the face of the earth, we'll see her again and—"

"But when?" There's a hunger in Ivy's eyes that has nothing to do with the treats surrounding us. The mere suggestion of a siren cure has her all riled up, and I'm honestly surprised she isn't standing on the table, demanding we continue the discussion on restoring her powers. Even the possibility of her regaining siren strength doesn't sit well with me; I can't forget how she tortured me for years, threw herself at my boyfriend just for spite, and abused magic in the stupidest ways possible, AND YET—what she did for her sister was truly noble; few mystically inclined creatures would be willing to completely give up their gifts like that.

"Soon, okay?" I try to reassure her. "I'm not gonna let Rose slip away; I need to stay in touch with her just as much as you do."

Ivy mumbles something to herself, slouching down in the booth.

"Well, I don't know about you all, but man, this sure has been a day!" Charlie says, loosening his tie.

"Yeah, there's no way I could've predicted any of this," Amani adds.

"And poor Jane! She seems so sweet and has had it so rough," Kim sympathizes.

"Yeah . . ." Being trapped in an environment where no one understands you is certainly not great and something I know all too well. But whereas my turf was the shop and all of Chicago, Jane's been swirling around the same little fishpond her whole life, having to stare at the faces she either matched or set a match to, day in and day out. To hear Rose tell it, Jane's parents tried to make her stop matchmaking altogether, not unlike how Amani's folks wanted to snuff out her fortune-telling. Because they didn't understand it, because it was different from what they knew. Even if I struggled when I was very young (and boy, did I struggle), my mom didn't take a hacksaw to my self-esteem just because I wasn't a witch. She may not have been #TeamMatchmaker4Life, but she didn't throw me down a well of shame either. Suddenly, my mom and her coven friends look like total saints.

And if thinking about all the therapy that little girl will need isn't enough, that nugget Rose dropped about fairy dust being a crazy deus ex machina has my head spinning. Could this be the answer I've been looking for? Sprinkle a little golden sparkle on myself and make my visions crystal clear? It sounds a lot nicer than working with Roscoe and his collection of magical nightmares, though if this is really true, I wonder why Mom never suggested it, seeing as how I know for sure that we used to sell it at Windy City Magic. It requires more research, so I guess I better put on my Giles tweed and head to my favorite supernatural library: the Sand-family grimoire collection.

Later that evening, I'm lying on the floor of Mom's office, piles of pillows under piles of books. I've lit every candle in the room, because supernatural snooping just seems more magical under candlelight, you know? I also have a bowl of hand-dipped chocolate-covered cherries, since I need to get in my fruit quota for the day.

I will never grow tired of looking through these grimoires. Even if their witchy stories and secrets don't necessarily pertain to me, I love the delicate parchment pages, and the inky drawings and loopy handwriting they hold. These tactile truths make me feel connected to something bigger than myself, and I like being part of the narrative, no matter how peripherally. Maybe someday I'll pass down my recipe book to a bright-eyed kiddo who will look at it with the same kind of wonder.

Mom sits on a rocker in the corner, hair braided into a high bun, a few gray strands cascading down her temples as she pores over the book in her lap. I told her all about Rose and how Ivy was practically foaming at the mouth to get her hands on some fairy medicine, figuring I'd slowly lead up to how I was drooling too.

"I will say that, of all the magical creatures, sirens are the most evasive," Mom huffs. "Because of the power they wield, most won't even reveal their heritage, and when they do, they are stingy with the details."

"I guess that makes sense. I mean, it'd be pretty scandalous if a world leader came out and said, 'Ha-ha! I tricked you all into putting me into a position of power! Suck it!'"

"Amber, don't say 'suck it,'" Mom sighs.

"Sorry."

"But yes, that's the general idea."

Which could be why I haven't found anything pertaining to sirens here, though to be fair, my witchy ancestors spent 99 percent of the time writing about themselves, seeing as how these are their diaries. There's the occasional spell mentioning banishing trolls or how to successfully replicate a vampire's agelessness, but nothing about sirens. Not to mention that sirens and witches have some sort of weird rivalry, made even more apparent by that creepo nix who terrorized Iris earlier in the year. I can still picture him, sitting in a pile of trash and resentment, going on and on about how all witches are the worst. Yuck.

After a few more minutes of unproductive page flipping, I ask, "Mom, do you think Ivy is okay without her magic? She seems . . . not herself."

Her forehead crinkles. "I can't definitively say. You know as well as I do how integral our magic is to us. It's a part of us, as essential as the blood in our veins. Think of Amani when she suppressed her precognition compared to now; she's living a fuller, more honest life, opening her eyes and heart to people and things like never before.

"And then there's Bob, who's had such a difficult rehabilitation, or even myself; abusing magic takes so much out of you. It's all about balance. Ivy's now missing a key component of her essence. That cannot be easy. But is she okay? I'm not sure." Yet the way her eyes cloud over as she turns the pages of her grimoire makes me think she knows more than she's letting on.

"Mom, what are you not telling me?"

She closes her book, folding her hands on top. Could it be she may actually tell me on the first ask? "This fairy you met? I'm worried she may have given you all false hope. She's right that fairy dust opens up many magical doors, but it's extremely volatile and not a simple solution to any problem."

"Why?" I press.

"Fairy dust works on wishes. Hold it in your hand, ask for what you desire, and it will make it so. Only, not always in the way you'd expect. You have to be very specific with the way you word your wish. If there is even a sliver of ambiguity, the dust will settle in the wiggle room. A member of Dawning Day used fairy dust once to wish for longer hair—a silly request, seeing as how she could've brewed herself a potion, but she thought fairy hair would be shinier." Mom rolls her eyes. "She wasn't wrong, but the hair grew from every inch of her body, and no matter how often she cuts it, it keeps growing back thicker and stronger. Had she wished for longer hair *on the top of her head*, she may have been okay. But since she didn't add that detail, she's basically a woolly mammoth now and she never leaves her house."

I try not to laugh, picturing Cousin Itt attending a coven meeting. "Why didn't she just use more dust to reverse it?"

Mom has no patience for this foolishness. "Because then she'd get sucked into a vicious, never-ending cycle. Every wish comes with a price: a consequence of equal magnitude to the wish itself. It's impossible to know what the aftermath will be. Sometimes it's minor, but often, the fallout is atrocious. Years ago, I made the mistake of selling fairy dust to a few of our supernatural regulars. I never had it out on the shelves for tourists to purchase, but I thought those who requested it could handle the side effects. Unfortunately, I was wrong, and stopped offering after too many customers literally fell apart." She tries to blink away the memories of mutant clients. "I don't even keep it in my private stash anymore. The risk is not worth the wish."

"What happened to the Wookiee witch?" I ask. "What was her consequence?"

"Her teeth fell out," she reveals flatly, my stomach dropping. "One body part for another."

"Oh my Gods!" My tongue runs over my pearly whites, comforted by their slick presence. No teeth? Never eating chocolate-caramel-covered pretzels again? THE HORROR! "So basically, fairy dust is not an option?"

Mom rocks in her chair, debating if she should say more. "Well, if you can find a fairy willing to grant your wish, then the consequence is waived. They are the only ones who can harness its magic without worry. Since fairies are responsible for harvesting the dust, they've built up an immunity to any negative repercussions."

Talk about burying the lede! "But we know a fairy! I'm sure she'd want to help!"

Mom tilts her head at that perfect "Oh, child, if only you knew" angle. "Don't be so sure. Fairies are very private and don't like flaunting their magic. Most fairies I know are very hesitant about granting wishes. Other magical creatures have abused fairy dust for years, causing a lot of mistrust. Why do you think they always hide their wings?"

Stupid me: I always assumed it was to avoid questions from boring old humans. I think of poor Rose pulling at her jacket. I don't know her that well, and while she may tout a tough aesthetic, her efforts to help her cousin paint her in a philanthropic light. "Even if we couldn't find a fairy to help us, could the dust by itself restore Ivy's powers?"

Mom thinks for a second. "Yes, but again, it's not a guarantee. And the consequence could be way worse than losing her powers in the first place," she warns, her gaze disappearing to a seemingly scary place. "Amber . . . I don't want you getting any ideas, okay? Not for Ivy, and not for yourself. I know you're worried about your matchmaking, but I'm still doing research. Please don't do something you'll be sure to regret."

Great. Well, this has been illuminating in the worst possible way. I guess that means using fairy dust for myself is also out of the question, so I'll need to befriend Rose, which for a normal person wouldn't be too hard, but since I've only made about three friends my entire life, I have quite a challenge ahead of me. Insert exasperated sigh here.

My eyes are tired from reading about stewing frogs and cauldron restoration, so I kiss Mom on the cheek and head back to my room, where my phone is waiting with a stream of texts from Charlie.

Hey girl hey

Thinking bout u

WOMAN I MISS YOU WHERE ARE YOU

I snort. I think it's hilarious when he randomly drops "woman" like he's some tough guy and not a total teddy bear.

Sorry! I was researching whether fairy dust is the answer to everyone's prayers

FINALLY GEEZ

Jk hi

So what's the scoop

It could save us all while also destroying us

Oh. Cool?

Not really. Magic is so annoying

You know what?

What

I keep thinking about that kiss from earlier

What kiss

jk yes it was good

very good

I'd even upgrade to great

Same 😍

Can I take you on a fancy date plz?

Sure. Is cake involved?

Obvs

I love you

I love you too

Eight

CHARLIE'S NOT THE ONLY ONE BLOWING UP MY PHONE. IVY HAS BEEN texting me nonstop, saying that she needs to talk to me ASAP. I told her to meet me at Windy City Magic, but honestly, all this wilting-siren, closeted-matchmaker stuff is dragging me down. I know I started my summer by almost entering a black magic contract with a West Loop weirdo, but that was to alleviate my worries so I could enjoy my break in peace. All year I've been busting my butt, working three different jobs and solving these endless romantic mysteries (a genre I somehow invented), and I don't want to be anti, but I've kind of had enough? College and adult life is waiting for me in three short months, and what I really want to do is watch trash TV with my best friend and make out with my boyfriend without these ginormous magical struggles constantly weighing me down. . . . Is that so much to ask? I want everyone to be safe and happy, but I also want Amber to be happy, and I'm having trouble finding that balance.

Especially because thanks to *Matchmaking Magic!* the demand for all things love is hot, hot, hot, and I've been forced to reopen my matchmaking table, accuracy be damned. It seems like all of Chicago has been stung by the love bug, and with summer tourist season in full swing, the masses are headed straight for us.

Mom is thrilled by the extra business, and has been hard at work creating new love-themed charms, spells, and tokens for customers to add on to their matchmaking experience. She's set up a display to the right of my station with things like first-kiss mints (improves both your and your date's breath), shots of bravery (little vials that give you the courage to talk to your crush), and enchanted quill feathers (to help you write an epic love letter to that special someone). Normally, I would not approve of such obvious cash grabs, but all these magical items do work, so it's not like anyone is getting ripped off. I've had to cut back my barely existent hours at the Black Phoenix and MarshmElla's just to help meet demand. I have never, EVER been this popular, though I know it's my services the masses desire, not my sparkling personality. Which I've been told by more than one less-than-satisfied customer.

"I thought you would be, like, sweet or something?" says a college-age girl sitting across from me. Even though I just spent the past ten minutes mapping out her happily-ever-after, my delivery doesn't seem to meet her standards. "You're kind of grouchy for a person who talks about love all day."

I close my eyes, breathing in deeply through my nose. I've been matchmaking for about six hours straight, and I'm on the verge. "I'm sorry, I—"

"Madame L'Amour is always so bubbly." The girl beams. Ha, if she only knew the scowly, pierced fairy hiding under all that stage makeup. "I just love how upbeat and positive she is! Did you see the episode where she matched that eighty-year-old woman to her high school sweetheart? She's the one who inspired me to come here today."

"That's great," I say through gritted teeth. I didn't see the episode, but I try to think of little Jane envisioning that match, and her faraway happiness gives me a sliver of strength. "Bob, is her sketch complete?"

I look at my accomplice, Bob, who is putting the finishing touches on this girl's described match. He turns to me slowly, dark circles under his droopy eyes. A quick glance at his sketch pad proves this is not his best work. Though what he's drawn technically resembles a human male, I'm pretty sure I could've created a similar end result, and I can't draw for crap. He gives me a miserable smile as he shakes out his drawing hand. We've always offered sketches as an additional service, but now that *Matchmaking Magic!* has made renderings part of the expected package, they are more popular than ever. He's just as exhausted by all this as I am.

"Yes, Madame Sand," he moans (ugh, yes—apparently now

I have to be *Madame* Sand, a right that used to be reserved for established witches like my mom). I snatch it from his hand and pass it to my patron, wanting to be rid of her. All I want to do is go home, take off my pants, and drown myself in a vat of cookie dough. Don't get me wrong; I'm all for spreading love around the world, but I'm not even sure if that's what I'm doing. Every single session today has suffered by some kind of interference, whether it be visions that play on rewind, are rendered like pencil drawings, or cut out after seconds.

The girl leaves, terrible drawing in hand, and I survey the line behind her: five more to go. Mom's been good about cutting off the crowds before I stab someone, but this afternoon her judgment is off. I give her big homeless-kitten eyes as she walks past, but she just shakes her head before diving back into her own sea of customer demands. The worker bees of Windy City Magic look pretty dang pathetic, except for Kim; her post at the register is filled with sunshine and rainbows. How she can swipe credit cards all day long with the same sunny disposition is beyond me. We've never hired a non-magical employee before, but maybe her ability to stay positive after hours of retail servitude is her supernatural quirk.

She bounds over to me between patrons, passing me a granola bar. While not exactly a sumptuous dessert, it does have chocolate chips, and I appreciate the gesture.

"How's it going?" she asks, jangling the collection of witchy charms she wears on her arms while working.

"Besides wanting to hang up my Cupid's arrows forever, great!" I whine.

"Aww, you've had a lot of people to deal with today," Kim sympathizes. She pats my shoulder like I'm a sad puppy, which I am. "Any interesting matches, though?"

There's been so many pairs that it's hard to keep them straight. "Well, earlier this morning an elf man was matched with a giant woman—Giant with a capital G, mind you—and the visual of that combination always just makes me smile." *If it's even true,* I think to myself, since the vision played out like a Pixar animation.

"That does sound cute." She giggles. "Are people being nice?"

I give her a look.

"I guess not. Oh, Amber, I'm sorry. Don't let the haters get you down, okay? I need to get back to the register." She bounces away and I swear a trail of glitter is left in her wake. To think that this real-life unicorn was causing me such anguish for so long is boggling. Life is weird.

"Finding love is magic!" sings a group of girls waiting next in line. *"Open your heart and seeeeeee!"*

"That's it!" I yell, throwing my hands up in a mock table flip. "I'm taking a break."

"Thank the Gods," Bob says, shaking out his drawing hand as I'm pushing in my chair.

"I'll be back . . . when I'm back."

My remaining customers let out a collective groan as I exit the store, one muttering, "I bet Madame L'Amour never takes breaks," as I walk by. Whatever. If these people want their love lives delivered with a spoonful of sugar, then I need a second to collect myself.

Except I don't get that either, because just as I walk to the lake's edge, I spot Ivy, waiting for me (I presume), tangled hair fluttering over her sullen face. After seeing me, she wipes her cheeks to erase any evidence of crying and, with great effort, pulls herself to her feet. As I notice her baggy shorts, smudged from sitting on the ground, I'm taken aback by how thin her arms and legs are; I guess her voluminous graduation gown masked her practically skin-and-bones frame. It's weird, honestly, to see her like this, a despondent dragon fallen from grace. I bite my lip to keep from saying something stupid.

We stare at each other, my brain too full of mashed-up matches to think of what to say. I need sugar and I need it now.

"So, want to grab a drink or something?" I offer with caution. Even though she looks like a breeze could knock her over, part of me still thinks she's going to randomly scratch out my eyes. I've yet to let down my protective shield; old habits die hard.

"Sure." She shrugs, moving at the speed of snail toward a kiosk. We wander around the carnival area of the pier, watching tourists spin around on swings and the merry-go-round. Her steps are slow, deliberate, and even though we're moving at a turtle's pace, her breathing is pained, like she needs an inhaler. I'm probably the world's most out-of-shape person, but I could run circles around her right now. To be fair, it's crazy hot today, with the kind of humidity that makes you sweat so hard so fast, you wonder why you even bother showering in the morning. I have a strict "no shorts" policy, even if the temperature climbs into the triple digits, which means my jeans are currently adhered to my legs. I'm contemplating dumping my iced coffee over my head when Ivy asks, "Ever been up there?"

She point to the two-hundred-foot-high Ferris wheel that beckons Chicago travelers to the pier. It looms above us, turning ever so slowly, the sun radiating off its silver spires. "Good Gods no," I say. "Have you?"

"Yeah."

Interesting. I automatically reject all things Pier. "It's so . . . touristy."

"But the gondolas are air-conditioned."

"Good point. Let's go."

As we wait in the horrendously long line, we play a fun game called Let's Not Make Eye Contact Ever! The rules are simple: stand in awkward silence for as long as possible with a person you have passionately disliked for years! For someone who has been begging me to talk to her, she's suddenly out of words, and I don't know the steps for getting a former enemy to open up. Neither of us are the talk-about-boys-over-mani-pedis type, nor the toast-marshmallows-and-tell-your-deepest-secret set (although I'm always down for s'mores). It's not like I'm Kim or Amani, who can flawlessly flow into the girl thing and cuddle up to someone in need. I'd like to know why Ivy missed so much school and what's happening to her, but short of shoving a truth serum down her throat, I'm out of ideas. All I can think to ask is "What is wrong with you?" but that doesn't feel like the right thing to say, now or ever.

Finally it's our turn to take a spin in the sky, and we're ushered into our gondola, completely encased in glass, even the bottom, which is in no way terrifying. Slowly we rise, higher and higher, over the rainbow-colored boats dotting the lake, getting an unbelievable view of the city streets and buildings curving against the water. From the south, the Shedd Aquarium waves; from the north, high-rises melt into three-story walkups. Sunlight floods the gondola as the pod sways gently in the Chicago wind, not at all disturbing my stomach or sense of well-being. The farther we climb, the more I dig my claws into my seat. I don't think I've ever dangled this high up in the air, and I'm not a fan of the sensation. We make our way around the giant circle, pausing at the top. I forbid my eyes from looking down, an order that they immediately disobey. *Gulp.*

Maybe Ivy is experiencing a similar adverse reaction to heights, as she's not as transfixed by the view as I thought she'd be. I'm about to make a stupid joke just to hear myself talk when Ivy says, "Have you ever heard the story of Gwendolyn the Greedy?"

"I can't say that I have." Random, but I'll go with it.

"Gwendolyn was a siren back in Renaissance times or something," Ivy starts, once-upon-a-time–style. "She rocked the whole Greek-goddess look: gauzy white gowns, blond waves down to her ankles, curves for days, that whole thing. Any guy who crossed her path instantly fell in love with her, and she loved the attention. She fed off it, and soon it wasn't enough for her to simply be loved, she wanted to be craved. Coveted. Pursued with such passion that men would literally die for her.

"So that was her goal. She started using her siren powers to drive her suitors mad with lust, gaining not only their hearts but their blood. Men fought to the death over her, and no matter the outcome, she was always the victor. This went on for quite some time, until one day when a man who had previously pledged his eternal soul to Gwendolyn left her side without explanation or warning. Others followed, until this once-desirable diva found herself all alone. No one would love her or even look her way. She went from town to town, sirening men to fall at her feet, but none would succumb to her spell. Unbeknownst to her, she'd used up all her powers and could no longer control another being for her own personal gain."

Ivy pauses, stopping to catch her breath. Her washed-out features appear even more pasty next to the vibrant blue of the lake. "Gwendolyn did not take this well. On top of falling into depression, her body started literally falling apart, losing all its strength and color. Without her magic, she turned into a zombie version of herself, until she was nothing but a pile of bones." Ivy looks to the sky, quickly blinking back the tears building in her faded eyes. "I always thought it was some BS fairy-tale crap my parents used to keep me and Iris in line, you know? Right up there with warnings to eat our vegetables and not stare into the sun. *Use your powers wisely, girls. Don't end up like Gwendolyn.* Well, as it turns out, this bedtime story was real and now I'm dying."

Wait . . . what? Did she really just say she's . . . dying? My heart skips a beat. I was worried about her post-siren state before, but I figured the dimming of her personality and appearance was mostly about her missing Iris or adjusting to her lack of power. I never thought her life was in danger. I struggle to find a reply. "Ivy . . . I'm so . . ."

"Don't apologize, I deserve this." She gestures to her ane-mic frame, picking up the ragged split ends of her once-lustrous locks. "That's why I missed so much school. My parents have been dragging me to every shaman and witch doctor across the globe, trying to figure out if I can be saved. Turns out that there's not a lot of sympathy for a stupid siren who used up all her magic, and most have laughed us away." Shoulders and ankles shaking ever so slightly, she wraps her bony arms around herself. "I'm running out of time, and we have no leads. My parents are currently running through some Brazilian rain forest looking for some kind of rare flower with magic pollen, if you can believe it." She chokes on a sad laugh. "When your friend brought up fairy dust, I had one last glimmer of hope. But then she left, and now it feels too late."

The Ferris wheel starts to move again, and I scoot over next to her as our gondola begins gliding downward. As we dangle in silence, the details of her story churn inside me, stirring up a feeling of dread. I'd be lying if I said I'd never daydreamed about Ivy disappearing forever, mostly during school when she went out of her way to bully and berate me, all because she thought my brand of magic was less than. But I never wanted her dead, just gone. I may not be a siren anthropologist, but I've never heard of this, ever—not for any supernatural creature. Magic is a part of us, sure, but more like a force that shapes who we are as people: the way we see the world and how we live our lives. Our talents are integral to our being, but they're not our lifeblood . . . unless . . . I'm understanding it wrong. Could it be that magic is more, an essence as crucial as air?

Though I've complained about my abilities more than once, it would be awful if they disappeared. Matchmaking has shaped me—for better or worse—and without it, I'm not sure where I'd be. How would I feel about love? Destiny? Fate? It's possible that I'd barely care at all; that's not the Amber I want to be. And that's nothing compared to what Ivy has relinquished; having the world no longer bend to your whim seems like a hard thing to get over, but now her life is on the line. I carefully pat Ivy's shoulder to let her know I'm here just as a terrifying and (admittedly) selfish thought crosses my mind: if my matchmaking problems are a sign I'm reaching the bottom of my well, what does that mean for me in the long term? I've viewed this issue as a total inconvenience, but what if it's deeper than that? What if this breakdown means a core part of my being is near extinction?

She turns to me, not as the vicious siren who could cut you with a glance but as a girl looking for a hand to hold. I can't think of a single thing to say.

"Anyway," she says with a shrug that's much too casual considering our conversation. "Sorry to dump all this on you. But hey, maybe you won't have to deal with me much longer, huh?"

"Gods, don't even talk like that," I snap. "Rose may have left, but she's not gone. We can go to her farm, and—"

Ivy looks at me like the trip would be more effort than it's worth. "I don't know, Amber. I'm so tired. I've been crisscrossing this stupid planet for months looking for hope, only to be served dead ends. I can't get my hopes up again."

There's too much on the line for her to say no. Maybe we can't use the dust ourselves, but there's no way Rose would refuse making a wish for someone if it's a matter of life and death, right? I frown at her with a *tsk tsk*. "The Ivy I know would not admit defeat so easily."

"Yeah, well, the Ivy you know is shriveling into the disgusting hell beast she was meant to be." Her head hangs heavy over her knees.

But I won't let her throw in the towel so easily. "Aww, Ivy, you've always been a hell beast in my eyes."

With just a hint of her former sparkle, she gives me a familiar death stare, accompanied by a sliver of a smile. "You really are the worst, you know that?" she says with some of her usual sass.

"I sure do!" I cheer, as our gondola finally reaches the ground. "Now, GET UP. We're going on a road trip."

Nine

WHAT DOES ONE PACK FOR A FAIRY-FARM ROAD TRIP? TO BE HONEST, the closest I've ever come to farm life was when Navy Pier held a disastrous petting zoo that resulted in a permanent policy banning animals from the premises. I'm definitely one of those Chicagoans who feels leaving the city limits is a huge inconvenience, so I'm not exactly a country girl. My knowledge of farms comes from pop culture stereotypes—meaning I know nothing at all. But meeting the Wisterias and learning about fairy dust has put an interesting spin on my previous understanding of fairies themselves.

Before seeing Papa and Mama Wisteria full of fire and fury, I couldn't even picture a fairy raising their voice, let alone creating a hostile home life. The brief encounters I've had with other fairies have always been chill, harmonious; I fully believe the fairy community is responsible for getting the general population to recycle, compost, use rain barrels, and all that jazz. But what do I know?

Maybe all that fairy dust has jacked up their brains. Gods know if I could sprinkle sparkles over all my problems and make them disappear, I would abuse the heck out of that. Though that "unforeseen yet comparable consequence" thing would definitely put a damper on things. Would I be willing to wish my matchmaker powers back to normal if it meant my sense of taste or something would be destroyed? Even the threat of not being able to experience baking flavors is enough to scare me away from that option forever. Ivy's on board to go full dust, though at this point, she doesn't have much to lose.

"Mom, do we have any more powdered sugar?" I'm packing up only the essentials for this road trip, meaning snacks. I mean, sure, I have a toothbrush and underwear in my bag, but Jane's family's farm is in Champaign, Illinois—about a two-hour drive. That means I need a healthy stash of portable treats, and by "healthy," I mean "plentiful," not "of nutritional value." I'm getting picked up any minute, but I need to put the finishing touches on this peanut butter puppy chow.

"How should I know?" Mom says from the kitchen table, where she's carefully cutting some periwinkle root for a memory potion. The demand for love-themed spells is still going strong, but she's also keeping regular inventory well stocked.

"I figured your witchy brain just magically knew the entire contents of our cabinets at all times."

Without looking up, she says, "Check behind the granola," and lo and behold, a fresh bag of powdered sugar awaits.

"See?! I knew it." Mom chuckles to herself as I dump my sticky cereal mix into a Ziploc bag and start shaking it up. In addition to this mix, I've also whipped up s'mores popcorn balls and dark chocolate trail-mix cookies, a few of which have wasabi almonds especially for Amani, who has graciously agreed to accompany me on this fairyland adventure so I don't accidentally smother Ivy or make matters worse for Jane. I mean, her parents apparently hate matchmakers, so what could possibly go wrong?

"How is Ivy handling all this?" Mom asks.

I let out a long exhale. "I mean, she's not great. She's looking at this like it's her last hope. We'll see what happens." I'm certainly not going to stand in the way of her mystilogical health, even if there could be an equally terrible side effect waiting for her. If she does get her siren powers back and becomes awful again, well, I won't understand the Fates ever.

Mom crosses the room, putting her hands on my shoulders. "I want to make something very clear: Ivy is taking a big risk here. Her situation is much different than yours. . . ." Worry creeps into the corners of her eyes. "I don't want you to get any ideas about what fairy dust could do for you. I know you've been struggling with your magic, but trust me: stay away from fairy dust." She squeezes me harder. "We'll find a different solution for you, somehow."

"Okay, okay!" I squirm, trying to get back to my snack prep. "I wasn't even thinking about using dust for myself." Okay, that's a lie, but I'm 87 percent sure I wouldn't use it, unless Rose or another friendly fairy decides she wants to help a girl out with her wish.

Parental warning properly applied, Mom sits back down and returns to her spell making. "So, you're sure the boys aren't joining you on this little road trip?" she asks, a hint of suspicion curling her lips.

"You know, actually, yes, you caught me. This whole fairy matchmaker story was all a ruse to have a giant boy slumber party in the heart of Illinois."

She sets down her knife slowly, which is somehow just as menacing as her holding it.

"I'm kidding!" I laugh. "Obviously, there will not be any members of the male species involved. Except for any boy fairies that live there, of course. It's just going to be quick: we go, say hello, save Ivy's life, give Jane emotional support, the end."

Mom gives me serious "I don't believe you" eyes but moves on anyway. "You've never gone on an overnight trip like this before."

"That you know of," I snort. She rolls her eyes. "Sorry, kidding again." For better or worse, we really have been two weird little peas in a magical pod for most of my life. Despite my struggles with being witch-adjacent, I've never really ventured too far from the nest, never sneaking out of the house or fighting furiously for later curfew. When you only have one friend and she's Mom-approved, there's no social-life drama. When I start at the Culinary Institute this fall, I'll still be living at home, so this excursion is really our first glimpse of post–high school independence or whatever.

"I want you to be safe," she says.

"I'll buckle my seat belt and look both ways before crossing."

"I mean with the magic."

"I will. For real." I cross my heart with my fingers for dramatic effect. "Besides, all Ivy really needs from me is a foot in the door. She is determined to see this through. We'll see what happens."

Mom frowns. "You haven't been great at keeping out of other people's magical business of late."

"That's true. When I was a lovable loser with only one friend, life was way less interesting."

"I don't expect you to have any trouble with the fairies." She cradles my face in her hands, stroking my cheek with her thumb, a gesture I can't ever remember her making, even when I was little. Not sure if she's more riled up by the dust or the idea of me going out into the world by myself, but either way, she holds me like I'm a fragile keepsake on the verge of shattering. "Just promise you'll stay away from the dust," she warns.

"My precious," I croak in my best Gollum voice.

"Amber!"

"I promise!"

"And no boys?" She raises an accusatory eyebrow. "You are eighteen now. . . ."

Ugh, gross. I don't even want to go where she's venturing. "Geez, Mom—no boys, no fairy dust . . . you're really cramping my style."

Our apartment buzzer rings, and I dash over to answer the intercom.

"We're heeeeeerrreeeeee," Amani's voice singsongs through our living room.

"Be right down!" I call back. Bags gathered, treats assembled, I give Mom what I hope is a reassuring kiss and trudge down three flights of stairs to kick off my first-ever parent-free road trip. Bless Amani for being the beautiful angel she is and agreeing to tag along on this special adventure.

"I call shotgun," I shout, dragging my stuff to the curb.

"Well, duh." Amani smiles, long dark hair pulled up in a bouncy ponytail. "I don't think you'd want to be in the back with Miss Havisham there." I peer through the rear window to see Ivy, bundled under a crocheted blanket, eyes closed.

"What is happening?" I ask. "It's like a hundred degrees out here. How is she not suffocating?"

"I don't know, but she looks . . . not great." Amani winces. "Remember when we used to wish her hair would turn into snakes?" Of course I do; it was my favorite visual for when she was torturing us, imagining a head of squiggling serpents screeching along with her. "I feel like she's actually shedding skin. It's scary."

We cannot get her that dust fast enough. "Cool, that sounds awesome to sit next to for . . . How long is this drive?"

"Three hours? Ish?"

I look at my baggie of puppy chow. "Sugar, give me strength."

"Gods-speed."

Climbing into the Sharma family minivan, I'm assaulted with the lingering smell of her five younger brothers—a mix of sweat, mud, and sour-cream-and-onion chips—as my sandal crunches into some stale popcorn on the floor.

"You would be the world's worst cabdriver," I snark. "This car is disgusting!"

"Whatever." Amani rolls her eyes. "At least it'll get us there. And there's nothing like riding in a swagger wagon!"

"I cannot believe you just said that."

"I did, and it was awesome."

I pull up the directions Rose texted me when I alerted her to our impromptu visit. Unsurprisingly, a fairy farm isn't something you can look up on Google Maps. She sent over a set of coordinates we entered in our GPS, along with a list of random "turn at the scarecrow" details that I'm sure will make more sense when we get closer. I turn to the back seat, offering Ivy some of my trail-mix cookies, but she groans in dissent, choosing to bury herself away. Wow. If she doesn't want my cookies, things are worse than I thought.

Amani starts the car and I sink down in my seat, taking a few bites of treats as my view transforms from tightly packed walk-ups to sprawling suburbs butting against the open expressway.

I hardly ever leave the city, so watching the terrain shift from urban cluster to sprawling land is mesmerizing. Once the remaining bits of Chicagoland are in our rearview, the road opens up to farmland for as far as the eye can see. Acre after acre of cornstalks and soybean sprouts, with giant tractors and picturesque red barns dotting the horizon. I'm always surrounded by people and concrete: taxis blaring their horns, crowds pushing and shoving to where they need to go. What's it like to have all this space, to not have smelly strangers breathing down your neck or spilling coffee on you as you walk? My apartment has like five feet of outdoor space on our back porch, but it overlooks a cement lot; everything out here is lush and green, open and free. I really must be a city mouse, because it's blowing me away.

"Ivy." I turn around and poke at our trip companion, who has yet to speak or move in over an hour. "Ivy, look at this."

She groans under her yarn cocoon and makes a half-hearted effort to swat me away.

"No, looooook." I pull the blanket off her head, and she ducks away from the window, hiding from the sudden influx of sunlight.

"God, what?!" she whines, struggling to open her eyes, like a mole finally burrowing out of her underground tunnels. "If you've woken me up to play the license plate game, I will gut you." At this point, I doubt she'd have the strength for physical violence, but I guess it's the thought that counts.

"We're in the country!" I cheer with a cheesy smile. "It's really pretty. . . . I thought you'd want to see."

She turns, slow as molasses, toward the glass, giving the rolling landscape about five seconds of attention before pulling her blanket back up. "Great."

"You're not psyched about corn and cows?" I feign surprise.

"Shockingly, no."

"But you must be pumped about possibly getting your powers back, right? So you can resume your terror across the land?" I say, hoping to lift her spirits, even a little.

Ivy runs a heavy tongue over chapped lips. "Because if anyone can help me, it's a matchmaker," she deadpans.

I try not to be offended, considering her physical state. "I mean, I'm trying to—"

"You know you've never even told me my match?" Ivy interrupts, gaze suddenly steely. "In all the time we've known each other."

Her comment catches me by surprise. "True, but you never really asked. When you were sirening it up, you looked pretty happy playing the field. Happily-ever-after wasn't really your focus, unless I'm totally wrong."

She waits for a long time before saying, "Yeah, well, the end never seemed so near."

"Don't say that."

"And besides, I'm not lovable. Oh, don't give me that look; we both know it. I'd pity anyone who gets stuck with me."

Her words hang in the air, circling 'round to the sounds of a soaring pop ballad before piercing my heart. I've never had anyone hope they don't have a match because of their own self-loathing. Even without looking into her eyes, I picture her match now—tall, quiet, peachy fuzz topping a gentle face—and in every vision I've had of them throughout the years, this guy has been nothing but caring and loving toward Ivy, offering calming companionship against a powerful presence. In a true opposites-attract pairing, he's destined to bring out the best in her, dulling her edges to a place where she can finally mellow.

It was always such a strange dichotomy for me—envisioning the future idyllic Ivy while dealing with present pain—but I still believed it. She drove me so crazy in school, I couldn't find a way to be the bigger person and give her the satisfaction of a happy ending. But she needs that now, and maybe sharing a glimpse into tomorrow will help her hold on today.

But I've taken too long to respond, and Ivy has disappeared back into her shell, letting her belief harden into her truth. Everyone deserves love—everyone—whether they believe it or not. Making someone accept it is a much different thing.

Ten

As we get closer to Fairy Family Fun Times, the mood in the car shifts toward somber. Amani's poptastic karaoke playlist gave way to an indie rock cryfest, and after we devoured all of my cookies and popcorn balls, all that remained was some sort of kale smoothie Ivy threatened us with that looks like the color of my nightmares. She's been emitting a sad, whimpering moan for the past thirty minutes or so, yet refuses to let us help her in any way. I'm trying to stay strong here, but I suddenly feel like we've been in the car forever and there's no escape.

"Not to sound like a toddler or anything," I whimper to no one in particular, "but are we there yet?" The magic of seeing farmland has faded, since it's all we've seen for hours now, and I'd really like this part of the journey to be over so we can get to the dusting. Sitting here, knowing Ivy is suffering yet unable to do anything, is torture.

Amani grabs my phone off the holder on the dash, big brown eyes squinting at the GPS pinpoint we're approaching. "It says we'll be there in five minutes, but"—she looks ahead of the steering wheel—"it doesn't look like there is any *there* to be had for miles."

"Ugghhh," I groan, slumping so far down in my seat I can barely see out the window. "I don't think I've ever been in a vehicle this long. I feel like my butt has fused with the uphol-stery."

"Tell me about it," Amani yawns. "My eyes are so tired, it feels like they're liquefying and running down my cheeks."

Now there's a visual. "How are you, Ivy?" She snorts like a warthog, which I guess means "Not great."

I turn back to Amani. "Sorry you had to do all the driving."

"Yeah, do you think you'll ever get your license?" she teases.

"Unlikely. Why learn to drive when there's the CTA?"

She nods. "Guess I'll be doing a lot of driving like this next year, though." Right, when she leaves the city to go to college hours and hours away from me. When I'll only get to see her sweet, beautiful face on holidays and breaks, instead of every single day. Amani is going to the University of Illinois, which is in the same town as this farm; I knew she was going to be far, but now, having experienced this drive, the distance squeezes my heart like an evil vise, turning the crank tighter with each additional mile. Chest constricting, I breathe through my pre-separation anxiety as best I can, remembering that we still have time before this painful divide begins. More than ever, I want to hurry and wrap up this mission, smoothing all the magical dirt that's been kicked up so I can be selfish and relish in the wonder that is my best friend for as long as possible.

Suddenly, there's a break in the stretch of farmland ahead. Out of nowhere, a forest rises above the surrounding corn, giant sequoias stretching to the sky above. It's jarring, for sure, to see nothing but flat acres for hours and then to drive up to mammoth trees packed into a tight radius. I didn't even think trees like this could grow in Illinois (not that I'm an arborist or anything), so if having a random forest sprout up like this isn't magic, I don't know what is.

With Rose's coordinates leading the way, we pull off on a dirt path between two rows of corn, tall stalks encroaching the car. After twisting and turning for a few minutes, we lose sight of the forest until it's right upon us, and we stop at the base of the biggest tree I've ever seen in my life. It has to be at least as wide as my apartment building yet four times as tall. Several gargantuan trees form a sort of barrier, though in the one straight ahead, I detect an arch-shaped carving with the words "Wisteria Farms" etched in a swirly font. With solid wood in front of us, and corn all around us, it appears we've hit a dead end.

"Um, what is happening?" Ivy croaks, peeking her head

into the front. Curious but tired eyes explore the space before us, a small glimmer of hope keeping her going. "This doesn't look right."

"Rose's text says: 'It'll look like you're in the wrong place.' See?" I flash her my phone screen, but she keeps staring outward. "Don't worry."

"Sure, why would I worry? We're just stuck in the middle of nowhere with no magic at all." Ah, Ivy. Never change.

A small, window-shaped section of the tree pops out, and a little man appears like he's a freaking Keebler Elf. He motions at us to come forward, and since we can't move the car any closer, we all pile out and walk over to his office space inside the tree.

"Is this weird?" I whisper to Amani. "It feels weird."

"What's weird about talking to a man living inside a tree in the middle of a farm that's completely off the map?"

"Right. Good point."

The man looks down at us from his perch, and I'm getting very strong *Wizard of Oz* gatekeeper vibes. If there is a horse in there that changes color, I am here for it. "Hello, travelers! I hope you haven't journeyed too far." He smiles warmly. "Sorry to be a bother, but we're actually not accepting visitors today. Harvest season keeps us very busy, after all!"

Amani stands tall, hands on her hips. "We were invited. By a Wisteria," she insists.

The guardian of the gate frowns, checking notes on his clipboard. "Hmm. According to my records, the Wisterias are not expecting any guests. I'm sorry, but I'll need to ask you to leave."

Taking a cue from my name-dropping boyfriend, I step forward and say, "We're here to see Jane, to help her with her"— I lower my voice—"matchmaking problem." I give him a knowing wink, effectively making me want to scrub my insides.

He leans out of his wooden window, all the color draining from his face. "Jane? Is she . . . getting the help she needs?"

"We sure hope so," I say, smiling warmly. "Can you please let us through?"

He hesitates, then reaches for the phone in his pocket. "I hope you know what you're doing," the guard warns, turning back toward his booth and hitting a buzzer. As his window shuts, a gateway carved into the sequoia before us slowly opens, and if you've never entered a fairyland via a magical wooden portal, well, you're missing out.

The farmland behind us melts away as a world that glows and shimmers beckons. We pass through the tree into an impossibly large open field surrounded by trees that form a leafy canopy. Near the top, countless rope bridges crisscross the sky, each leading to clusters of bright, rainbow-colored blossoms with glittery centers. Oven-sized petals curl back as twisting stamens burst all around, each spilling a steady stream of sparkle into large wooden barrels tied to the branches. There have to be hundreds of these flowers, each more remarkable than the next, and yet for every exploding bloom, there's a fairy in flight, iridescent wings dancing against the vibrant reds, greens, blues, and purples. It almost feels like there is glitter in the air, as everything from the dirt at our feet to the tiny cabins dotting the perimeter takes on an otherworldly sheen.

"This is amazing!" I exclaim, barely able to take it all in. "How does this exist?"

"It's like something out of a movie!" Amani twirls around, arms spread wide. "I've never seen anything so beautiful! These flowers . . . their sparkle . . . I'm dying!"

Even Ivy in her emo state looks around in wonder. "This is crazy," she mutters, still clutching her crocheted blanket like a cape. "What is this place?"

I shoot some texts to Rose letting her know we're here as we continue to roam around the compound. Although the patch of forest didn't seem terribly expansive from the outside, now that we're inside, the grounds don't appear to have an end. Like the contents of Mary Poppins's bag, Wisteria Farms just keeps going, revealing a small village of homes, storefronts, and community areas, including the most eco-driven patch of land I've ever seen, with a series of rain barrels and solar panels that work together in a singular quest to save the planet. Everything that's not colored green is rainbow bright, and there are so many turns and hidden corners tucked into the trees, it feels like it'd take days to uncover all the secrets hiding within. I quickly pull out my phone to snap a shot and send to Charlie:

If dragons do exist, I bet they live in fairy trees

Almost immediately, he texts back:

DO NOT PLAY WITH ME I WILL DRIVE THERE RIGHT NOW

I send back a kissy emoji, and return my attention to this new world around us. We continue to stroll over a crushed-limestone path, weaving through modest, moss-covered homes, each with signs displaying a family name and specialty like CARPENTER, SEAMSTRESS, and BUTCHER. A bakery sign catches my eye (of course), and I make a mental note to stop in later. Rose said this was her family's farm, but it's so much bigger: an entire fairy community snuggled away under a magical canopy of flora and fauna.

"This is all a little too hippie for me," Ivy groans, stomping beside me like a sleepy T. rex. Compared to the Technicolor all around us, she looks even more like a ghost. A crabby ghost, at that. "Everyone is smiling. And wearing so much hemp. Blech."

Before I can respond, a pack of fairy children flies by, chasing after a running target. She trips, curling herself into a protective ball once she hits the ground, shielding herself from the sticks and tiny rocks her airborne bullies drop on her from above. Even with sea-foam green hair covering her face, it's not hard to tell who they're picking on: it's Jane.

"And they all lived happily ever after!" one of the pint-sized terrorists taunts, too much glee on his smug little face. How anyone could want to hurt sweet Jane is a mystery to me, but this tiny tyrant sure seems to be enjoying himself.

"Hey!" I yell, sprinting over to their circle, Amani and Ivy in my wake. But before I can swoop in and save the day, a flash of lavender whisks by, sending the cruel cluster into a flurry. Most of the fairy pests fly away in panic, but Rose catches one of them by the wings, making him drop to the ground.

"You little creep!" Rose yells, admittedly terrifying in her fury. She sticks her pierced nose in his face, effectively evaporating his previous grin. "You think it's okay to pick on someone? Just because she's not like you? What is wrong with you?" The boy whimpers an apology, and she releases his wings in disgust, bending over to help her little cousin as the bully buzzes off.

"Are you two okay?" I ask, on the verge of tears myself. Rose and Jane look up at me, both faces brightening upon seeing me.

"You made it!" Rose smiles, truly happy at our arrival. Lavender wings perk up behind her as she helps Jane to her feet.

"Amber!" Jane cries, wrapping her tiny arms around my waist. "You're here! Rose told me you were coming, but I didn't believe it until now!"

I resist the urge to pet the top of her cute little head. "Yes! We meet again, my matchmaker sis!" At this, she beams, sunlight warming her freckles as she snuggles into me harder. I pick a few leaves out of her minty strands, wanting so badly to crush those pint-sized jerks. "What happened? Why were those kids after you?"

Keeping her cheeks buried in my stomach, she mumbles, "It was nothing."

"No, it was something," Rose corrects her, still flush with anger. "Those kids were in the wrong, Jane. I want you to remember that."

"Seriously, I don't know them at all, but I can tell they're terrible," I agree, squeezing her tighter. Jane doesn't respond, so I look to Rose, who is shaking her head.

"This is the kind of crap she has to put up with," she fumes. "This is why we do *Matchmaker Magic!*, to show her there is more to life than this."

I know how Jane feels. I've walked in her shoes. I vow, right then and there, to be her ally in whatever ways I can. "It'll be okay," I whisper. "Things will get better." Sad brown eyes look up at me.

"You promise?" she asks.

"I promise."

Rose runs her fingers through her fauxhawk, trying to shake off the confrontation. "What a terrible first impression of our farm!" She sighs. "Welcome, I guess?"

"It is incredibly beautiful here," Amani says, trying to help ease the tension.

"And isn't this where fairy dust comes from?" Ivy asks, not subtle at all.

The fairy nods. "I mean, it's not the only place. There are other farms. But see those flowers?" Rose points up, but really, how could you not see them? "They are called coruscents. Their pollen is the dust." I shake my head, feeling stupid. I guess when

I thought we were coming to her family's farm, there'd be, like, chickens or strawberries or some kind of market-worthy produce. I didn't realize fairy dust was their crop. "Coruscents grow about thirty feet up in the air, so only someone with wings can access them easily." Her face falls slightly, another example of how her little cousin doesn't fit in here.

Ivy trudges over to a barrel nearby, its glittery contents close to spilling over onto the ground. The dust casts a warm glow on her pale skin, and she leans in, eyes hungry. It's the most animated I've seen her all day, but before she can dive in, I pull her back.

"You shouldn't touch," I forbid in a whisper. "Let's see if we can get a fairy to make the wish first." I explained the whole "dusty consequences" thing in the car ride here, but while I know for sure Amani heard me, I'm not sure if Ivy listened to—or cared about—what I had to say.

"But I thought that's why you brought me here!" Ivy sneers in my direction. "To help me! Remember?"

"I know. But trust me, we have to take the proper steps."

She grunts, crossing her arms in frustration. The sooner we can help her the better, because I'm not sure how I'm supposed to divide my attention between babysitting an ex-siren and nurturing a young matchmaker.

"Jane," I say, turning back to my little pal. "Let me introduce you to my friends. You already know Amani"—my BFF gives a cheery wave—"and this is Ivy."

The two lock eyes, and after a few seconds, Jane gasps,

eyebrows meeting her minty hairline. She looks like she's just seen a ghost and not because of how pale Ivy is. But Ivy doesn't even notice.

"Hey," Ivy manages, before laying her security blanket out on the ground. "If we aren't doing this dust thing now, I'm just gonna lie down for a bit." Not waiting for approval, she sprawls out at our feet as Jane tugs on my shirt.

"Amber, what's wrong with her?" she whispers, light brown eyes full of worry. I wrap an arm around her shoulders, guiding her away from the slumbering siren.

"She's . . . not well," I say, unsure of what kind of details an eight-year-old can handle.

"Tell me everything you know about her."

Everything? Yikes. Is there a PG version of Ivy's existence? "What do you want to know?" I ask. "Is this about her match? I know you just saw him."

"Just . . . tell me," she pleads.

What can I say? "Well, she used up all her magic trying to save her sister, and now she's . . ."

"Sick?"

"Um, worse than sick . . ."

"Dying?!" Jane's hands fly up to her face. "No! She can't die!" While it's sweet that she's so concerned, her sudden intensity puzzles me.

"Seriously, Jane—what did you see when you looked at her?" I demand.

"I can help her," Jane responds, two moves ahead.

"Help her what?"

"Get her powers back. Get healthy again!"

Since Jane's relationship with her family seems iffy at best, I can't imagine she has much pull in granting magical wishes. "Why would you do that? You don't even know her." And if she did, I don't think she'd be making an offer like this.

"Helping her would . . . help me too." She bites her lip.

Okay, now I'm completely confused. "Because . . . ?"

Her face flushes underneath her freckles. "I have to help her. Ivy is my brother's match."

Eleven

THERE WAS A TIME WHEN THIS WOULD HAVE MADE ME LAUGH, WHEN just the thought of being matched with Ivy would seem like some sort of cosmic joke. Something I wouldn't wish on my worst enemy, which is . . . Ivy. Although that's not true anymore. My worst enemy is probably broccoli.

"I've been seeing Ivy my whole life," Jane says, sneaking a peek back at the sleeping former beauty behind her. "But seeing her now . . . she is not what I expected. In my visions she's fierce, tough; in person, I almost didn't recognize her until I saw my brother, Peter, in her eyes." Her face scrunches up, trying to reconcile the two different Ivy images. "I want him to be happy; she's gonna make him happy."

If I wasn't a matchmaker, I'd assume a siren like Ivy could

only really ever love herself. But I've had the visions, I've seen this boy of hers, and I know it's meant to be.

"Well, I am not one to stand in the way of true love," I tell Jane, who looks at me optimistically. "It's against the Matchmaker Code of Ethics, after all."

"There's a code of ethics?" she asks eagerly.

"Ha, I don't know. Sure? We can write them together."

"Thank you," she sighs. "I can't use the dust, but if I talk to Rose—" Her plotting is cut off by the arrival of a male fairy with bright orange wings, swooping down. I instantly recognize him as Peter, Jane's brother, and—holy crap—Ivy's match. He looks just like I've always envisioned, with short peachy hair and kind brown eyes, and looking at him now, I see Ivy echoed back to me, though the picture starts to swirl like batter in a mixer, twisting from the center and radiating out until I can barely make out the image. It doesn't matter; I know it's him. I geek out a little, instinctively looking over at Ivy to see if she's noticed her future beau, but she's still napping. Peter hasn't taken note of her either, focused entirely on greeting his little sister, but I'm hoping to spy the moment they spot each other for the first time. It's a magical thing, seeing two halves of a whole come together, and so rare to witness for the first time. I can count on one hand the number of couples I've personally introduced, and the results have varied from instant attraction to immediate repulsion (like with Amani and Vincent).

"Finally!" Rose exclaims, giving Peter a shove. "I texted you like ten minutes ago!"

"Sorry, I was dealing with a difficult coruscent that was sputtering dust everywhere," he says, brushing sparkly remnants off his overalls with thick gloves. "Is everything okay?"

"I handled it. Again." The two share a charged glance, Peter sheepishly turning back to Jane.

"I got here as quickly as I could. I'm sorry those kids were bothering you again," he says gently. She shrugs, trying to be brave for her big brother. "You know you're my favorite sister, right?"

"I'm your only sister," she says with a giggle.

"Then you win in a landslide!" He picks her up and twirls her around, wings spinning the pair a few inches off the ground. Jane squeals with laughter, all happiness and light, a changed girl when she lands. Peter takes notice of Amani, Ivy, and me for the first time, blushing over his lack of manners.

"Janey, you made some friends?" He smiles warmly.

"Yes!" She bounces on her heels. It's the first time I've seen her genuinely happy and I love it. "This is Amber—she's a matchmaker, like me!"

Peter breaks into a toothy grin. "Really? That's wonderful!" He removes his gloves to shake my hand, clasping my palm like a clamshell. "How exciting to meet another matchmaker!" Orange wings flap happily behind him, intricate swirls shining in the sunlight.

"Likewise!" I say in a high-pitched voice, unaccustomed to being greeted with such enthusiasm. "And this is my best friend, Amani, and our friend Ivy, who is . . . very tired from our trip." Peter takes a quick look at the sleeping girl beside us, but in all the excitement, I don't think her bundled-up form registers.

"Well, this is truly something!" Peter beams. "And you came all this way to visit Jane! You must be hungry. I was just going to grab something at Mama and Papa's. You should join me!"

Rose holds up a hand in protest. "Whoa, you think that's a good idea?"

"Why wouldn't it be?" He blinks in innocence.

"Peter, don't be dense. Did you not hear that Amber is a matchmaker?"

"Of course I did!"

Her jaw drops in a "Hello? What are you thinking?" expression that makes me feel super comfortable for whatever situation we're about to walk in on. "And you think they're just going to be fine with that?"

He considers this. "I think they'll be happy Jane has made some friends, especially considering what happened to her today."

Rose takes a quick flight around us, cursing under her breath. I wonder if, when fairies get mad at each other, their arguments escalate not only in intensity but distance aboveground. Do insults hurt more at higher altitudes? "Fine! Whatever," she concedes. She takes off, hovering above us to cool down, while Jane and Peter lead the way, hand in hand. I rustle Ivy as we head off to what I'm sure will be a very awkward meal.

I turn to Amani. "So, how are we feeling about things?"

"Not great." She shakes her head, long lashes blinking thoughtfully. "I mean, Peter seems psyched to have us here, but Rose's reaction makes me think his parents will be less so."

"What are the chances they agree to grant some wishes and we'll be on our way tonight?"

Amani snorts. "Something tells me it won't be that easy."

"It would be nice, for once, if something was."

"Yeah, but you're not that lucky."

"Hey!" I feign resentment.

"It's okay. Challenge builds character. Or something."

"I think I have enough character, thank you."

The Wisterias' cottage is at the end of the path, almost identical to the others we've passed, with large heads of hydrangea nearly engulfing the front door. As we pass through the entry, I realize the home is much like the farm itself: deceptively small from the outside, but surprisingly expansive within. Rose holds me back at the door.

"Just so you know, my aunt and uncle are not over Jane's trip to the city," she warns, stating the obvious.

"Yeah, I picked up on that."

"It'd be great if you could help me on the 'matchmaking is not a horrible life profession' campaign," she continues. "They don't listen to me, but even though they don't trust outsiders, maybe you can change their minds."

Gee, no pressure at all! But since I need her to like me, I flash her some pearly whites and find a seat, already self-editing in an attempt to present as pleasantly as possible. I comb through my choppy peacock hair with my fingers, smoothing it down as much as sweaty palms can, and retie my Converse, because I don't know what else to do.

Everything in the Wisteria living room is just a pinch smaller than common measurements. Not Tinker Bell–sized or anything (it's not like the house is made of acorns and mushroom caps), but enough to make my limbs feel out of proportion with my surroundings. The wicker coffee table sits lower than most; my butt is extra cozy in a compact armchair. Sunlight pours in from multiple windows, and we settle in as Peter disappears into the kitchen, where the familiar sounds of meal prep greet my ears.

"Amber, do you want to see my room?" Jane asks, full of excitement. Tiny fingers clutch the arm of my chair, begging me to come play.

"Totally," I answer. "Let's say hi to your parents first, though, okay?" I don't want them to think they have a random eighteen-year-old home intruder roaming the halls. She nods, pulling over a mini pink polka-dotted bean bag chair next to mine that must be her special seat. Just as she plops into the pouf, dishes clatter from the other room in a not-happy way. Amani shoots me a worried look as Rose's wings rise in defense, a woodland creature sensing danger.

Papa Wisteria enters the room, icy-blue brows stern. He leans on a wooden cane, taking in the bunch of misfits loitering in his living room, both hands clutching the walking device as if it might reveal what is going on here. Mama shuffles in behind him, carrying a tea tray across her plump body, as Peter peeks in over them, grimacing in the doorway. What the trio before us lacks in height, they make up in splendor, wings towering high above their frames. They all have Jane's same smattering of freckles down the bridge of their noses, each with hair in a different shade of sherbet.

Peter wiggles past them, unknowingly taking a seat next to his match, Ivy, and I hold my breath as the two exchange their first glance. Peter, with his peachy-orange fuzz and gawky, lanky frame, is the perfect male specimen for a meet-cute: he is just destined to fumble with his teacup, turn three shades of red, and get all flustered offering Ivy sugar. Normally, the ex-siren would have spotted him immediately, preening like a peacock and turning his boy brain to mush, but today, when he gives her a shy grin, she doesn't immediately pounce. Instead, Ivy self-consciously smiles back, tucking a lackluster curl behind a pink-tinged ear. I don't think I've ever seen Ivy do anything without total confidence before, so the bashful behavior is truly telling. They both look down at their feet, suppressing smiles, and it's so precious I want to scream. Jane looks up at me, smiling extra wide and bouncing slightly in her seat as we watch the two of them awkwardly squirm.

"This is so great," Jane whispers. I beam down at her, sharing the joy of our secret knowledge.

"I have to admit, they are pretty dang cute," I whisper back.

Mama sets down the tea tray, silently pouring herself a cup. It's not exactly the warmest welcome, but they didn't immediately chase us away with brooms or anything, so . . . good start?

"Uncle, I want you to meet—" Rose starts, but Papa Wisteria stoically holds out a palm to silence her. His expression gives no indication of his thoughts; he could just as easily throw us out for trespassing as pour us a cup of tea.

"Jane, are these your friends?" he asks. His cold treatment of Rose is as icy as his hair, but he seems open to his daughter's words, face softening as he looks at her.

"Yes, Papa." She stands up from her beanbag, hands clutched in front of her. "They came to visit me."

Papa glowers at us, as if he's using heat vision to determine the worthiness of our souls. I don't help the matter by twitching like a guilty perp, but the tension of it all is killing me. Obviously we're not fairies, and since I get the sense Jane doesn't leave the farm very often, there's only one place she could have met us. Does he recognize us from the *Matchmaking Magic!* set? That exchange happened so quickly, and their attention was solely on Jane, but it's not a huge intuitive leap.

"You met on your little . . . excursion, then?" he asks, throwing Rose additional shade. She grits her teeth, doing her best to stay calm. Starting an argument won't help anyone right now.

"Yes, they are good people," Jane continues, voice soft as a feather. "I'm really happy they're here."

Mama Wisteria pipes up. "That's so nice, dear, but—and I don't mean to be rude—aren't these girls a bit old to be your friends?" Pink curls bob as she sips her tea. I try not to take offense—it's not like I'm seconds from the grave or anything—but from a parent's perspective, I guess it would be weird if a teenager suddenly befriended your second-grade child.

Jane looks back at us, not bothered by the age gap. "I don't think so. We have a lot in common."

"Such as?" Mama asks hopefully. "Why don't you tell us more about our guests, sweetheart?"

"Of course, Mama." Jane beams. It's clear this poor little sprite has never invited friends over before, and she's relishing the moment. After witnessing how that pack of demon children treated her, I wonder if she's ever successfully made a fairy friend her own age. It saddens me that I think I know the answer. "This is Amani; she's a precog."

At this, the parents' wings stand straight at attention, heads snapping toward my bestie. "You can . . . see the future?" Jane's mom asks, worry in her throat.

"Um, sometimes," Amani tentatively responds, sensing the sudden shift in the room. "It's kind of unpredictable. My visions choose when to reveal themselves, not the other way around." A nervous grimace crosses her face as Mama and Papa exchange a suspicious glance. As magical powers go, Amani's are very tame:

cool, but not "you will crumble under my whim" or anything. As far as I know, none of her visions have altered the course of humanity. Being fearful of a precog is like getting worked up over a Magic 8 Ball: pretty pointless.

"How interesting that you happened to find such a unique friend," Mama says, words taking on a shadowy tone as Papa remains silent at her side.

"All my friends are magical," her daughter replies, joy seeping out of her like a leaky balloon.

"All?" Mama reaches for Papa's hand, and I don't like the sudden pearl clutching. It's not like Jane brought serial killers into the house, or worse—telemarketers—and what's the drama with having magical friends? What's more magical than a fairy?

Jane keeps the show moving, fast-forwarding to the main event. "This is Amber. She's a matchmaker, like me."

Mama actually does a spit take, which I didn't think happened outside of network sitcoms. Apparently Jane just uttered the magic word, but not in a fun-favor kind of way. Her parents go completely white, and for a second, I suspect they've frozen to stone.

"A matchmaker, isn't that cool?" Peter says tentatively, throwing his sister a lifeline. "I know you always hoped to meet one, Janey." Her face brightens a shade at his effort, and I do my best to keep the positivity train chugging.

"Hi!" I stand, extending my hand to Papa. "It's really nice to officially meet you all. Your farm is so—"

Papa, still as a statue, leans on his cane and glares at me. He forces us to hold our breath an excruciatingly long time before he speaks, as if he were waiting for the pony express to deliver his thoughts. Amani mouths an "uh-oh" my way, and I can't help but concur.

"When we brought you home from Chicago," he says to Jane finally, his words slow and deliberate, "we talked about this. How this . . . foolishness is holding you back."

"Foolishness?" I blurt out, covering my mouth with my hand as Jane buries her face in hers. Her father transfers his withering stare to me.

"Yes, foolishness," he repeats harshly. I'm sensing he's not a guy used to repeating himself. "Jane's endeavors go against our way of life."

Huh? Feeling dumb, I ask, "So you're against love?"

Offended, Papa scowls. "Of course not. Fairies cherish love and peace above all else. We've been committed to harmony since the beginning of time, and we consider it our sacred duty to maintain balance. There are consequences to using magic—you have to show restraint. Jane doesn't wield her magic properly and acts like the world is ending if she can't make her matches. She has to learn balance, timing. Stop flaunting her so-called abilities."

"But it's not like with dust," Rose interjects, instantly attracting all the vitriol in the room. "There aren't huge side effects to what Jane does."

"No side effects?" Papa bellows. "What about when she told Pastor Jacob that Rebecca, his wife of thirty years, was not his match? Or when she stood up at Thanksgiving and announced that cousin Jeffrey's fiancé is destined to marry a werewolf?" He snorts like a bull, lips pursed and quivering at bad memories. Behind him, Mama nods solemnly while Peter wrings his hands. "Jane stepping in and toying with people's hearts is simply unacceptable."

Living with a witch means I've heard similar logic before; Mom's all about making sure her spells aren't throwing off some sort of cosmic plan. But his views are way skewed and misinformed.

"That's not what matchmaking is," I counter, unable to stop myself. I won't let someone tarnish the magic and optimism of matchmaking, especially when Jane is crumbling beside me. "Jane doesn't force people to fall in love against their will. We're not brewing love potions or holding hearts hostage. Matchmakers are like love conduits, just helping things along. What we do is beautiful, it's hopeful, it's—"

"Enough." Papa doesn't have to yell; his blue wings reach full span, filling the room with his command. "I will not be lectured in my own home."

"Papa, maybe we should hear Amber out, get another perspective," Peter tries gingerly. Ivy watches from the corner of her eye, a sliver of a smile on her lips. "We've never met another matchmaker before; maybe she can illustrate Jane's situation differently."

"No. We've talked about this more than enough. Jane needs to learn how to respect magic and the dangers it can create. And she's not going to learn that by hanging around with those who don't see the repercussions of their actions." He looks at his daughter, a mix of concern and frustration swirling in his eyes. "You will stay in this house until these people have left the farm." We're all dealt a major case of side-eye as he turns, Mama jumping up at his side, before he adds, "Love is not something to be trifled with."

Twelve

"I NEVER THOUGHT I'D MEET SOMEONE WHO HATES MATCHMAKERS more than I do," Ivy says as we sit outside the farm bakery. I figured we could all use something sweet to wash out the ugly taste from our mouths, but this is a far cry from MarshmElla's. Everything is made with ingredients grown on the premises, meaning the choices are über healthy and therefore über unsatisfying. I'm sorry, but sugar-free vegan zucchini brownies aren't exactly my first choice when I want to eat my feelings.

"Well, it's a good thing we didn't mention your whole siren thing; they probably would've lost their minds," I say, spitting out a chunk of vegetable. "I know all supernaturals have drama about overstepping the Fates, and I guess that's what they think matchmaking is, but, like, you're telling me these fairies never use the dust they're harvesting? Or sell it to others who could then abuse the crap out of it? How is giving someone access to powerful magic like fairy dust any different than revealing a match?"

"It doesn't add up," Amani agrees, pushing her plate away. "I thought they were going to lock me up for being a precog, and yet this whole place is literally sparkling with magic."

"Fairies are pacifists," Rose mumbles, head buried in crossed arms on the table. She looks up, rubbing her temples. "We don't actually have any magic of our own, and we distrust those that do."

"But those wings—you can fly!" I exclaim.

Rose frowns. "That's not magic; it's biology. And the dust . . . it's from the earth. It's natural. They see it as a duty to take care of the coruscents, which are so rare. They harness the earth's bounty . . . they don't view it as magic, per se."

Amani and I exchange a look. "That makes NO SENSE. Fairy dust is like the most magical substance in the world! It can do almost anything! I mean, what does your family do with all this dust once they've performed their sacred rites or whatever? There is a ton of it lying around here."

"Most of it gets stored away, kept for magical emergencies or whatever. Very small portions get sold to vetted vendors, but getting fairy-approved is nearly impossible."

Amani has to physically stop me from pulling my hair out. "But it does happen, and clearly dust gets in other people's hands!" I yell. "This is why black magic markets exist!" I think of Roscoe, salivating as he runs his tattooed hands over his precious dragon eggs. He would probably cry himself dry seeing all this dust.

"Obviously I don't agree with any of this," Rose says, wings drooping behind her. "I'm just telling you how things work here. Fairies have serious trust issues, and they push away what they don't want to deal with." My heart swells with a sudden rush of appreciation for my own mom. She may not have understood what I was going through, but she didn't make matters worse by pushing me away. She never shunned me or purposely made me feel less than. There was so much I wanted to say to the Parents Wisteria, but I didn't get the chance. And what's worse, I got next to zero time with Jane, who is now locked away Rapunzel-style, unable to leave the house. I was hoping we could hunker down for some serious shoptalk, swap some matchmaker war stories, and maybe, just maybe, pick her little brain about why my visions are going all wonky. All I want is someone to tell me what's wrong with me. Is that so much to ask?

"Well, you're better off without them," Ivy declares. Rose turns to her, annoyed. "I mean, why bother with people who are clearly idiots?"

I sigh.

"What?" Ivy asks.

"That's her family." Though I don't know why I have to explain it, especially after all the drama the Chamberlains have been through. "Rose is trying to make things better between them. And besides, they weren't *all* idiots, were they?" I do a suggestive eyebrow waggle in Ivy's direction.

Ivy's taken aback. "Ew! What? Why are you doing that?" She blushes, which is saying a lot considering how pale she's become. "God, why are you always so weird?"

As if on cue, Peter finds us, approaching with the gait of a guilty puppy who just chewed up all his owner's shoes. He holds a bouquet of wildflowers—the non-fairy-dust kind—and after a few awkward attempts, finally places them down in front of his cousin.

"Rose, are you okay?" His wings shudder behind him.

She shakes her head, fat tears rolling down her cheeks. He kneels down beside her, gently patting her back. "I'm sorry," he whispers. "I know you're just trying to make things better for Jane, to make my parents see the error of their ways. But fairies are nothing if not stubborn idealists." Rose chokes on an abbreviated laugh and wraps her arms around her cousin. Both pairs of iridescent wings float upward as they embrace. I sneak a peek at Ivy, who watches the exchange with silent adoration.

Rose pulls back, holding Peter's hands. "What are we gonna do with them, Pete?"

"Scrub their brains with dust and hope for sparkling results?" He quickly looks at the rest of us, giving a shy smile. "May I join you all?" Rose scoots over, patting the space next to her.

Peter sits, shoulders bowing forward. "Well, that was a completely terrible first impression, wasn't it?"

"Pretty bad." Amani grins.

"The worst," I one-up. "And your fairy snacks are gross." Peter takes our teasing in stride, though I notice that Ivy, who was happy to bash on the whole scene moments ago, remains suspiciously quiet.

"I don't believe I caught your name," Peter says to her, extending a hand.

"Ivy," she says, in a tone so soft and gentle, I didn't think her vocal cords were capable of it.

"Lovely." They shake hands, lingering at each other's touch, eyes locked. "And can I assume you're magical too?"

"Well, not exactly. . . ."

He gives her a lopsided grin. "That's okay, neither am I. Not really."

"Your parents must really love you, then." I regret it as soon as it comes out; Amani's pinching the bridge of her nose in embarrassment. When will I ever develop a filter? But Peter just nods sadly.

"They love Jane too; they just can't get past themselves. They have to want to see things differently, though. No one can do that for them."

"What do you think will be the best way to get through to them?" I ask. "Because besides a karate chop to the face, I can't think of any solutions. I need to talk to your sister, and since she's trapped in your house, that seems a little difficult to achieve."

"Since when have you ever karate-chopped someone?" Amani asks, amused at the thought.

"All the time. In my head."

"Right."

Peter sighs. "Well, they can't keep her in there forever. Tomorrow is the summer solstice, and there's no way they'll let her miss that, even if they are mad." Tomorrow?! No! I hadn't planned on this trip being an overnighter. I'm not exactly psyched to hang around. "You all can stay with me," he continues. "It'll be cozy, but we'll make it work."

Ivy straightens, flashing her best ex-siren smile. "In the meantime, maybe you can show us what this fairy dust is all about?" Even though *I* know these two are meant to be, I'm surprised Ivy's focused on Peter and not—oh, I don't know— badgering Rose to grant her a lifesaving wish? Unless she's thinking she'll convince this boy to do her bidding like in the old days instead, which could work to my advantage. If getting face time with Jane is going to be a nonstarter, maybe my new buddy Rose would be willing to cover me in gold and wish my malfunctions away. I know I promised Mom I wouldn't use the dust, but if a fairy did it for me . . .

Peter returns Ivy's cheerful expression. "I'd be delighted." He offers her his arm, and as she snuggles into his side, we head off for a guided tour.

"Looks like siren habits die hard," Amani observes, nodding at Ivy clutching Peter's arm.

"Yeah, but he has no idea what he's getting himself into," I say.

"What do you mean?"

"Oh Gods! I haven't told you yet!" I shout, pulling her in conspiratorially. "Peter is Ivy's match!"

"WHAT?!"

"YES!"

Amani chuckles, shaking her head in surprise. "A fairy taming a siren. What a world."

"Stranger things have happened," I laugh.

The farm doesn't seem as enchanting the second time around. These fairies have created a perfect little utopia (well, aside from the snacks), but it's completely cut off from the rest of the world, shutting them off from anything they don't want to see or deal with. Their Swiss-cheese logic toward magic use is pretty hypocritical, and I feel awful that Jane is growing up in a community that would rather suppress magic than let it thrive. No wonder Rose helped her create a safe space to share her gift.

We approach a sequoia with a spiraling staircase carved into its trunk. Peter points up to the maze of rope bridges crisscrossing above at dizzying heights, saying something I can't hear. Apparently he's been giving a little tour spiel along the way, though only Ivy is listening. I'm not really interested in the historical highlights of a place that I want to leave as soon as possible.

"This here is the only way earthbound individuals can access the canopy area," he says, proudly gesturing to the passageway.

Amani frowns. It doesn't take a genius to tell she is over fairyland too. "Earthbound individuals?"

"Erm, those who can't fly." Peter's ears turn red, his wings cowering behind him. "We don't use this entrance much."

"Then why do you have it?"

"Emergencies, I guess." He quickly turns to grab a basket filled with work gloves and paper masks. "Here, I'll need you all to put these on. For protection."

"Protection from what?"

Peter blinks rapidly, suddenly unsure of himself. "Didn't you want to see the dust? The canopy is the best part."

"Wait . . . we're going up THERE?" My voice cracks. Staring at the twirling staircase with no end in sight, my legs liquefy, wobbling on the limestone below. Do I really have to go up to the top? Is this truly necessary? I don't think I'll look back on this time in regret if I just sit here quietly while the rest journey upward.

"It'll be okay." Rose squeezes my arm. "Despite everything, it really is beautiful. You should see it." I want to believe her, but I also want my brain to remain safely in my skull, and not splattered from an inevitable thirty-foot fall. "I won't let any-thing happen to you." She presses a pair of gloves into my hands. "Just put these on. For safety."

"Safety for us or the dust?" I ask, wary of doing anything the fairies want me to.

"Both actually. We try to keep the dust in its purest state possible, free from any skin oil or germs," Peter recites. He sounds like a nerdy voice-over instructional video on how to stay safe in the workplace. "But it's also highly volatile. Fairies can handle its power, but you all . . ." He trails off, eyes clouding.

The thought of interacting with dust visibly perks Ivy's interest. "What happens?" she asks innocently, but her question doesn't land well with her match.

"Just . . . don't," he warns, tone hardening. "If you have dust on your person, and even *think* about something you're wishing for, it could be activated." Pearly wings splay sideways, a pseudo stop sign preventing the topic from going further. The authoritative vibe doesn't sit well on his gangly frame, but we all let it go, not eager to have a second showdown today.

Amani snaps her mask on her face, leaning into me. "If he's secretly taking us up there to lock us up for being magical, I'm going to be super pissed."

I didn't even think about that! Great, another thing to worry about. As if the frightening height was not enough. "You and me both, sister."

We wind our way up the tree, climbing higher and higher. For someone with wings, the distance aboveground wouldn't even faze them, but my nerves are getting the best of me. There's no handrail (I mean, why would there be), so I press my left shoulder into the trunk, wanting to feel something solid as the world spins below. Everyone else is way far ahead of me, but I could care less. Last place and alive works for me. My breathing quickens, possibly from the change in altitude, but more likely because everything inside me is screaming, *THIS IS SCARY, WHAT ARE YOU DOING?!* I wish Charlie were here. To hold me, keep me steady. He's always so good at making me feel safe, even just thinking about his sweet mushy face puts a little more strength in my step. *Don't die,* I tell myself. *So you can kiss Charlie again.*

Getting to the top offers no relief, as the rope bridges sway constantly in the breeze. A never-ending labyrinth of walkways expands before me, swooping under and over each other, each leading to a glittering collection of coruscents. Now that we're on their level, it's clear these flowers must have prehistoric roots. They are even larger than I thought—probably as tall as the fairies who tend to them—stamens swaying on their own to an inaudible rhythm, baskets of shimmering gold perched at the petals. Though it'd be smarter to keep my gaze on this once-in-a-lifetime view, my stupid eyes peer down, spinning over the skyscraping height. I cross one bridge at the speed of snail, then decide I've had enough sightseeing. I sit down on the wooden planks of the bridge, wrapping my arms around the rope for security.

Rose takes a seat in front of me, maneuvering the height without worry and doing her best not to shake the bridge more than necessary. "You doing okay?"

"Besides being on the verge of vomit, perfect."

"We won't stay up here long." She hugs her knees to her chest, lavender wings fluttering in the breeze. "It's pretty, though, right?"

"Mmm-hmm." Though currently my eyes are closed, trying to recall all the calming meditations Mom forced on me over the years. I zero in on her voice, hoping to leech some of her impossible tranquility.

"Did you get a good glimpse of the dust?" Rose asks, trying to distract me with something sparkly.

"Not really. I'm kind of in survival mode right now."

"C'mon. We'll go together." She helps me up—an impressive feat considering I'm like a baby deer attempting to cross ice—and guides me to the nearest barrel full of twinkling dust. Even though it's now twilight, the granules continue to glow, somehow even more shiny without the sun's reflection. Taking a tentative step closer, I hold on to Rose's hand for balance and peer over the edge. Instantly I'm drawn in, entranced by the glistening powder. It calls to me, begging me closer, in some intense, Ring of Power–level mind control. I haven't even touched it and can practically feel its sorcery coursing through my veins. I stagger back, shaking away the feeling of alchemic allure. Dang, there's no way I'm touching this stuff. But Rose can.

Sensing an opportunity, I begin, "Hey, can I ask you a favor?"

Rose crosses her arms, stiffening. "I'm surprised it took you this long."

"Huh?"

"Most people can't wait to ask a fairy to grant them a wish," she says, disappointment in her eyes. Her wings lower behind her, the tips curling around her waist protectively. "I thought you'd be different."

What? That's not fair. She's the one who wanted me to help her first! "Wait a minute, it's not like that. . . ."

"Sure, sure." She swats my comment away. "I get it. Why else would someone come out to a fairy farm?" Looks like Wisteria distrust runs deep, and I am not here for it. After another crestfallen stare, she flies off into the treetops, leaving me to stew. But just as I'm about to call after her, Amani pops up from behind, scaring me half to death.

"Hey!"

"Gah! You do not sneak up on someone when you're thirty feet up in the air!" I yelp.

"Sorry. It's just . . . I had a terrible vision." Her stony expression alarms me further.

"Oh Gods, are we going to plummet to our deaths? Please say no."

"No . . . well, I hope not . . . but no, it was about Ivy. And maybe Peter, I don't know." She shakes her head, rubbing at her temples. "The vision is really unclear. . . . More like a feeling than a picture. Maybe all this dust is somehow interfering. But it's bad." Her dark brown eyes widen in worry. "Something bad is going to happen between them."

Trying to calm whatever demons are dancing in her head, I rub my best friend's upper arms. "Like what? Is she going to use the dust to become a supersiren and rule over us all?"

Amani bites her lip.

"Even so," I continue, "it's not like we can prevent her from saving her life. Are these the choices: a dead Ivy or an evil-mastermind Ivy?"

"I don't *know*," she emphasizes, gripping the rope handrail. "What I'm feeling now . . . it's bad. Like, 'Warning: Danger Ahead.' But there's nothing we can do except watch the storm roll in."

We look toward Peter and Ivy, off in the distance a few bridges away. Moonlight and flowers halo the couple, the surrounding dust adding to the glow of blossoming romance. They chat happily, Peter's wings anxiously fluttering as he awkwardly tries to get closer to her, and Ivy, calm and mellow, doesn't pull out any of her usual male-melting tricks. She just stands and smiles, listening to his nervous chatter, and doesn't even take stock of the fairy magic around her—the whole reason she's here—because she's completely bewitched by Peter's presence. It's innocent, sweet: she doesn't appear to be setting a trap, or if she is, she's fooling us all.

From this view, there doesn't seem to be any impending danger, but clearly I'm not seeing the whole picture, because Amani looks on like she's seen a ghost. Or worse, a monster.

Thirteen

THE NEXT MORNING, IVY SNEAKS AWAY TO SPEND TIME WITH PETER, while Amani and I play dress-up in borrowed clothes from some of Jane and Rose's cousins. It's all strapless dresses and halter tops (clothes that easily accommodate wings), which veer wildly outside my strict T-shirt-and-jeans aesthetic. My girly-girl bestie is in fashion heaven, though, eating up all the flowy bohemian vibes.

"Maybe I should have been a fairy," she says, twirling around in a floral-print backless dress as we walk aimlessly through the farm. Her long, dark hair catches the sunlight, looking impossibly shiny and beautiful. All around us, fairies fly by with various party supplies, starting to prep for tonight's solstice shindig. A long trail of golden ribbon flutters past my head, flapping in the warm summer breeze.

"I would be crazy jealous if you could fly," I say. "Would you carry me around, fly me from place to place, my own personal supernatural ride-share service?"

"Absolutely not," she laughs. "Besides, you hate heights."

"True. Also, I hate it here. I could never be a fairy. I've eaten more vegetables in the past day than I have in the past year. My insides feel so clean, it's horrible." I kick a rock for added effect.

"You are such a baby."

"Yes. Also, I miss my boyfriend. Wah."

"Me too." Amani pouts. "But we just have to make it till this party tonight."

"Blah." I pull awkwardly at the strapless dress Amani made me wear. Why does this kind of garment exist? I'm afraid I'm going to flash someone at any second. "I'm beginning to think no one here will ever help me, and I should just sign my life away to Roscoe."

"What? Don't be stupid."

"I'm serious!" I slump down in the grass, tucking my feet under me in the most ladylike move I've ever performed. "This fairy angle is going nowhere. Rose got all anti even though I didn't so much as breathe the word 'wish,' and Jane's practically locked away in a tower." Rose doesn't live on the farm, and she conveniently failed to mention where exactly she resides. I sent her a couple "Hey, can we talk?" texts, but she's yet to answer. I get that there's a lot of weird fairy mojo surrounding wishes, but

I don't think I did anything wrong here. It's not like I barged in, demanding favors like "Yo! Fix me, fairies!" No. While I hoped maybe someone would be willing to help, I genuinely came here to make sure a siren didn't die on my watch, and that a fellow matchmaker knows she's not alone in the world. Hmph.

"Yeah, well, it's better than being beholden to a dark warlock!" Amani shoots back. "Have some hope."

My hope jar is running dry, but I guess trying to stay positive for a few more hours won't hurt. At least I'm with my best friend, even if it's not my ideal locale.

We lie under the canopy, looking up at the sky, which seems to shimmer with the surrounding dust. "Vincent would like it here," she observes after a while. "If it weren't for the whole burning-up-in-sunlight thing."

I poke her ribs. "Man, vampires are so high-maintenance."

"Seriously. Yet it's weird how normal watching your boyfriend drink blood can become."

"Okay, Buffy," I laugh, and she joins in.

"No higher compliment!"

Watching Amani's face light up about Vincent, it's like her heart is actually aglow, radiating a brightness throughout her entire being. It's beautiful.

"You love him," I whisper, nudging her shoulder.

Every last pearly white shines at the trees above, palms clasping her cheeks as if they're about to burst. "I do," she admits. "I really do. And you don't have to say it—"

"Told you so!" I beam. But it's not my superior matchmaking skills that have me giddy; it's seeing my best friend blissfully happy, as she so deserves to be. Her joy means more to me than the satisfaction of being right, especially considering my matchmaking has been on the fritz.

"What about Charlie?" She turns to me, propping herself up on her elbow.

"What do you mean?" My heart flutters at the sound of his name.

"I bet he'd geek out over a place like this," she says. "Aren't you guys doing some sort of 'fancy date' challenge for each other? How could he possibly top a summer party at a fairy farm?"

I sit up. "Amani! You are a genius! There's no way he could outdo me if he came here, even with all his Blitzman bling." I roll the idea around, thinking of how cute he'd be seeing all the wings and dust. "I did tell my mom there'd be no boys, though."

"Well, it's not like he's sleeping over or something," she reasons. "Plus, what Mama Sand doesn't know won't hurt her."

I make a dismissive sound with my tongue. "Please. She'll know. She always knows. Sometimes I think her eyes are actual crystal balls."

Amani grimaces. "That sounds uncomfortable."

"I know. Especially for me." But she does have a point. If we're stuck at this farm until nightfall, I may as well have a handsome boy at my side. I dial his number before I can talk myself out of it.

"What's wrong?" he answers.

"Hello to you too. Why does something have to be wrong?"

"Why are you calling me instead of text? Are you on fire?"

"No, I . . . I miss you." The words tumble out without thought, but hearing them aloud cements their truth. I want him here, I want him now. His musky boy scent, his nerdy laugh, his fingers tangled up in my hair: I want it all right now.

My honesty surprises him as much as it did me. "Say no more," he replies after a beat. "Well, actually I need you to say a little bit more. I have no idea where you are."

A set of GPS coordinates and a few hours later, Charlie arrives via helicopter, which is apparently something the Blitzmans have access to (#richpeopleproblems). I convince the grumbly gatekeeper to let him through, and the sight of his glasses and bumblebee-printed button-down propels my feet toward him, and before he can finish saying, "What is this place?" I'm kissing him, long and deep, gripping the back of his neck. Thanks to my fairy couture, his hands run over my bare shoulders, causing him to pull back in shock.

"You're wearing a dress." He smiles. "A strapless one."

"You like?" I reply, never before realizing how flirty two simple words could be.

His lips press to my right ear as he whispers, "Very much."

I lean my cheek into his, maintaining my grasp on my beautiful boy. "I missed you. Like, a lot."

"Same. So much the same." He pulls me even closer, and I wish I had an invisibility cloak so I could just keep kissing him. "So, this place seems insane. Give me the tour; I need a distraction." It's the last thing I want—I'm over this glittering nightmare and want to hightail it out of here with a cute boy in tow—and glossing over all the drama brewing underneath is not my style.

"There's really not much to see," I say.

"Be serious, Sand. This place is literally glowing."

"Gah, fine." I point to the canopy (no way am I going up there again) and blab about the coruscents, his eyes sparkling. For so long he lived in a world where magic didn't exist, and now that I've opened that door, he can't get enough.

We approach a patch of wildflowers tucked into an outer corner of the commune, and spy Ivy and Peter snuggled on a two-person swing, her head resting dreamily on his shoulder.

"Holy crap, is that Ivy?" Charlie gasps.

"Shh!" I grab him, pulling him down behind a boulder so they don't see us.

"She looks so . . . tranquil! How is that possible?"

"That's the power of love, baby."

"I always thought she'd be matched with, like, a minotaur or something. That dude looks so chill."

I shrug. "Opposites attract, I guess."

"But we're not opposites, are we?"

I climb onto his lap, stroking his cheeks with my thumbs. "We defy clichés." Peering through his lenses, I see again the static of his match, a pixelated jumble of images and feelings. Gods, I'm beyond tired of this. For all my visions, but especially with Charlie. I came here full of hope, thinking a fairy who understands my matchmaking sorrow would be kind enough to lend a magical favor. But years of people abusing fairy friendships have led to deep-rooted distrust, and now I'm back to square one. I promised Mom I wouldn't use the dust on myself, but now it seems I'm out of options. Either I make a wish on my own and wait for the Fates to roll the dice, or I place my needs in the hands of a madman, whose deal is sure to be laced with misfortune. Neither is great, but I have to do something. I can't spend my life toiling in this uncertainty, wondering what is wrong with me and if my faulty magic will lead to bigger problems. I have to act, but I don't know what's best.

At the very least, I hope to get one question answered tonight. Even if my matchmaking troubles can't get resolved, I'm hoping Jane can reveal once and for all if Charlie is truly my match. We've defied the odds for so long now, but can we do it forever?

Fourteen

THE SUMMER SOLSTICE HAS ALWAYS BEEN ONE OF MY FAVORITE pagan holidays. On the longest day of the year, Dawning Day meets to honor the sun, with festivities including a bonfire by the lake and lots of summery foods. Last year I made strawberry panna cotta and watermelon macarons, and we danced and sang until the stars appeared. It's a night of magic and wonder, of relishing something beautiful and sharing it with people you love.

But tonight, so far away from home, I'm not in the party mood. Amani tries to make the best of things, weaving daisies into my choppy hair. Peter's cottage is not exactly a Sephora, but somehow she's managed to gather up every blossom and ribbon she could find to get us all flower-child glam. She excitedly helps Ivy and me prep for the celebration, but I can't help feel disappointed over how this trip has gone.

"Word on the street is that for the summer solstice, fairies will cover themselves in a layer of dust for a sunshiny effect," Amani says while spritzing us with rose water. "But they can do that since they're immune to its magic. It's probably best for us to steer clear."

"Well, not me," Ivy croaks from the corner of the room. "I'm getting some dust tonight." She's sprawled lethargically on a bench, hair faded to a silvery white, skin almost translucent. For someone who used to be positively obsessed with her appearance, she's made zero effort to join our girly party prep. Amani tried to put some lipstick on her, but she resisted, preferring to stay curled in a ball. If this whole siren thing doesn't get resolved soon, she could just vanish into the ether completely.

"Oh really?" I ask, curious as to how she thinks she'll pull this off.

"Yes. I'm going to ask Peter to grant me a wish," she slurs slightly, eyes unfocused.

"Have you explained to him what's happening to you?"

Ivy's head wobbles. "No, no. He won't look at me the same."

"You're right; he'll probably admire you more for what you've been through and what you did for your sister," I say.

Ivy looks over at me, eyes glassy.

"You talk about it like I was some noble unicorn," she

grumbles, body heavy with self-loathing. "I did it for selfish reasons. I didn't want to lose my sister."

Regardless of her reasoning, being up front with Peter about her wish is the only way to go. Based on my experience with Rose, maybe he'll be more willing to help if he understands what's at risk. I don't know if Rose thought I'd wish for something dumb like fame or fortune or what, but I don't want him rejecting her without knowing the whole story. "Just be honest with him," I tell Ivy. "I can tell you care about him; he deserves to know what's going on."

Ivy props herself up on her elbows with much effort. "Seriously, Amber, I know what I'm—" But she's interrupted by a coughing spasm that shakes her whole body. Sharp, violent coughs fill the room, and when she finally stops, it's like she expelled part of her soul, her cheeks devoid of any color. Amani and I exchange worried looks.

"C'mon, let's get you up." Amani rushes to Ivy's side, being patient and sweet with her despite her precognition of impending doom. It's impossible to know how Ivy using fairy dust will play out, but it's clear that time is up for the ex-siren. My stomach flops like a fish out of water. I want to help but I'm worried what the outcome may be.

There's a knock at the door, and Charlie walks in with daisies pinned to his shirt. I love how he can just roll with whatever situation he's thrown into. What a pro. "Are we ready to party or what?"

Outside, evening sunlight streams through the canopy, and the whole farm takes on an ethereal glow, thanks to hundreds of candles and strands of fairy lights (ha, get it?!) strung from the rope bridges above. A folksy band plays banjos and fiddles, while couples do-si-do, half in the air, half on the ground. The fairies themselves are slathered in dust, wingtip to toe, looking like golden gods and goddesses on holiday. Every surface, every guest, is gilded in powder, making it exceedingly challenging not to accidentally bump into something and get dust all over ourselves. Amani guides Ivy by the arm, taking slow, deliberate steps, and we part ways upon seeing Peter, looking handsome in summer linens. He waves them over, and I give Amani's hand a squeeze before continuing to stroll with my sweetie.

Unsurprisingly, I find my way to the dessert table, despite having been burned by all my previous fairy food offerings. A stack of cute cookie boxes catches my eye; inside are several quarter-sized granola bites, and while the treats themselves are less than memorable, I nab the little box to bring home and show to Ella. "How lucky this dress has pockets!" The top flaps of the box fold into a swirling flower, eliminating the need for stickers or ribbon to keep it closed. She's been looking for portable ways to share her desserts at street fairs, and this may do the trick.

As we munch on almond butter tarts and sugar-free banana bread, I keep my eyes peeled for Rose and Jane. I'd like to leave things on a high note, though I'm worried I won't get the chance to say good-bye. After searching through the crowd, being very careful not to brush up against any of the abundantly scattered dust, Charlie and I decide to sneak away to a cozy spot on the outskirts of the celebration, forever outcasts resuming our natural post.

"Did I tell you how beautiful you look tonight?" Charlie says as we're seated under an archway of honeysuckle and lights.

"You didn't, actually." I feign offense.

"You look radiant." He takes my hand. "I love you in jeans, but this fairy peasant look really works for you too."

"Is that so?" My lips inch toward his.

"Very," he breathes before moving in for the kiss. I feel intoxicated, bubbles of joy rushing through my body, making me warm all over. Kissing my sweet boyfriend, I suddenly remember my quest to have the best fancy date ever.

"You know what?" I take Charlie's hand, leading him into the golden crowd. "We should dance." He smiles in agreement, glowing from cheek to cheek.

A slow, string-tinged ballad creates a hush as couples wrap their arms and wings around each other. A few pairs take flight, tangled together while feet drowsily dangle in bliss. The sun has finally set, so the world is nothing but a twinkle, flickering embers and winking stars casting a luminescent blessing. Though dozens of fairies dreamily sway and twirl around us, in this magical moment there's only Charlie and me, holding each other with hearts wide open. Feeling his skin on mine, breathing in his warmth, I can almost push away my matchmaker worries completely, plunging myself so deep in the present it drowns out the future entirely. How could anything be better than this, truly? How could anyone make me feel so safe and yet so electrified at the same time?

I lean on his chest, his heartbeat echoing through my veins. If Jane reveals Charlie's not my match, would that change the way I feel? Would I want him less? We've been through so much, at this point I feel like we could conquer anything, especially when his lips meet mine. I know I can't predict my own match, but this just has to be it. I feel it deep in my heart, my veins, my soul. I love him to the ends of the world and back, and besides, how could something this good not be right?

At the end of the song, I spy Jane's minty head swerving through the crowd, and my heart leaps. I call out to her, grabbing Charlie's hand as we swerve through the dancing couples to meet her.

"Amber!" She reaches out for a hug, looking adorably sweet in a floral sundress and crown of wildflowers.

"You're free!" I (only kind of) joke. She giggles, happily swinging back and forth so her pretty dress can twirl around her.

"Yeah! My parents wouldn't let me miss the summer solstice, no matter what." She grins. A few steps behind her is Rose, the only fairy dressed in black, though she has styled her short lavender hair with streaks of sparkle.

"Hey," she says, purple wings flat against her back in guilt. While her lips bend in remorse, she keeps her eyes steely just to remind us that she's tough. "Sorry about before. I may have jumped to conclusions."

May have? Okay. "No worries." I smile, keeping it light.

"It's just that I've had a lot of relationships fizzle out due to people using me," Rose admits, eyebrows pinched. "And since you were being so sweet with Jane, I didn't want that to be true of you."

"I get it." And I do. How many classmates approached me just because they wanted to know if their crush was The One? People rarely ever talked to me for me, a truth that got old real fast. I was always eager to share my magic, but it wasn't great being treated like a destiny vending machine. "I want you to know that I am here for Jane, though. No matter what."

"Good." Rose smirks, wings fluttering with satisfaction. "Then we're cool." Yes! Friendship achievement unlocked!

"Amber, who is this?" Jane asks, innocently pointing at the fella beside me.

And now, the moment we've literally been waiting for. "Jane, this is my boyfriend, Charlie."

"Pleasure to meet you, Jane." He takes her tiny hand, lightly kissing the top, bringing a rush of color to her freckled cheeks. I consciously block out the lights, music—everything—around me so I can hyperfocus on this meeting and how Jane reacts. As they take each other in, I examine her face, searching for a sign, a hint of recognition in her little eyes. Does she see me when she looks at Charlie? Is what she saw in me echoed behind his frames? She stares at him, a warm smile spreading across her face, and my fragile heart does somersaults in my chest. Would she look that happy if she saw someone other than me looking back at her? No, no way, right? Unless she's one of those hopeless romantic types who geek out over any example of love. At her age, I would've lost my mind if a couple I envisioned was standing right next to each other. Heck, I *still* would freak out. The expression on her face is pure joy, and for a few enchanted moments, I let myself believe in my own happily-ever-after.

But we're interrupted by loud coughing behind us. We turn just in time to see Ivy collapsing from her seat, fainting into a bed of moss.

Fifteen

PETER KNEELS AT IVY'S SIDE, GLOWING MORE SHERBET THAN EVER. Just like his fairy family members, he's completely covered in dust, giving him an otherworldly presence. But now his party enjoyment melts away, and he crumples beside her, careful not to touch her with his golden fingertips.

"Ivy!" He's panicking, looking her up and down.

Jane clutches on to me, sobbing into my dress. "Amber," she cries. "She can't die!" But I don't know what to say. Did Ivy get the chance to tell Peter about her history, to ask for a wish to save her life? Her unconscious body makes me think not, or he would have helped her already. Will he be willing to save her now, or is this really the end for Ivy Chamberlain? Heart in my throat, I stroke Jane's tiny head, hoping my attempt to calm her will help soothe the churning dread in my gut.

Amani joins our circle of fear, clutching a mason jar of fairy punch. Eyes wide, her free hand covers a gasp; was this the danger she envisioned? There's no time to ask as Peter's hands hover over Ivy's fallen body. Scared, desperate, he looks like a prince poised over his Sleeping Beauty, a mixture of love and fear in his eyes. "Has she ever used dust before?" he asks us.

"No," I answer. Up until she lost her powers, I don't see why she would've needed it. "I don't think so."

"Well, there's no time like the present." Peter flies to the nearest fairy dust barrel, grabbing a heaping scoop in his hands. He quickly shakes the sparkles over her fallen body, not unlike how I use a sugar sifter at home. Then he leans in with intense focus, cupping his hands around her jawline, thumbs resting on her cheeks. He takes a deep breath and exhales. "I wish for her full health to be restored." Instantly, the dust ignites, bringing color to her pale skin. The warmth spreads, setting her face aglow, trickling down her neck, shoulders, arms, all the way to her toes. Amani takes my hand, and we watch to see how and if fairy dust really can cure all. Will Ivy awaken a snarling, heinous beast, or will the dust simply revive her to the regular amount of siren evil we knew? Whatever the outcome, it's too late to go back now, as Ivy's ghostly skin has returned to her usual golden tan, blond locks full of luster. When she opens her eyes, dazzling baby blues greet us all.

"Ivy? Are you okay?" Peter questions, breathless at the transformation before him. "You look . . . you look . . ."

"Yes?" she asks expectantly.

"You look . . . well." He blushes, bewitched by the radiant creature before him.

"Thank you."

"Do you feel good enough to stand?"

She smiles, the kind of grin able to melt boys' hearts down to butter. "Let's dance instead." Ivy stands, fluffing out her shiny hair. She puts her hands to Peter's chest, getting more dust under her nails, and presses her lips to his. He shrinks back a bit, surprised by her sudden forwardness, but still wraps his shimmery arms around her waist. He kisses her again. And again. And the more they make out, more of his dust transfers onto her body, empowering her further. They come up for air, and Ivy, equally covered in dust now, pulls Peter to the dance floor, a dopey expression on his face.

Fairy dust works. It totally works. Not that I doubted it, but seeing the stuff in action is a lot different than having its powers described. The immediacy of watching a problem solved by this fairy magic fills me with longing, and against my better judgment, I find myself inching toward the nearest barrel, staring into the glittering possibilities. Would it be so bad, dealing with a dusty consequence? Could it be any worse than the constant confusion and worry blurring my visions, driving me crazy day in and day out? I lean in, billions of shimmery golden granules tempting me, my fingers aching to reach in, make a wish, and see my troubles melt away. . . .

"Well, that just happened." Amani pops up next to me, breaking the spell of the dust below. I gasp, heart racing over how close I was to giving in, and how much I didn't care what happened next.

Face flushed with wonder, Charlie adds, "That was some kind of miracle, right? Now Ivy's a siren again?"

"I guess so," I reply, breathing deep to tame my runaway heart. Ivy's alive. We did it! Her magic has been restored.

But my relief doesn't last long. The peaceful summer solstice vibe suddenly transforms into something deeply uncomfortable. It's not uncommon for supernaturals to suss out others in the community, and Ivy's resuscitation sounds the alarm. Like a telekinetic game of telephone, one by one the crowd takes notice, sensing an intruder in their midst. The awakening of a siren ripples through the farm, fairy wings standing at attention like a dog's ears sensing danger. Charlie and I watch as confused, mistrustful eyes peel away from the party and toward Ivy and Peter, whose celebratory affection has caught them red(gold?)-handed.

Before the masses pick up their pitchforks and torches, I scurry over to the endangered couple, still blissfully unaware of the attention they're garnering. I tap Ivy on the shoulder, careful not to touch any of the dust that is now all over her neck, arms, and waist, who turns to me with her movie-star glow, all lashes and lips and glamour.

"Hey, um, how you feeling, champ?" I ask, unable to get the words out quick enough.

She laughs, touching her hand to her chest like she's about to thank the academy. "I have to tell you, this fairy dust is no joke. I feel better than I ever have in my entire life. And that's really saying something." Peter leans in to kiss her cheek, setting off a string of giggles. "I feel like I could do anything, Amber. Anything." The way she savors the word "anything" drops my stomach.

"Cool." I pull her just out of Peter's earshot. "Have you talked to him about the siren thing?" Judging by the sappy look on his face, I'm guessing no.

Ivy purses her lips, tapping a finger to her cheek. "It hasn't come up. We've been a little preoccupied."

Gross. "Well, I'm no Amani, but I see a quick exit in our future."

"What do you—"

Just then, Mama and Papa Wisteria fly over, purposely landing right in between their son and his siren.

"Peter, what is the meaning of this?" Papa demands, gesturing wildly at Ivy like she's a circus freak. She crosses her arms in defense, holding her head high. "You gave this girl fairy dust, without supervision?"

Peter looks down at his speckled hands, unable to refute the golden evidence. "She fainted, I—"

"So take her to the apothecary!" Papa bellows, wisps of ice-blue hair falling over his forehead. "Do you even know what you've done?"

Shocked by this response, Peter scans Ivy, trying to uncover what he's missed. Ever since they met, he's been smitten, filtering out any issues or flaws in his potential new partner, something we all do when relationships begin. Full of possibility and hope, we focus on what's good, putting blinders on against anything we don't want to see so we can just relish the moment. But now he takes a step back, out of the siren's snare, and reason sinks in. Peter's magical radar lights up, cluing him in to who she really is. Color drains from his face as the realization congeals.

"Ivy, you're . . . a siren?" Fairies murmur as the hurt in his words fills the air. "Why didn't you tell me?"

She tries a few innocent "Who, me?" eyelash bats before realizing those tricks won't work here. "Well, technically, I wasn't until a few minutes ago. . . ." She trails off, acknowledging her own lame excuse.

Anger rolls into his eyes. "But you were, before, and you knew what would happen if you had access to dust."

"Not . . . officially." Ivy bites her lip, ashamed. "But I had hoped."

Peter's peachy wings flutter out to his sides, incensed. "You played me."

"No!" she cries, and the tears are falling so fast, I worry she won't be able to properly explain herself. Surely crazy, I intervene.

"She couldn't manipulate you, Peter. She didn't have her

powers. And more than that, she was dying," I reveal, transforming Peter's expression from rage to confusion.

"Y-you . . . what?" he stammers.

Ivy nods, cheeks wet. "It's true," she whispers, wiping her face. "Without my magic, I was fading away." The fairies chatter among themselves, unsure of how to react to this news. Clearly they're uncomfortable with a siren being restored, but they wouldn't just let another magical creature die, would they?

Ivy takes a tentative step toward Peter, but Papa stands firmly in the way.

"You're a siren. You knew exactly how to get what you wanted, and you used my son and my family to get you there," the patriarch insists.

"It wasn't like that," she vows. "I mean, yes, I did come here hopeful for a cure, but then I got to know you and . . . things changed."

From the crowd, Jane appears, peeking out like a frightened woodland creature. She tiptoes over to her brother, a crown of flowers sitting atop her minty strands. "Pete, try to hear her out."

He glares at his own sister, unsure of who to trust. "Why should I? All she wanted was a wish!" He flaps his wings, floating a few inches above. The heat of the moment is taking over, our arguments losing steam.

Keeping her eyes on her brother, Jane stands strong despite the chaos. "You don't understand what's going on. You don't see what I see!"

"And what's that?" Peter crosses his arms with a cocky air. The sassiness does not suit him.

All eyes turn to Jane: the weirdo, the outsider. If she reveals his match to be a siren, one of the most mistrusted magical beings there is, that'll be it. The final nail in her coffin. She'll be crucified—not literally, but no one will ever want to listen to her ever again. To be an abomination, and then match her brother to one? No. That would not sit well. And yet that is the truth. Not something she chose, but something that's real. And something that needs to be known.

So I step in, taking a bullet in the name of love, as I've done so many times and will certainly do again.

"This siren is Peter's match," I announce to a horrified crowd. You'd think I'd said "Babies taste delicious!" the way everyone recoils in disgust. A couple of fairies actually cry out in shock, but I don't let their repulsion stop me. "The two of them are destined for each other. I've seen it in both of their eyes, and it's beautiful. Peter saving Ivy today was an important step in their love story. As their relationship continues to flourish, they'll need your support. Your acceptance." Mama Wisteria buries her blubbering pink head into Papa, whose face freezes like he just saw Medusa. Peter, losing the will to stay airborne, slowly touches down, eyes glazed in an unreadable expression. Excitement? Abhorrence? Embarrassment over my totally broadcasting his meant-to-be in front of literally everyone he knows? Whichever it is, he's dumbstruck; I could probably knock him over with a feather.

Ivy, on the other hand, is all lightness at the revelation. She covers her mouth to conceal her joy, but there's no shading the sparkle in her eyes, which dance my way with a silent "thank you." Two halves of a whole stand inches apart, miles of questions and unknowns between them.

"I know some of you may be wary of matchmaking and how that magic works," I continue, "but this is a good thing. No matter the union, nothing bad can come from two people in love."

"That's enough!" Papa yells, silencing the crowd with his raised cane. "I won't let this recklessness continue. You all need to leave, immediately." He turns to his shell-shocked son, voice dropping several octaves. "Including you."

This demand snaps Peter back to life. "I had nothing to do with this!"

"You had everything to do with it!" his father screams back. "You let yourself get tangled up in this mess, blinded by a dark kind of magic. This is not how we raised you." Papa swings back to the rest of us, rage burning from ear to ear. "Get out! Now! All of you!"

Without a second thought, Peter takes off, flying straight toward the canopy until he disappears into the night. It's kind of overdramatic, to be honest, yet I'll give him points for tantrum flair. Rose takes off after him, as the rest of the fairies freak out, shrieking and crying out like the floor is suddenly made of lava. In the panic, Charlie and Amani manage to grab hold of Ivy, protecting her from the yelps of confusion and hysteria. But I can't leave without checking on Jane, the only being standing still in the frenzy.

"Hey." I crouch down, placing my hands on her tiny shoulders. Her lip quivers, but she bravely forces a sad smile. "Are you okay?"

"I guess. I don't know," she says, her small voice hard to hear among the commotion. "I didn't think revealing my brother's match would happen like that."

"Matchmaking is nuts," I try to reassure her. "The reaction is hardly ever what you'd expect." She looks at me, long and deep, and I know my future partner is dancing through her mind. I desperately want to know what she sees, but with everything that just happened, it's not the right moment at all. Jane hardly looks ready to deliver romantic fates, what with all the confusion swirling around us. As much as I crave my match, I don't want to pressure her, especially if the outcome isn't what I'm hoping for. I know what it's like to watch an adult's hopes and dreams fall apart; I can't pass that burden onto her tiny shoulders. I don't think any of us could handle any more bad news at the moment. As much as I'd want her to, I understand now that she's too young to help me.

"Amber," she whimpers, lip trembling. "What's going to happen to my brother?"

"I don't know, but I'm sure he'll be okay." I force a smile, knowing I have to be strong for her.

"Can you help him?"

I swallow down a groan. "Jane, I barely know him, and he just flew away to . . . Gods know where!"

"But if anyone can help him, it's you and your magical friends!" she yelps, tears forming in her sad little eyes.

Curses! I knew having friends would get me into trouble in the long run. I dig deep to keep calm in the presence of a child. "He's eighteen, though. Can't he take care of himself?"

"I just want to know he's all right, that's all," she sobs. "Please? For me?"

I sigh. Saying no to Jane would be like smothering a baby kitten, and I don't need "cat killer" added to my long list of transgressions. "Fine! Fine. I'll see what I can do. But I can't make any promises."

She wraps her tiny arms around me, squeezing tight. "Thank you, Amber!"

"Yeah, yeah," I grumble just as her parents call for her somewhere in the distance. She waves me away, and I run toward the exit, twinkling lights pointing the way. Rose catches up with me, grabbing my shoulder from behind.

"Hey, are you okay?" she asks, wiping sweat from her brow. From the way she's breathing heavily, I'm guessing she didn't have luck chasing down Peter.

"Yeah, um, sorry for ruining the party. Wish I could say it was my first time."

Half her mouth curls in a smile. "Well, fairies are pretty good at ruining good things anyway."

"Did you find Peter?"

"I caught up to him, but he told me to buzz off." She sighs. "Whatever. Jane's my priority, not a pouty man-baby." A flock of panicked fairies fly by. It's really time to go. "Keep in touch, okay?"

"I will," I promise, resuming my exit. But just as I'm about to bid fairyland good-bye forever, another barrel of dust catches my eye, its gleaming treasure stopping me in my tracks. So much power shimmers below, taunting me with its life-changing abilities. So close and yet out of my reach, the threat of consequence keeping me from making a wish. I wanted so much more out of this trip, to walk away whole and free from magical dilemmas. But I'm leaving right where I started, with no answers and nothing to offer.

Offer . . .

Out of wishes and out of time, I decide to make what I'm sure will be an Amber Sand Top Five Worst Choice Ever and take some dust to offer to Roscoe in exchange for his services. Fairy dust has to be a good payment, right? It's not a dragon egg, but he could use it to wish for one! Or for anything his gross little heart desires. While I didn't think it would come to this, he really and truly is my last resort.

After tossing out the treats, I carefully scoop up a one-wish portion of fairy dust with the little cookie box I'd tucked in my pocket, making sure not to physically touch the granules with my skin. It's harder than it looks, but once I have a decent amount (I'm not actually sure how much it takes to make a wish come true, but based on the handful Peter used for Ivy, this looks about right), I shake off the excess, securing the top before tucking the glowing container back in my dress. Will I give this to him? I'm not 100 percent sure. But I'd rather have the option.

Everyone's ready and waiting in Amani's minivan, with Charlie in the driver's seat. I slide into the passenger seat, sparkly contraband at my side. No one says a word until the giant sequoia gate slams behind us. We careen onto the highway, staring off into the miles and miles of dark farmland stretching on every side, looking even more eerie after days of rainbow bright.

Amani and Ivy lie in the back seat, exhausted. "That was nice of you to step in and speak up like that," my best friend says to me.

"Well, I thought maybe it'd be easier if it came from me." The wreckage of the scene plays violently in my head. "Guess not, though!"

"You really know how to kill a party, babe," Charlie teases from the driver's seat. "That may have been your biggest match-making disaster yet."

"Hmm. Top five at least." I flip my barely shoulder-length hair in an act of pride. "I don't like to brag, but I am Queen of Catastrophes."

"Well done, Your Highness," my boyfriend says with a laugh.

"I thought it was amazing," Ivy pipes up, unable to dim her megawatt smile. "I mean, I've always thought matchmaking was complete and utter garbage, but man . . . the spectacle! The drama! I loved it."

"Probably didn't hurt that you were at the center of it all," I say.

"Obvs, that was the best part. Everything's coming up Ivy!" We stifle a collective groan. While I'm happy she's psyched about her match, leave it to Ivy to find the joy in a total train wreck of an evening. "But, like, how does this work now? Peter is my match—which I'm definitely into, BTW—but how do we make it happen? What's the next step? Does the happily-ever-after just kind of start automatically, or . . . ?"

I snort at her cluelessness. Of course Ivy has no idea how to engage in a relationship; almost everyone she's ever hung with (present company excluded) has been forced into friendship by her sireny will. "That's all you. Jane and I just see the ending, not the journey. You'll have to get there on your own."

She thinks on this for a minute. "It shouldn't be a problem, right? I mean, he could barely keep his hands off me back there . . . see?" She wiggles around in her seat, showing off Peter's golden fingerprints all over her body.

"Barf," Amani says.

"Double barf," I repeat, burying my face in my hands.

"What's the problem?" Ivy asks. "You had no issue being all up in our love life back at the farm."

"Hey, I have an idea," Charlie begins. "Let's play the quiet game. Give everyone's hearts a chance to return to their regular rhythm?" He turns the radio to a jazz station, and seemingly seconds later, the back-seat passengers fall asleep, an unlikely pair snuggled and slumped against each other. With one hand, I lightly touch the box of dust in my pocket, hoping the shimmer within won't glow through my garment. With the other, I take Charlie's hand, piano riffs mixing in the dark, as headlights guide the way, and try not to worry about Jane and Peter.

Sweet home Chicago, here we come.

Sixteen

IT'S PAST MIDNIGHT WHEN WE FINALLY ROLL UP TO MY APARTMENT
building. "Exhausted" doesn't even begin to reach the depths
of our collective fatigue. I feel like a three-ton sack of potatoes
getting out of the car. With dead legs, I'm dragging myself to
my door when Charlie calls out, "Hey!" from the passenger-side
window.

"What?" I laugh deliriously.

"Can I see you later?"

"It's like one a.m.; it *is* later."

"I mean for dinner."

With everything that just happened, I can barely think past
taking off this dumb dress and snuggling into my sweatpants,
but I appreciate where his head's at. "I kind of need to decom-
press for a bit? But after that, sure."

He blows me a kiss. "Okay, love you."

Once I survive the three-story stair trek, I open my apartment door just a crack, reaching to disengage the witchy alarm system my mom devised: a bell that detects magical DNA. I rub the brass fixture, located to the left of the doorframe, letting it sense me. Ever since Mom's evil witch-nemesis, Victoria, tried to storm the castle, Mom figures we can't be too careful.

It's so dark, I wish I could snap my fingers to make candles flicker like all the cool witch kids can, but instead I stumble over a stray shoe and go crashing into the hardwood. Seconds later, Mom flies out of her bedroom, sleep-mangled braid trailing behind, broomstick wielded like a baseball bat. She's wearing her "Resting Witch Face" pajamas I bought her last Christmas.

"Amber?" she cries, shaking away dream remnants. "What in the world?"

I pick myself up off the floor. "A broomstick? Really, Mom? Can you be more of a cliché?"

She looks at her weapon as if she's seeing it for the first time, then sets it aside, drowsy eyes examining me. "What's wrong? What's going on?"

I strategically place a hand over my right dress pocket, hoping to hide the bulge of stolen fairy dust. "Well, I'm on the no-fly list in fairyland now, so I needed to make a quick exit," I explain.

Mom's expression hardens. "What happened? Are you okay?"

"I'll give you the scoop, but can I get some jammies on

first? This is the most uncomfortable thing I've ever worn."

"Yes. I'll go start some sleepytime tea."

"Blech!" I scowl as Mom's slippers scurry off to the kitchen. Quietly locking my bedroom door behind me, I pull out my contraband, a slight golden halo emanating from the cardboard packaging. Now, where can I put this without Mom accidentally discovering how I completely went against her rule? Under the bed seems too obvious. . . . My closet is pure chaos. My desk has gone virtually unused since school let out, so I pull open the bottom drawer, burying the world's most powerful magic under unused notebooks and knickknacks. The perfect crime! I slip on some sweatpants and a hoodie (good-bye forever, strapless peasant dresses!) and get ready to raid the fridge.

Mom's messing with the teakettle as I pull out my secret stash of dark chocolate peanut butter cups from the back of the pantry. After all that crunchy granola fare, I enter a state of euphoria as the candy crosses my lips. All hail processed sugar!

"I don't know why you made a whole pot," I say once I've downed a few treats. "I'm not drinking that tea."

"Well, I need it. You scared me half to death." Mom yawns. She pulls out her hair band and starts shaking out her braid, long gray waves framing her tired face. "A text would've been nice."

"As if you would've heard it! You're one foot in the grave when you're asleep. Besides, my phone died. It doesn't run on fairy dust."

Over a steaming mug, Mom asks me all about our adventure, frowning as I describe the Wisterias' weirdness toward magic. She props her cheek in her palm, head (and heart) heavy.

"Their feelings toward magic are not without merit," she observes sleepily. "Fairies have had to endure misconduct for centuries. Magical creatures used to enslave them, forcing them to harvest fairy dust for their own devious spells. Witches, warlocks, and even more peaceful creatures have gone over the edge after getting a taste while fairies have been forced to watch from the sidelines, witnessing self-destruction and perilous paths caused by their own dust. Even today, fairies hide their wings to avoid danger, to keep themselves from getting pulled into supernatural traps."

I nod, thinking of Rose trying to stay on the DL while out in public.

Mom continues, sipping her tea. "It's certainly true that fairies have had it rough, though they're not alone. Every magical bloodline has had to endure some sort of persecution or unethical behavior over the generations."

"Totally! I mean, hello? Salem, anyone?" I ask.

She doesn't smile, clearly too tired for my wit. "Witches have been tortured, feared, and misunderstood, not to mention how even the word 'witch' is synonymous with 'evil.' So I sympathize with what the fairies have been through, and understand where their strict views on magic use are coming from. I don't like to judge other parents, though I worry their overbearing rules will lead to their children making rash decisions."

My thoughts go to Peter, disappearing into the canopy the second he used magic without approval. Where is he now? And how I am supposed to find him?

"Yeah. I told Jane I'd look after her brother, though I'm not super sure how to achieve that."

This does make her grin. "I'm proud of you, you know?"

I almost choke on my chocolate. Mom is not one to dole out praise, especially before dawn. "What?"

"Unless you're exaggerating, it sounds like you really stood up for both Jane and what you believe in." She chuckles to herself. "Your professors are going to love you next year."

"They'll definitely love my baking. . . . Jury's out on what they'll think of me."

"Jane needs a friend like you, someone to look up to."

"Her fairylike height means she pretty much *has to* look up to me," I quip.

Mom rolls her eyes. "You know what I mean."

"Yeah." I squirm. It's not that I don't appreciate the compliment, but praise is so rare, I never know what to do with it. Flattery makes my insides all twisty. When you're accustomed to insults and ridicule, good sentiments need to break through a thick outer layer of protection before they can land. Still, her words make me feel nice, in the most awkward way possible.

I've never been someone's role model. How does one fill those shoes?

Mom gets up, kisses me on the top of my head, and pads back to her bedroom, leaving me in my now-wired state. When you've consumed a week's worth of sugar in a few minutes' time, that manic energy needs an outlet.

Seventeen

By dawn, I've whipped up cinnamon-sugar pancakes, Nutella beignets, and vanilla peach scones, all of which I've laid out on the kitchen table like I'm the proprietor of the world's most dreamy bed-and-breakfast. And honestly, that imaginary life sounds pretty amazing: I love bed, and breakfast is the birthplace of such gifts as donuts, waffles, and coffee, so what's not to love? I'm already planning to take some business classes so I can find the best possible way to release my culinary gifts into the wild. While I've always envisioned owning a bakery like MarshmElla's, maybe a decadent B&B would be the way to go. Or a food truck, spreading smiles and sugar across the land. Or maybe I'll steal Jane's idea and become an Internet personality with my own cooking show. Only the Fates know for sure.

I'm pouring my third cup of French press when Mom the Zombie stumbles into the kitchen, still wearing her jammies, sleepiness lingering in her lashes.

"Good morning, starshine!" I sing in the too-chipper tone of a madwoman who stayed up all night baking. "Coffee? Beignet?"

She wipes some sleep from her eyes, yawning. "Yes, please."

I guide her to my bountiful table like the gracious chef I am. "There's syrup, honey, jam, powdered sugar—everything." Mom wraps her hands around a freshly poured mug, taking it all in. "C'mon, now, someday people will be paying for all this splendor, and you're getting it for free!"

Mom bites into a pastry, lips instantly spreading into a smile. "Oh, wow," she garbles through vanilla glaze. "That's amazing."

"Thank you, thank you." I actually bow, which is ridiculous. Someone needs to shoot me with an elephant tranquilizer. "The secret is to use vanilla bean shavings in addition to extract."

"You were shaving vanilla beans before sunrise?"

"Yeah, well, some people go for runs before five a.m. That's *truly* crazy."

She laughs. "Agreed." We load up some plates (not that I need any more sugar) and plop down to eat. A thought makes her pause before grabbing another scone. "Oh, you got a letter from the Culinary Institute," she continues through a mouthful of pancake.

"What? Where?" She nods toward the living room, where we usually drop our mail after walking through the door. I dash across the apartment, fueled by caffeine and delirium, returning with the envelope in no time flat. If my gym teachers could see me now! I'm going to crash so hard later, it's going to be tragic.

The letter doesn't say much—some basic information about orientation and how to log on to the school's student portal—but thoughts of the fall rile up my nervous system (though maybe it's the countless cups of coffee—hard to tell). I'm excited to start school; no, excited is putting it too gently. I'm ECSTATIC to finally spend my days doing what I love instead of suffering through a curriculum I could care less about. High school was a curse to my existence, and college is my reward for surviving. Still, this is probably my last summer to linger in the kid world, as starting school will unlock the door to all the responsibilities and burdens of adulting. Yay? Now that I've successfully aided in preventing Ivy's death, I can focus again on fixing my own magical drama so I can then FINALLY achieve the slothlike levels of laziness I intended for this summer. #goals

Speaking of random messages, I hear my phone start buzzing incessantly from my bedroom now that it's once again charged. Heavy with the pounds of pastry in my belly, I trudge back across the apartment to grab it, scrolling through a stream of texts.

Oh good Gods.

"What's up?" Mom asks when I return.

"It's Rose. Peter reached out to her. He . . . hurt his wing somehow. He needs help." Laughter is the wrong response, but I can't help it. "And now she wants a favor." *Oh, really, Rose?*

Now YOU want a favor from ME? I want to type back, thinking of her super-judgmental eyes the second I started to ask for help. "Apparently he has *no one else to turn to.*" I flop to the floor in dramatic fashion, posing for a chalk outline. I don't have time for any more supernatural nonsense right now! I need to sleep for like five days straight. But I did agree to be there for Jane, and, by extension, Peter. "Mom, do you have something?"

"To repair fairy wings?"

"Maybe? Or at least to help with the pain, assuming he's in any. I don't really know about the central nervous system of wings. . . ."

Mom, purveyor of all that is right and just, purses her lips in thought. "Maybe if you help him, and that news gets back to his parents, they'll all see that magic isn't that bad," she suggests. A pinch too much smugness, if you ask me.

"Yeah, and maybe if I wish real hard, a unicorn will appear at the front door!" I snark back. Mom stands over me, syrup bottle in hand, threatening to pour it all over my face. Joke's on her, though, because that'd be awesome. There is no part of me that wants to get up and assist a runaway fairy. I'd rather him stagger around, wingless for the rest of his life. See how he likes it!

"We're obviously going to help him, so you may as well just get up," Mom says. I press myself into the floor, willing gravity to pull me down harder so I can stay here forever. "Find out where he is and we'll bring him a magical remedy, whether he likes it or not."

Eighteen

TURNS OUT THAT AFTER HIS TANTRUM, PETER FLEW ALL NIGHT and conveniently ended up in Chicago. Since modern-day fairies don't usually fly such long distances anymore, his wings gave out from his weight, nearly tearing in half. How he was able to fly the whole way without being seen is my real question, since seeing a fairy blaze through the sky would make anyone do a double take, including me, and I'm enlightened to fairy existence.

I had hoped today would be filled with binge-watching crap TV with Amani, but instead she agrees to help me with this Peter mess. We meet him at a cozy coffee shop in Lincoln Park, and it's instantly clear he's in rough shape. While he's hidden his tattered wings under his shirt, he's positively wrecked, battered and bruised from what I can only assume was a massive fall from above, looking like he hasn't slept in days. Last night at the solstice, he was handsome and happy, a literal shining knight rushing to the aid of his lady love. Now he looks like he's been slain by a dragon, dragged to the ends of the earth on a quest gone terribly wrong.

"Oh, there you are, Peter," I say, smiling at my *Hook* reference as we slide into his booth. Honestly, I should get a trophy for going this long without constant Peter Pan and Tinker Bell jokes.

Dark brown eyes with even darker under-eye circles greet us, and I'm flooded with images of him and Ivy together—this time, everything's pixelated, like they're in a 1980s video game, but from what I can tell, they're enjoying a candlelit dinner, lovers glowing against twinkling tea lights. I know we've only been home a few hours, but I wonder if Ivy's tried to contact him yet. Her cluelessness over how to be in a relationship without magical manipulation still makes me chuckle, but despite her uncertainty, this vision proves that their destiny remains unchanged: they will fall in love, somehow, some way. And it won't be due to siren seduction; that kind of magic can't make someone fall in love. Lust, for sure, but love is too pure to stem from wizardry and tricks.

"Thanks for coming," Peter croaks. After a long sip of coffee, he tries to reach for my hand, but I pull away, causing him to wince further. I don't know this guy; I don't want him to hold my hand. I'm only here for Jane. His every movement seems pained, slow and deliberate, as if all his limbs are about to snap, not just his fragile wings. "I didn't know who else to call."

"Definitely not the Ghostbusters. This end of the supernatural spectrum is not their specialty." Peter looks at me like I'm an alien, and I shrug at my own joke. They can't all land! "Anyhoo, we brought you a tonic that should help. Calendula, elderberry, and horse chestnut, mixed with pomegranate juice and a little secret sauce. Made for those with aching supernatural body parts: wings, tails, horns, and the like." I hand him a water bottle with my mom's brew. Carefully, he screws off the lid, sniffing the contents before wrinkling his nose.

"Where did this come from?" he asks, suspicion lodged at the back of his throat.

"My mom's shop. Well, technically our kitchen. She brewed it fresh this morning. None of that stale healing potion, pshh."

"A witch's potion?" Peter pushes the bottle away, spilling some of the liquid on the table. Droplets land in heart shapes before quickly evaporating.

"Hey!" I grab it before the whole thing falls over. "What's wrong with you? Don't you want to feel better?"

"Yes, but not by the use of magic." His tone is infuriating. He's refusing a surefire cure while hunched over the table in pain. I don't know whether to force the potion down his throat to heal him out of spite or to just let him suffer forever.

Amani, playing good cop to my bad cop, adds gently, "Her

mom's a witch. This will work. I've taken her potions before."

He scowls in disgust, shoulders hunched in an unnatural position. His wings must be hanging heavy, though I can't say I feel sorry for him. "I want a natural remedy."

"Then go suck on a dandelion and lie still for six months. See how that works out for you," I spit. "This was a mistake. Let's just go." I stand, but Peter emits a frustrated growl, scratching his fingers through his messy sherbet hair.

"No, don't go," he pleads.

"Then drink the potion," Amani instructs, more forcefully this time. She's giving him concerned caretaker eyes, while I'm sure mine could cut glass.

Peter recoils into the booth seat.

"You want our help? This is how we help. Drink. The. Potion," she repeats. "Or we leave." She crosses her arms for extra dramatic effect.

Trapped between his dumb ideals and his aching body, Peter breaks, grabbing the bottle before he can second-guess himself. He takes a minuscule sip—so small I'm not even convinced he consumed any liquid—then shudders with delight, reflexively releasing a sigh of relief. With only a drop of potion on his tongue, he already looks ten times better.

"Imagine if you drank the whole thing," I coax.

And that suggestion is all it takes: he guzzles it, draining the entire bottle in seconds, tiny dribbles of raspberry-colored liquid trickling down his chin. It reminds me of the first time I tried fondue; it was like the melted chocolate became air, and I couldn't get enough. Peter quivers, a current of healing power coursing through his veins. Gone is the exhaustion and suffering, replaced with a man who looks strong—capable—his wings practically beating through his shirt.

Amani's jaw drops, fingers at her cheeks. "I . . . I didn't think you would actually do it!" she gasps.

"Neither did I!" he replies with a shocked laugh.

"How do you feel?"

He stares at his hands, opening and closing his fists like he's freaking Peter Parker post-spider-bite. "Amazing."

"See? See?" I clap, riding this sudden wave of positivity. "Not all magic is demonic curses and sociopathic quests for power!" But I've said the wrong thing (shocker), because now he's back to giving me major side-eye.

"How do I know this isn't some trick, an elaborate ruse to lure me into your coven and make me do your bidding?"

I snort. "Um, first: Who talks like that? Second, I'm not in a coven. I am not a witch. And third, I helped you because you're Jane's brother. I don't want anything from you, except maybe for you to stop being such a total tool."

But he's barely listening to me, eyes dilated and far away. "I've never used magic before. Ever. Not even that time I fell through the canopy hanging Christmas lights. . . . I was hanging upside down, tangled in one of the rope bridges. . . . My leg was definitely broken. Mom and Dad said it had to heal on its own, giving me the most minimal of remedies. I had to fly everywhere; I couldn't walk until spring." His eyes glaze over. "But the dust could've healed me. It didn't have to be that hard. . . . None of this had to be that hard. I . . ." His forehead drops to the table. "I don't know how to feel right now."

I bite the inside of my cheek, unsure of how to offer comfort, or if I even should. But before I can make a choice, a voice calls from behind us. "Peter?"

The fairy pops up, and we turn to see Ivy, glammed out with giant Audrey Hepburn sunglasses and a venti Frappuccino. She pushes her shades up on her once-again-lustrous locks, flashing a perfectly lip-glossed grin. It sickens me how amazing she looks, and if there was any doubt over whether her siren powers were restored, well, mystery solved. With a tank top tied to reveal a tanned and toned midsection, bikini strings dangling from her neck, it's a wonder Peter manages to keep his eyeballs in his sockets. "It's really you! I didn't know where you disappeared to, silly!"

Jaw on the floor, Peter stumbles on his first attempt to respond. "Uh . . . uh . . . yeah. I guess I just needed to blow off some steam."

"Understandable." Ivy slides into the booth without invitation, snuggling right up to her match. "Listen, I . . . oh—" She pauses, just realizing Amani and I are also sitting here. "Um, can you give us some privacy here, please?"

I have no intention of leaving—I want to monitor how Peter

does post-potion—and luckily he responds with "They can stay."

"Fine," Ivy huffs but with less venom than I'd expect. She takes a deep breath, and I can almost see her trying to breathe in white light and push out her regular poison. "Peter, I've been thinking about it, and I'm really sorry I didn't tell you about being a siren. I really liked you from the start, and I guess I didn't want you to think less of me, given your family's whole . . . thing." She scrunches up her nose like something smells rotten. "I honestly was not trying to trick you into getting my powers back. The truth is, I was dying. You saved my life, my handsome hero." She strokes his forearm, and I notice goose bumps spreading over his skin. Cheeks flushed, he fakes a cough to cover his grin. It's a different approach for this siren to be straightforward and sweet instead of seductive and sultry, and it's more than clear he's melting under her touch. Against his better judgment, he's spellbound by her, their attraction tangible. I can't say for sure, but I think his hand is on her leg under the table. . . . Gah, now I kind of wish I did leave the conversation. "Can you ever forgive me?" she coos.

"You were really dying? That wasn't just for show?" he asks, barely able to speak. She nods, batting her lashes innocently.

After an uncomfortable amount of less-than-subtle PDA, Peter clasps his hands over hers to stop her from driving him the good kind of crazy. "I'm still processing everything that happened. . . . I have a lot of mental hoops to jump through." He squeezes Ivy's hands but looks up at me. "But perhaps my family and I have been too rigid. I need to open my heart, and I hope you all will help me."

I don't believe for one second that he's done a total 180, but fine, whatever. Though while I'm in his good graces, I decide there's no time like the present for a favor. "Hey, so now that I healed you with the wondrous powers of magic, do you think you could help me with a wish?"

He tilts his head, curious. "Like, a fairy-dust wish?"

"Yeah, like what you did for Ivy. Only less life-and-death, more happily-ever-after."

His mouth twists around, trying to find his response. "I don't know, Amber. What I did for Ivy . . ." He stops to lock eyes with his lady love. "That was my first time. And clearly it didn't go so well."

"What are you talking about? Your wish came true! Look at her!" I gesture, prompting her to strike a princess pose.

"I mean, yes, it did work, but look how my family reacted. I don't want to disappoint them further."

Ugh, these fairies and their morals! "They won't have to know. It's just a tiny wish, to help a fellow supernatural."

"I don't have any fairy dust with me, anyway." Peter shakes his peachy head. "And besides, I think I need to really figure out how I feel about granting wishes first."

GAHHHHHHHHHH. Amani puts a pastry in my hand before I explode into the sun from rage.

"So!" Ivy jumps in, anxious to regain attention. "When are

you taking me out on our first official date?" She leans forward, the contents of her tank top demanding an answer. I roll my eyes. *There's* the Ivy I know.

Peter burns bright red, averting his gaze to the ceiling. "Um, soon. I need to figure out what I'm doing first. Like where I should stay now that I'm here. I didn't really plan for any of this."

I offer up Charlie's place as a crash pad. "I'm sure it'll be fine; he has the space. And his dad loves to cook for guests. I'll text him right now."

"I appreciate that. Thank you."

"Well, once you're settled, come get me, okay?" Ivy says, planting a kiss on her beau's cheek. Slowly, she walks away, shorty-shorts dangerously close to revealing another pair of cheeks.

"Subtle, isn't she?" I laugh before killing off my coffee.

Peter, completely overwhelmed, wipes his face with his hands. "And she's really my match?" he asks.

"Yup!" I say with glee. "Good luck with that!"

Nineteen

"CHEERS!" I CLINK GLASSES WITH CHARLIE, AMANI, AND VINCENT at an adorable Italian spot in Lincoln Park. Summertime in Chicago means that every restaurant suddenly has an outdoor eating area, stringing a few lights and lanterns over as many tables as they can legally cram onto the sidewalk so our little midwestern hearts can soak up as much sunshine as possible.

Peter got all settled at Charlie's, and then my boyfriend got his wish for more romantic fun times. We had to wait for sunset so Vincent could join, which meant I was able to squeeze in a much-needed power nap beforehand.

"It feels soooo good to be home," Amani sighs, somehow defying the index-crushing humidity in a blush-pink halter dress. I tried to take it up a notch by wearing a gray T-shirt dress, but I can't even come close to my trio's level of glam. Charlie's rocking a gingham button-down that coordinates perfectly with his dragon tattoo, while Vincent (not in a tux for once) is very *GQ* in white linen and khaki. The three of them could easily be inspiration for an "Effortless Summer Fashion" photo shoot, while mine would be titled "How to Achieve the Bare Minimum." It's a carefully curated aesthetic.

"It sounds like you all had quite an adventure," Vincent muses, swirling his sauvignon blanc.

"Slightly disappointing, though." Charlie frowns. "Those fairies were kind of a bummer."

"Kind of? Try *completely*." I laugh, ripping off a chunk of breadstick.

Vincent nods. "It's too bad they can't relax and just reap the benefits of that dust of theirs."

"Oh reeeeeeally?" Amani's eyebrow curves in suspicion. "And what kind of benefits would those be, hmm?"

Her boyfriend grins, revealing some extra-pointy canines. "All that power . . . endless possibilities . . . I've seen some things, but it would be ungentlemanly of me to divulge further."

"C'mon, Vincent, I've candied pig brains for you; you can tell us," I say. We all stop eating until he agrees to share.

"All right, well . . . from what I've witnessed, fairy dust makes you unstoppable. Like you're holding the world in your hands. But that's the problem; some people don't know how to stop."

"So you've partaken?" Amani asks.

"No." Vincent's tongue touches the tip of his right fang. "But I can't say I haven't been tempted. It's hard to look a dream in the face and pass it by. That instant gratification isn't for me, though. I always craved something real, less fleeting." He reaches for his girlfriend's hand, and she sighs with content, candy-coated hearts radiating from both pairs of eyes.

"Ugh, you two are so gross sometimes, you know that?" I tease.

"We learned from the best." Amani smirks, and my head snaps in Charlie's direction as our mouths drop in fake shock.

"Are you talking about us?"

"PLEASE!" Amani rolls her eyes. "Don't even get me started." I decide against shooting a meatball across the table (mostly because I want to eat it) and instead reply by very maturely sticking out my tongue at her. We settle back into our entrees, but I take a second for a mental snapshot of this moment: good friends, good food, and fun times in the summer. This season is so fleeting, and with college looming on the horizon, there are so few of these moments left. When we come back together after weeks or months apart, will it be just like this? Will we be able to talk and laugh like no time has passed, or will our separate adventures create craters in the conversation, making it seem like we were never once whole? I want to believe the Fates brought us together for a reason and those ties will only strengthen as we move on. I can't see the stars, but I know they're up there, shining down on us, a double date with the best people in the best city.

"Well, this has been delightful," Charlie says once the bill's been paid. "But I'm afraid you'll have to excuse us, because I have a surprise for Miss Sand." He offers me his hand.

"Is it pie?" I ask.

"It's better than pie."

"What's better than pie?"

"Just . . . come with me, okay?"

Amani winks at me, and I wonder if she's had a vision about whatever Charlie has planned. She knows I don't like being caught off guard, so I'd hope she warn me if something insane was about to happen. But she just grins at me, snuggling into the cold-blooded arms of her vampire beau.

We walk through the neighborhood, passing by brown-stones and eateries, each one vying for the attention of Chicago foodies and families alike. Block after block, the city is crawling with people looking to get crazy, hang out, or fall in love. Fingers intertwined, we talk about anything and everything, from an upcoming camping trip he's taking with his dad, to which classes we're most excited to start in the fall (me: Intro to Sauces; Charlie: Sociology 101). Even though the sun has set, summer humidity rages on, and we stop at a Popsicle truck to help ward off sweat. I choose a pineapple-fig pop, while Charlie goes with coconut-blueberry-basil, and we find ourselves at the gates of Lincoln Park Zoo, a small, meandering animal park nestled into winding, tree-lined paths. I thought the zoo closed after dark, but the gate attendant waves us through, giving Charlie a knowing nod. We pass by zebras, gorillas, and lions, but the farther we go, Charlie grows increasingly weird, body stiffening, hand clammier than usual, even when accounting for the heat. His breathing becomes a concentrated effort, like he's trying not to vomit, and I feel like I've missed some key turning point in his demeanor.

"Hey, um, you all right there, Blitzman?" I ask, nervous he could vomit at any second. "You look really pale."

Jittery, too-loud laughter escapes his lips. "Gee, thanks!" His voice is all wrong, eyes looking anywhere but at me.

What is happening to him? "Was it the Popsicles?"

"No, I just . . . let's sit down a sec."

"Okaaaay." If his surprise is a behavior transplant, then he's succeeded. We find a bench next to a merry-go-round with spinning leopards and pandas instead of ponies. Faint carnival music fills the night air, along with a cinnamony-sugar scent wafting from a nearby churro cart.

"So, Amber, we've known each other for how long now?" Charlie asks, wiping his hands on his shorts. His question is odder than odd, but since he's clearly imploding, I go with it.

"Um, forever? Since our parents had us do playdates in diapers?"

"Right. Forever. Forever is a pretty long time, right?"

I'm doing everything I can not to have major WTF face. "Yes . . ."

"Some people are afraid of forever. But not me. I say, 'Bring it on, Forever! I'm ready!'" He raises an imaginary sword into the air.

"Charlie, what—" But I stop myself as a stabbing realization of where this could be heading solidifies. But no, he wouldn't, would he? Charlie is so much more romantic than me, but he wouldn't—he couldn't—be proposing . . . right? I mean . . . no. No! We're too young! We're only eighteen! And while for some strange reason that means we're legally adults, I know I am nowhere near being ready to be someone's wife. WIFE. The word doesn't sit right in my brain. I love Charlie, more than I love chocolate, but this cannot be happening. Not now . . . not yet. Oh Gods, now I'm clamming up, looking for the nearest trash can in case my spaghetti needs to make a reappearance.

"We're going to different schools next year," he continues, a legit river of sweat trailing from his temple, "and while we'll still be able to see each other lots, it's going to be harder. We'll both get busy with new classes, new routines, new people—"

"New people?" No matter what changes are headed our way, Charlie needs to remain fully mine. The idea of him having fun without me adds additional stress to this already-uncomfortable exchange.

I don't know if he can sense my freak-out, but he shifts toward me, finally able to look me in the eye. I shake away the static as he rubs my cheek with his thumb, finding a sudden reserve of serenity. "I want you to know that no matter what, I'm committed to you." As he reaches into his pocket, my heart beats so hard I worry it will rupture against my ribs. What is this boy thinking? He cannot be serious right now! I love him with all my heart but this—THIS—is just . . . AHHHHHH!

He does, in fact, pull a small ring from his pocket, but before I can faint, he says, "I know what you're thinking; this is not a proposal. That'd be crazy, right?"

I can't tell if I want to kiss him or punch him. "Oh my Gods, Charlie!" I sharply exhale. He chokes out a shaky laugh too, the pressure of the buildup subsiding.

"I wanted to give you something—a symbol of how much I care about you." He smiles. "I mean, I know I'm a pretty great boyfriend, but I'm not husband material yet." I let out another stilted breath as he extends the ring, a simple silver band with tiny etched stars. I don't wear much jewelry, but if I did, this is exactly something I would choose: understated with a hint of personality. I love it, and I love him for getting it right. "It's a promise ring—a promise that I'll always be thinking of you, and you'll always be in my heart. I know things are messed up with your magic, and your visions for me are all confused, and while I know you'll never stop worrying about it, I want you to know I'm not. Because I see us together. Forever."

I don't even realize I'm crying until he slips the band over my right ring finger. Tears blur my vision as I whisper, "It's perfect. You're perfect." His palms on my cheeks, he pulls me in, and we kiss to the soundtrack of circling zoo creatures, enveloped in the evening's warmth.

Charlie stops, dark green eyes gleaming behind his glasses. "Let's go for a ride," he says, nodding toward the carousel. "I call the dragon."

We run, hand in hand, laughing as we each choose a beast to carry us on the journey. With him perched on a dragon and me on a unicorn, we spin in circles, a flurry of lights and love. Charlie reaches across the ride to squeeze my hand, my new ring pressing into my skin. It feels good, solid—a promise I can touch and hold on to, regardless of what the Fates have in store. Never in the history of summer nights was there one as perfect as this; I want to live in this bliss forever.

Which is why I decide right then and there to sign Roscoe's contract and be done with my magical drama for good.

Twenty

I STORM INTO ROSCOE'S RUNES, APPOINTMENT BE DAMNED. I NEED my magic fixed and I need it now, and I'm hoping my form of payment will accelerate the process. Is giving a dark warlock a heaping scoop of the most powerful substance ever a terrible idea? Maybe. Who knows what kind of sick, twisted wish a dude like this could dream up? But based on how obsessed he is with collecting coveted objects, there's no way he'll be able to resist using it, and hopefully his consequence will be so colossal, no one will ever have to deal with him again. BOOM! YES! AMBER SAND FTW!

Gripping my cookie box of fairy dust, I blow past the cases of perfectly lit horrors and start pounding on Roscoe's office door. I get some stares from random customers perusing the selection of deadly snakes, but whatever. "Hello!" I shout, purchasing power giving me a boost of confidence. "I know you're in there!"

Roscoe's feline assistant creeps up from behind, stealthy paws crushing the sneak-attack game. Frustrated that I've bypassed her precious scheduling system, she glares at me, furry ears flattening against her head.

"Excuse me," she hisses. "Do you have an appointment?"

"No." I keep my chin up, mirroring her high-and-mighty air. "But I have something Roscoe will want to see."

Her tail stands straight in anger, fur puffing up. "He's very busy, I'm afraid. You'll have to come back later."

"Too busy for this?" I pop open the box, and golden light bursts forth. Her amber eyes widen with wonder as she stumbles backward, grabbing the doorknob and disappearing into the office without a word. Looks like somebody has the golden ticket after all!

Seconds later, Roscoe appears, wearing a different fedora-vest-distressed-jean combo, but still evoking the same douche-bag vibe. His gaze goes straight to the box, and I swear a tear of joy rolls down his carefully groomed face. He reaches for it, like a tiny child grabbing for Santa Claus, but catches himself before his tattooed fingers brush the dust.

"Amber!" he exclaims, unable to contain his enthusiasm. "What a remarkable find! However did you manage this?"

I shrug. "Doesn't matter how," I say, invoking my inner badass. "It's here, and I'm ready to make a deal."

He ushers me inside, shutting the door on Catwoman, much to her dismay. I sit on a royal-blue floor cushion, carefully setting my treasure at my feet.

"I must say," Roscoe begins with a laugh, keeping his eyes on his soon-to-be prize, "I'm quite impressed that someone as young, and, no offense, barely magical as you found fairy dust." Considering the amount of drool on his chin, he really should be nicer to me. Nobody in this room has time for backhanded compliments. "I have been searching for dust for over a decade to no avail. Those fairies . . . they really keep a low profile."

"Yeah, well, not if you know where to look," I throw back, enjoying my superiority.

He waggles a knowing finger, checking himself. "You Sands . . . you are tricky!" He chuckles. "Like mother, like daughter."

No one really ever compares me to my mom, unless it's in an "Oh, isn't it sad Amber's not a witch?" kind of way. I don't mind it, though, especially since he's musing on our dastardly tendencies, which I enjoy.

"Anyway." I shift, eager to get this done. "So, what's the timeline here? I give you the fairy dust, and you bust out a cure?"

He scratches his stubbly chin. "As I mentioned before, I'll need to do some research. As I'm sure you've discovered, uncovering answers to uncommon questions can be difficult. I don't want to give you an estimate and have it be wrong. It could be days, weeks. . . ."

Weeks? "I'm not giving you fairy dust to have this go on for weeks. Maybe I should take my business elsewhere." I start to stand, but he desperately lunges forward, pressing my legs back into the pillow.

"No, no, no," he says, lust in his eyes. "I'll do everything I can. Put my best people on it, work myself around the clock. I will find you what you need."

I huff in agreement. It's not like I actually have other options. Convincing a fairy to grant me a wish has been like asking a troll to share a sandwich (just trust me, the struggle is the same), and even Mom, with all her magical connections and resources, has come up empty. I need this, just as much as he does. And this time, when he unfurls the shimmering scroll before me, I know this is truly the end of the line.

I skim through the mystical verbiage, but even if I could read these words in their hyper-swirly font, I wouldn't understand what they mean. I feel like Ariel, signing her voice away to a devious Ursula but ready to put everything on the line for what she wants. Before I can chicken out again, I sign on the dotted line. The parchment quivers with my acceptance, and Roscoe rolls it up tight, turning to me with predatory hunger.

Yikes. Alarm bells rattle in my brain, but it's too late now. I hand over the box, which he cradles like a bubble, not wanting it to burst. I can already see the wheels turning in his wicked head, cooking up what I'm sure will be a truly wretched wish. I just hope the Fates will check him with an equally brutal side effect in return. Of course with my luck, that'll be the day they're asleep on the job.

Coming out of his lovestruck trance, he locks the cookie box away in his cabinet, securing the key on a leather cord around his neck. "I'll send my assistant, Kasia, to check in with you from time to time," he says. "She'll keep you posted on my status."

Ugh, can't he just text? I don't want that whiskery woman following me around. "Sounds . . . great."

He leads me out to the showroom, pausing at a wall display with rows and rows of tiny glass vials that are filled with a dark, viscous liquid that can only be blood. I don't even want to think about whose or what DNA is lining his pockets with cash. "Amber, before you go, I have to ask: Why didn't you just use the dust yourself? Weren't you tempted?"

"Sure," I admit, recalling how the barrels hypnotized me. I came really close to giving in, screwing it all just to find relief from this constant worry. But being with Charlie last night made me realize that while I want to feel secure in my matchmaking magic, I want my future more. Putting my fate in the tattooed hands of a creepy warlock may seem like an illogical choice, but it's better than grappling with an unforeseen consequence that could completely alter who I am. I may be a mess, but it's a mess I know and love. I don't want anyone taking that away from me. "I didn't want to deal with the aftermath."

He smiles, the kind of grin that makes you wish you hadn't. "Well, we all have limits on how far we'll go."

I think of everything I've been through in the name of love. Hunting for leprechauns, chasing down goblins, battling against witches, tangling up with mermaids and werewolves. None of these adventures were for me, but I threw in my heart just the same, hoping for happily-ever-afters. Now I deserve closure too, and I think I've gone pretty damn far to get it.

Twenty-One

AFTER DEALING WITH THE DARK MAGIC SCENE, IT FEELS STRAIGHT-UP comedic to head over to the carnival colors of Navy Pier. All the shops are having a summer sidewalk sale, which is hilarious and dumb because most stuff here is so overpriced that any savings received will just be eaten up by the hourly parking rate. It's not like anyone casually meanders over to the pier in hopes of catching a sale or event; this place is a destination, so if you are here, it's for a specific reason, and I can guarantee it's not for discounted tchotchkes. Windy City Magic is contractually obligated to participate in things like this, though, so I've set up a table just outside the door with some of our less popular potions and knickknacks, including this sour-smelling incense that in no way embodies its "Natural Spring" namesake, and mood-sensitive lip balm that unfortunately turns most mouths blue. Bob has been manning this station for most of the morning, but it's one of those rare summer days where it's warm without being suffocatingly humid, so I'm taking a break from my still-busy matchmaking table to soak up some sun.

"Hey, Nancy." I wave at the vendor down the way. Our next-door neighbors are one of three "I ♥ Chicago" shops, selling T-shirts, backpacks, and anything that can be screen-printed with their namesake. The owner has set up their sale with a collection of Cubs, Bears, and Sears Tower snow globes (I don't care if it's called the Willis Tower now—Sears Tower forever). Nancy, an older woman who has always treated us like we have leprosy, scowls at me, turning the other direction. Cool. Her rude behavior makes me want to sacrifice a goat just to annoy her, because I'm sure she assumes that's what we do.

I rearrange my sad assortment of discount items for the tenth time, trying to make them more alluring, when Kim comes out to join me.

"I'm bored." She pouts, pulling at a unicorn necklace we sell that quickly became her favorite. I love unicorns forever, but I can't seem to pull off that happy-rainbow vibe like she can. "What's happening out here?"

"Oh, nothing." I sigh. "Nancy thinks we're the devil incarnate."

"Right." Kim attempts to throw a dirty look in Nancy's direction, but it's like a baby kitten trying to roar. I tuck my face into my shoulder to hide a laugh. "So, I was thinking of planning a sleepover at my house. A big girly explosion of snacks, movies, and makeovers. Sound fun?"

She's my friend, but I'm not even sure I would enjoy the party she's describing. Except for the snacks: I'm always down for food. "Um, sure."

Kim claps her hands excitedly. "Yay! I know I wasn't part of the fairy road trip, but it sounded pretty crazy. We could all use a good time. You'll be in charge of desserts, obvs, and I'll have Amani bring her makeup trunk. For the movies, should we go rom-coms or horror marathon?"

Hard pass to both. "Let Amani pick."

"Perfect. And . . . should we invite Ivy?"

Hmm. I wonder how that'd go down. Ivy used to force random bands of harpies to follow her around at school, but I don't know if that devotion ever carried over outside Manchester Prep. Did she do sleepovers and "girl time"? I always pictured her sitting alone in a dark room, reciting satanic rituals and building her siren strength on the weekends, but I guess that's not fair. Ms. I ♥ Chicago over there probably thinks the same thing about me. "Yeah, go for it." I shrug.

"Awesome. Do you think your mom will mind if I use some spare parchments to write down party plans?"

"Nah—" I stop myself. "Well, just check there aren't any symbols or scribbles in the corners. Sometimes she leaves really abstract notes that look like nothing but are her own little witch code."

"Got it! This is gonna be so fun!" She skips off, and once again I'm alone to observe a sea of strollers, shorts, and Slurpees. I space out, watching an infant repeatedly throw her pacifier on the sidewalk, her tired mother wiping it off every single time, when a hand waving in my face snaps me back to reality.

Peter smiles down at me, kind and warm, back to his regular self. "Hey there."

"Oh! Hey, Peter. What are you doing here?" I'm glad the potion has him all perked up, but I didn't expect him to come by the shop, like, ever.

"Ivy told me I'd find you here. We were up all night talking." He winces, pulling his shoulders back awkwardly. It must be really uncomfortable tucking wings into your pants. "She told me all about your shop, and I'm hoping you can give me a tour . . . show me what real magic looks like." He smiles hopefully.

While I'm not completely ready to forgive his past behavior, at least he's trying. "Sure, why not?" I turn to my left. "Hey, Nancy, don't steal anything while I'm gone, okay?" She waves dismissively. Ha, ha.

The shop isn't busy—it's too beautiful to be indoors shopping—and happily the store is as presentable as it can possibly be. No children have knocked over our figurine display, and the Brew Your Own Potion station is relatively spill-free. I walk him around, showing the precious gemstones, bird feathers, and herbs, finishing with the gaudy selection of "authentic" witch hats (in that they were stitched by a witch, but witches don't actually wear them). Kim waves cheerily as we pass by the register, but Peter looks more confused than impressed.

"So, that's it," I say, propping my hands on my hips.

The fairy's sherbet eyebrows furrow. "But . . . there's no bubbling cauldron. No animal blood, no pentagons."

"Oh, we do have some pentagon charms over there." I nod at our jewelry stand. "Were you in need of something bigger, or . . . ?"

He shakes his head. "No, nothing like that, I . . . It's all so different than I expected."

I click my tongue. "Yeah. You can't believe every stereotype." I fail to mention our giant cauldron at home, but that's okay.

"Everything is so bright . . . positive. I thought there'd be wizards dueling or werewolves scratching the place apart to get their paws on magic." He self-consciously tucks his hands under his armpits.

"Nah. The closest we ever get to something like that is when we have a fifty-percent-off sale." I pause for him to laugh at my joke, but he's not picking up what I'm putting down. "But seriously, we hardly ever have trouble. Most magical folks know how to handle themselves and are only looking for supplies for fun stuff. And if someone does cause a ruckus, we refuse service and Bob here kicks them to the curb." I gesture to my mending magus friend as he lumbers by, looking incredibly menacing as he dusts the crystal balls.

Peter coughs out a nervous laugh. "Are all magic shops like this?"

"Do you mean, as awesome as this? Unfortunately no. There are those that will assist anyone, even those with less-than-righteous intentions." I think of the pile of venomous scorpions crawling around at Roscoe's Runes and try not to shudder. "But honestly? Those shops are so few, because they are scary as hell and most magical people don't want to deal with that scene."

He considers this, head swirling with questions. "I am pleasantly surprised. By all of this." Walking around some more, comfort levels rising, he asks, "Do you have the ingredients for that potion you gave me?"

I shrug. "Um, I'm sure they're scattered around. Mom was the one who made it, though, and she brewed it at home."

"I was just thinking . . . it may be good to have some extra, in case the pain returns," Peter says cautiously.

"Are your wings okay?"

"Oh, yes, they're great," he says, glancing around. He awkwardly reaches back to touch the tops of his concealed wings, a skittish smile crossing his lips. "I'm just being overly cautious."

"I don't exactly have the recipe, nor the ability, to make another batch. But you could grab some of our premixed tonics." I guide him to a small refrigerator near the back, which contains several five-ounce bottles of easy remedies for headaches, cramps, stuff like that. There's nothing in them that has to be refrigerated, and the magical contents are very small, but they taste better cold. "Let's see . . . maybe an Aches and Pains tonic? I've used this before. It's kind of like drinking an Epsom salt bath."

Peter's eyes grow wide with wonder as he reads through all the labels: Mood Booster, Instant Nap, Heartburn-Be-Gone. He's unusually excited to see the wide variety, like a kid in a toy store. But I guess if you've gone your whole life without any magic, anything and everything seems amazing.

"I'll take one of each," he announces, swinging open the door. He enthusiastically grabs every flavor, proudly carrying them to the register.

"Did you find everything you were looking for?" Kim chimes, ringing up his purchase.

"Yes, thank you," he says, eyeing the small add-ons cluttering the counter. "I'll take one of these too." He grabs a tin of magic mints. "And this." Permanently Trimmed Toenail juice. "And why not this too!" Vampire sunscreen. Weird choice. All in all, he walks away with twenty-five magical concoctions, a veritable magic starter kit. Excitedly, he grabs his bag and dashes out the door, barely remembering to wish us good-bye before disappearing into the summer day.

"Well, that was one satisfied customer," Kim says.

"Yeah. I never would've guessed."

Twenty-Two

"Amber, truth or dare?"

I fill my mouth with M&M's, giving myself a few more seconds to choose which is the lesser of two evils. Why is a game where you have to either share your innermost secrets or be forced to perform ridiculous feats of bravery a thing? Sigh. Maybe this is why I avoided group sleepovers my entire life— that, and the complete lack of invites, I guess. But staying at Amani's while her brothers went bonkers in the background was more civilized than this.

"Dare, I guess," I finally answer to the groans of the group. "What?"

"You can't keep picking dares," Kim sternly informs me, arms crossed over her lavender sleep tank. She worked really hard planning this event, making sure the menu, activities, and even candle fragrances would all blend in one cohesive night of magical memories, and right now, I'm not playing into her vision. Hell hath no fury like a party planner scorned! "Eventually you have to pick truth."

"That's not a thing. I demand to see a rule book."

Amani glares at me from the other side of the circle, giving me her patented "Amber, stop being annoying" face. Man, I will really miss this expression when she leaves for college. How will I know when I'm being the worst?

"Ugh, fine!" I throw my hands up. "TRUTH."

Kim churns up the most mischievous look I've ever seen her conjure, and I'm frightened of what's about to come out of her mouth. "What is the most romantic thing Charlie's ever done for you?" Oh. There was a time when hearing his name from her lips would've put me into a tailspin, and even though we're past that drama, I'm still not the most comfortable sharing the private details of my relationship with anyone but Amani. You'd think that someone who's spent her years creeping on other people's love lives would make me more open, but no. My BFF and our hostess stare at me expectantly, as possible answers swirl through my head, each more precious than the last.

I spin the silver band on my ring finger; that was definitely a top-five romantic moment for sure, but honestly, the memory that makes my heart grow three sizes is less obvious, a little moment that meant so much. Back when I was waiting to hear from the Culinary Institute, my impatience was mounting (shocking, I know). Every day I waited by the front window for mail delivery, practically flinging myself down three sets of stairs the second the mail carrier left, falling into a pit of despair every time there wasn't a letter for me. Eventually the deadline for acceptance passed, and my lack of correspondence resulted in assuming I'd been rejected, a theory I took really well.

One afternoon, I was perched in my regular stalker spot (because my foolish heart would not let go), when Charlie roller-skated—yes, roller-skated—into my line of sight. He waved up at me, an additional pair of skates dangling around his neck. He forced me out of my apartment before the mail arrived, and we skated around the Wicker Park neighborhood, falling over every crack in the sidewalk, since neither of us are athletically gifted, but also laughing at how dumb we probably looked. I don't know where he got those skates, or even how he pried me from my post, but for a few hours, he made my worries skate away and gave me my first chance to smile in weeks. When we returned, there was an acceptance letter in my mailbox, and I'm still convinced his magic made it happen.

It's silly, maybe, but it feels like the most quintessential Charlie moment. Still, it's not as flashy as the promise-ring thing, so I go with that. The girls eat it up, responding with a chorus of "Aww!"'s meaning it's my turn to exact pain.

"Kim: truth or dare?"

She sits up straight on her giant fluffy floor pillow, dark hair falling down her back. "Dare."

"What? How come she can choose dare again but not me?" I ask.

Amani throws a handful of popcorn at me. "Stop being such a baby!" She laughs.

"Fine!" I fake-pout, shaking a kernel out of my peacock hair. "Um . . . I dare you to stick an entire cupcake in your mouth at once." Weak, I know, but whatever.

She grabs for my plate of honey-butterscotch cupcakes, choosing the one with the most frosting (respect). "With pleasure." She smiles, cramming the whole thing in, impressive not only because her mouth is not exactly large, but also my cupcakes are crazy dense. We applaud her effort, and when she finally manages to swallow all that sugar, she turns back to me. "Amber: truth or dare?"

Ugh! "Why me again?!"

"Because it's fun to torture you."

I release a deep groan to the heavens. "Truth, apparently."

With a twinkle in her eyes, she asks, "Do you think Charlie is your match?"

The room goes silent, and I almost choke on the brownie I'm chewing. Amani's face looks like someone just pulled a fire alarm. It's an emotionally loaded question coming from her, and I'm doing mental gymnastics trying to decide whether she's trying to be evil or what. Kim's a sweet person; I doubt she'd purposely do anything to make me feel bad. Yet she knows about everything I'm going through with the matchmaker biz. I've put a lot on the line to have this mystery solved, hoping to find out once and for all if I could text Charlie to say, "Hey, guess what? We're meant to be!" or "It's over; forget I ever existed." Now I'm waiting for a warlock to brew up answers, and there's not a second that goes by where I'm not obsessing about it. Finally, I yell out, "Not sure!" and dash into Kim's kitchen.

Seconds later, Amani has a hand on my shoulder. "You okay?"

"Yeah, I just . . . A lot of sharing back there."

"Pretty sure Kim wasn't trying to give you an aneurysm," she says. "You doing okay with all this matchmaker stuff? I know you were hoping Jane would be more help, and the dust turned out to be a bust."

My lip trembles against my will. "Yeah, I . . . did something."

Amani raises a brow. "Something bad?"

"It depends on your definition of bad."

"Let's go with the traditional one."

"Okay, then probably yes," I admit. There's no way she'll let me off the hook with this, but there's also no way I can keep my deal with Roscoe a secret. "I signed the contract."

For a second, she freezes, locked in a stare somewhere between disappointment and disgust. "You . . . what?"

I look around the kitchen, making sure there are no hard

objects within arm's reach that she can hit me with. "Listen, okay? I know he's gross, and I know we agreed to find another way. But there isn't. Every lead has turned cold, every option exhausted. Mom can't help, the fairies *won't* help, and the Fates are jerks who won't even give you a vision of me to relay. There's literally nothing else I can do."

She chomps on a chip, irritation sounding in each crunch. "Does Charlie know about this?"

"Yeah, I told him." That was a fun chat. Though I couldn't tell if he was more disturbed with me signing a deal with a dark warlock, or that I was in the vicinity of dragon eggs without him.

Her hands fly up in frustration. "Well, it's done. Can't go back now. Do you really think he'll be able to help you?"

What does she want me to say? Obviously my answer is yes, or I wouldn't have gone through with it at all. "Gods, I hope so! I just want some answers."

"Like if Charlie is your match?"

"Yes! I mean, sure. That would be great. I've been dying to know my match ever since my powers became a thing. But honestly at this point, it's more than that. Yes, I want to know my fate with Charlie, but I want to know my fate with myself. If my magic is drying up, what does that mean? Who will I even be? Will I just turn into someone boring and normal?"

Amani pinches her lips together in a tight smile. "I hate to break it you, but you'll never be normal."

"I AM TRYING TO DROP TRUTHS HERE!"

She laughs. "I know, I'm sorry. But this Roscoe stuff makes me nervous! I want you to be happy and whole, I just hate that it's come to this."

"Well, I'm not exactly psyched about it either."

My best friend leans back on the counter, staring at an impressive collection of copper pots hanging from the ceiling. "So now we wait to see what's next?" I nod. "Okay. Let's talk about something else, or I'm gonna go crazy thinking about it. What do you think the chances of my parents letting me take their old Camaro to U of I are?"

Bless my BFF for her solid subject change. "Um, zero? Negative zero? Isn't that their datemobile?"

She makes a *blech* sound, sticking out her tongue. "Yes, yuck. But it hardly ever gets used, especially compared to the swagger wagon. And how will I ever get around Champaign without a car!? It's not like they have a CTA!"

I stroke an imaginary beard. "Hmm, yes, sounds like you haven't really thought this through. Guess you'll just have to transfer to the Chicago campus."

But she will not be deterred. "No, no. Being a precog means nothing in my life has been normal, and I want to do the typical college thing. Join a sorority, live in a dorm, learn how to do a keg stand . . . you know."

I sigh. "Kids these days." My phone buzzes with a notification. "Speaking of which . . . looks like Jane and Rose are back at it with a new *Matchmaking Magic!* video." We pull up their latest episode, and I can't stop smiling thinking about scowly Rose under all that Madame L'Amour makeup. It's really impressive how she's able to slide into this happy, bubbly personality, when her reality could not be more different. But I'm glad she's keeping Jane busy; it must be strange for her not having her brother around. *Finding love is magic. . . .*

The doorbell rings, and we hear Kim welcoming another guest. Shortly after, Ivy comes waltzing in, all short-shorts and bunny slippers.

"Sorry I'm late, all," she says breezily, scanning the snack table. "I got caught up with Peter."

Kim makes a kissy face with accompanying smoochy sounds, much to my dismay.

"No, it's not that," Ivy says, though a sly smile betrays her statement. "Okay, it was a little of that." Amani pretends to vomit. "We're just getting to know each other better. He's . . . different than he was on the farm."

"Different how?" I hand her a cupcake to coax her further.

"Like, I don't know. I guess I haven't spent a lot of time actually talking to boys, so whatever, maybe my view is a little skewed, but Peter definitely has a lot going on. He's kind of a handful." She pauses. "Not like that."

Color drains from Kim's face. "I may need to leave this conversation."

"Ivy, cut the innuendo and tell us what's up," I demand.

"It's hard to explain. When we met, it was under the weirdest of circumstances, right? I was on my deathbed, and clearly he was in some sort of mental prison. In the past couple days, there have been lots of emotional highs and lows. Now I guess he's on some kind of journey to find himself?" She grabs a handful of popcorn, shrugging. "All I can say is, it was much easier to just love 'em and leave 'em. Who knew boys were so high-maintenance?"

"Ladies and gentlemen, I think that's what's known as personal growth," I say, gesturing to Exhibit Ivy.

"Whatever." She rolls her eyes. "Enough about dumb boys. Anyone want to make voodoo dolls?"

I laugh, never expecting the sleepover activity I'd be most interested in would be suggested by my former nemesis. Ivy starts unpacking an impressive collection of doll-making supplies as Kim pulls me off to the side.

"Hey, I'm sorry about earlier," she half whispers. "I didn't mean to upset you with the match thing; I was just curious. I ship you two hard-core."

I wrap my arms around my friend. "Don't worry about it."

From my embrace, she mumbles, "Do you think Peter's okay?"

"With Ivy? No one's safe."

"No, I mean, what she was describing, about him being really emotional. Obviously I didn't know him before, but based on what you all told me, his Windy City shopping spree seemed kinda weird."

"I guess." I shrug. "He's living in a whole new world now, and I'm sure it's a lot to process. Plus he's dating Ivy, which is basically like living in a real-life horror movie. Don't worry too much; he's staying with Charlie, so the Bliztmans are keeping an eye on him. John's pretty tough. . . . I wouldn't want to mess with him." Kim smiles at this. "But for now, who in your life deserves to be a voodoo doll?"

"I could think of a few people," she says with a giggle.

"Only a few?" I laugh. "You are so precious."

Twenty-Three

IT'S BEEN A FEW WEEKS, AND NOTHING CATACLYSMIC HAS GONE down of late, except for the fact that I've received ZERO information from Roscoe. I know he said it may take a while, but this is pretty ridiculous. He also said Kasia would be touching base, and while I'd be happy to never see her kitty-cat face ever again, it would be helpful if she'd at least give me a status update. More than once I've started the trek to his store, only to turn around in a huff. To keep my antsy brain occupied, I've picked up some extra shifts at the Black Phoenix, because what's better than serving goblins and witches deep-fried beetle shells and scalding-hot bat soup? My Summer of Sloth has turned into anything but, and I. Am. Over. It.

After tying on my apron, I disappear into the kitchen, which is loud and busy prepping for dinner. Cooks run back and forth, yelling at each other and clanging pots with more force than necessary. The scent of simmering butter and searing flesh invades my nasal passages, and I'm instantly treated to an extremely close view of a bowl full of squirming earthworms. Great, just what I wanted. Time to make some creepy desserts, I guess.

"Hey, Amber, good to see you." Marcus waves from the corner of the room. He looks content, somehow calm with all the clamor around him, and it makes my heart pinch in happiness. His romantic feelings for me have cooled since last winter, and we've settled into a comfortable friendship. I'm so glad. Besides Ella, he's one of the only people who gets my food geekiness, and I didn't want to lose him from my life. Charlie and I have even double-dated with him and his new girlfriend, Hazel, who I am mildly convinced is his match, even if my visions are making it hard to tell.

I make my way through the commotion, excited to see my culinary companion. "Hey! Oh! Were you able to get that strawberry huller I was hoping for?" I ask. "I was thinking I could use it to extract fish eyeballs before I whip up my under-the-sea dessert soufflé."

Marcus laughs, unable to contain his excitement. "That's what you wanted that for?" He pulls the gadget from a drawer of infrequently used tools. "Man, your professors are really going to love you."

"You know, you're not the first person to say that to me, and I'm starting to develop a complex about it."

He smiles, toothy and bright, as he starts to season an iron skillet. "No, it's just . . . there's a lot of people at CCI who try making weird stuff just to prove they're some kind of food wizards or something." He frowns. "Not actual wizards, you know, but like, innovative. Provocateurs. People trying to be edgy for the sake of it. But you are genuinely psyched to do new stuff just to see if it tastes good. Kitchens need that kind of heart." He nudges me with a spatula, and I can't help but blush.

"Sheesh. Thanks, Chef. I can't wait to start."

"Well, you can go crazy by breaking open that pile of pomegranates over there. I hate tearing into those things."

"On it!" I give a small salute, though I agree that pomegranates are super annoying and not entirely worth the struggle of stripping all those seeds. Whoever decided this should be deemed a "superfood" and in turn increased its popularity should be forced to cut into one of these messy beasts every hour on the hour.

Soon enough, I fall back into the kitchen rhythm, recalling the menu items and uncommon special requests, weaving in and out of the furious chopping, drizzling, and plating. I'm totally in the zone, artfully placing tiny rose apples on top of a caramelized vulture breast, when Alessandra, Black Phoenix's hostess, pokes her elegant sphinx self in behind the scenes.

"Psst! Amber!" she whisper-shouts, barely audible over the kitchen clatter. "AMBER!" I jerk up to see her wildly motioning for me.

Wiping pomegranate juice from my fingers, I ask, "What's up?"

Wearing a formfitting cocktail dress, with golden hair accessories matched to her gilded wings, she looks completely out of place in the chaotic kitchen. "Your friend Ivy is here. . . . I recognized her from a few months ago. She's on a date with a fairy gentleman, and he's causing a bit of a scene."

"Like how?"

"Like . . ." She bites her lip. "Just come see. Vincent is getting upset."

Gah. I holler to Marcus that I'll be right back, and hit the dining room floor. A large group has gathered around one of the center tables: vampires, trolls, warlocks, and the like all laughing hysterically at some kind of spectacle. As we get closer, it's clear they've assembled around Peter and Ivy's table, where the fairy of the hour is letting it all hang out, orange wings and all, regaling his audience with some sort of swashbuckling tale that I can't imagine ever actually happened to him.

"And then I said, *'See you in Neverland, jerk!'*" Everyone cracks up at his mildly lame joke, but Peter is loving the attention, a smile as wide as his wingspan. He throws an arm around Ivy, who's equally thrilled to be in the spotlight, beaming like a recently crowned pageant queen. Totally glam, she's dressed in a mermaid-blue sequin dress paired with starlet blond waves, while Peter almost looks like a different person; sherbet hair cut short and mussed with product, wearing a tailored suit that could've been swiped from John Blitzman's closet. To the casual observer, they're just a beautiful, popular couple living it up on a night on the town, but Peter's never struck me as a "life of the party" kind of guy, and while I'm impressed he's indulging in magic culture, hobnobbing with so many supernaturals is not something I ever expected of him.

I give Alessandra's shoulder a pinch and then squeeze into the lively circle. "Hi! Hello! Can I get anybody anything?"

"Amber!" Peter leaps toward me, kissing both my cheeks like we're European BFFs. "How are you, darling?"

Darling? Wow. That's quite an improvement over his previous opinion of me. I haven't seen him much in the past few weeks. Maybe absence really does make the heart grow fonder. "Peachy. And I can tell you're golden."

"Definitely, definitely!" Gripping my biceps with Hulk strength, his eyes dance all over my face, unable to settle on a destination. I try to make eye contact, but he literally cannot focus, like he's existing on a separate plane. Something is not right at all. Peter quickly loses interest in me, turning to an ogre on his right, giving me a chance to slide in next to Ivy, who is casually stealing the cherry from her date's martini.

"Hey, uh, what are you guys doing?" I ask.

Impossibly lush lashes flutter my way. "We're on a date. What does it look like?"

"It looks like Peter's gone manic."

She shrugs, twisting a golden curl. "Or maybe he's finally acting like himself. Did you ever think of that? He was trapped in that hellish family hole that poisoned him toward the magical community and now he can finally breathe." Our eyes follow Peter as he heads up to the bar; after ordering another round, he does a flying backflip off the countertop to rousing cheers. I cringe when I spot Vincent near the front looking extremely displeased at these shenanigans.

"Ivy, has Peter been playing around with more magic?" I ask, watching as he hovers over his newly acquired fans, wings shimmering against the golden countertops. "I mean, we've given him potions to help heal his wings, which look perfectly fine now, but has he had access to other stuff?"

"I don't know what you're getting at," she says flatly.

"It's just . . . his behavior seems like a complete one-eighty, and magic could be playing a part." I pause, not even wanting to insinuate further, but I know I have to. "Unless *you* have something to do with how he's acting . . ."

At this, she throws her napkin on the table, jumping out of her chair to loom over me. "What, you think I'm sirening him to be the life of the party? That I'm forcing him to be this giant personality for my benefit?"

Well, yes, that's exactly what I was thinking.

Ivy presses her glossy red nails into her temples, making an active effort to calm herself down. I can almost hear her inner monologue, reminding herself not to take vengeance on innocent plebes. "I've learned my lesson, okay? Maybe the old me would've pulled tricks like that, forcing my boyfriend to be something he's not, but I'm not doing that ever again. Per your matchmaking,

Peter and I have a long life ahead of us, and I'm not going to waste my powers on stupid crap when I just got them back."

"Okay! Okay. Sorry. Calm down," I say, holding up my hands. "I was just asking."

Ivy takes a deep breath. Fire and fury subsiding, she sits back down. "Besides, I want this to be real," she adds with a much softer tone, which makes me feel horrible for accusing her of anything.

"I'm sorry," I say. "As a matchmaker and . . . friend . . . I'm invested in your relationship too. I just thought since Peter's hanging from the ceiling that I should check in."

"Thanks, I guess. We're fine." She keeps a steady glare on me, red lips pursed like she has something to say but doesn't know how to form the words. I consider bolting, lest they be filled with venom. "Also, since you're here or whatever," she continues, "I wanted to say thanks for taking me to Wisteria Farms in the first place. You didn't have to do that, especially after everything I've done to you, and . . . well, you're a bigger person than me, Amber Sand. I owe you one."

That is definitely the absolute last thing I expected to come out of her mouth. I guess we're now officially friends. What a world. "Um, sure. Any time."

Uncomfortable in our bonding moment, Ivy stands, crossing the room to Peter, who leans her back for a very passionate kiss to whoops and hollers all around. I shield my eyes.

Ivy being nice, Peter being . . . whatever that was . . . What's going on? I think as I head back to the kitchen. The Peter I've come to know is not this loud, showboaty person who flaunts his wings and makes out with his girlfriend in public. In all my visions of him, he's always appeared quiet and kind, more comfortable with a night in than going wild in the city. I get that he may be battling inner demons, trapped between the life he was taught and the possibilities before him. And that's not the kind of turmoil to just quickly and easily sort through.

I have an itchy feeling that magic is playing a part here, as much as I don't want that to be true. He took those healing potions a while ago, and any possible side effects would have left his system by now. Magic affects everyone differently, but at worst he would've felt the extreme relaxation common with painkillers, not this hyperactive personality reversal.

I text Rose, feeling like she should be kept in the loop here.

Hey I'm worried about Peter. He's used some magic, and now he's not himself.

A few minutes later, she responds:

And?

And? Sheesh.

And I was thinking you could help? Advice? Anything?

Peter's a big boy. He can deal with this himself.

Wow. Wonderful. Why should I care if his own family doesn't? I throw down my phone, but I already know the answer.

Because I made a promise to Jane, and matchmakers stick together.

Twenty-Four

THE NEXT MORNING, I WAKE UP TO ANOTHER TEXT FROM ROSE:

> Hey can I ask you a favor

For real? She cannot be serious. I love how when I ask her for literally anything, she gets all up in arms, but she has no problem turning around to see how I can help her. It is too early for this kind of hypocrisy. I type and delete several raging responses before replying with a simple:

> **Sure**

It took real restraint not to add an eye roll emoji. I'm treating myself to a donut later for my maturity.

> Jane's birthday is coming up and with Peter gone and her parents all in a huff, she's feeling kinda anti about it. Would it be cool if I brought her up to Chicago for a quick visit today?

Hmm. I told Ella I'd take a double shift at MarshmElla's today, assisting her while she takes care of some custom orders. I can't back out on her, especially since I haven't been around as much this summer. But I guess there really isn't anywhere better to celebrate one's birthday than in the world's most delicious bakery, right? I agree to meet up, and send off some texts to Charlie and Ivy, seeing if they can get Peter to drop by for an extra-surprise visit. That should earn me some Big Matchmaker Sister karma points for sure.

A short while later, I'm in MarshmElla's kitchen, boxing up an order of iced diamond-shaped sugar cookies for a bachelorette party while Ella nervously rushes around, taking stock of any and all baking tools that could be intriguing to a small child.

"And you promise you're not bringing a pint-sized demon into my store?" Ella asks, putting the pie weights on a high shelf so little fingers can't be tempted to throw them around. Her panic is justified, if not a little bit over the top: last spring, she added "Cake Decorating Birthday Parties" to her menu of offer-ings, thinking it'd be a fun way to bring new customers into the store. Unfortunately, the first and only party was a total disas-ter, causing sugar-fueled monsters to smear frosting all over the walls while their parents stood idly by, too busy sipping wine coolers out of water bottles. Ella and I were finding runaway sprinkles under the booths and display cases for weeks, bleaching food-coloring stains out of all our aprons and linens. Ella vowed never to host anything for anyone under voting age again.

"I promise," I say, forcing her to put down her collection of cookie cutters. "I personally vet anyone I bring to this sacred space."

She eyes me, blowing a stray blond strand out of her face. "Good! You better. Last time I was afraid someone was going to lose a finger in the stand mixer!"

"I know, don't worry. I've got this under control." Luckily, Ella had bought a ton of party supplies before nixing that particular business plan, so I have plenty to work with. I string up some streamers and a birthday banner over our biggest countertop, and fill the workspace with containers of rainbow-colored frosting, sprinkles, and candies that are just aching to top the dozens of vanilla, chocolate, and strawberry cupcakes I baked this morning. The setup looks pretty awesome, if I do say so myself, and I make a mental note to ask for something similar when my birthday rolls around.

The doorbell chimes, and I hope it's Peter, here to celebrate with his sister. But the second I peek my head out front, Jane comes running toward me, mint-green hair flying behind her like the mane of a happy Shetland pony frolicking through the fields. How can you not smile at that?

"Happy birthday, my friend!" I cheer as she wraps her tiny arms around my waist.

"Thanks, Amber!"

I pull back, giving her a quick once-over. Her pastel polka-dotted dress helps her blend right in with the sugary confections all around us. "Wait, have you gotten taller since the last time I saw you?" She preens, tilting her chin up in an attempt to grab some extra height. "Yup, you did. I can tell."

Rose saunters up behind Jane, smiling over the birthday girl's happiness. Dressed in tattered cutoffs and a floor-length black trench coat, she's rocking a completely different vibe than her little cousin. She gives me a quick nod, arms crossed in what could either be approval or annoyance—it's hard to tell with her. All I get is a quick "Hey," which kind of bugs, causing my spirits to dip for a second.

But Jane, mesmerized by her surroundings, doesn't notice. Brown eyes dart excitedly from pudding to pies, unsure where to start first. "This place is so cool!" she exclaims. "It smells soooooo good in here!"

"Doesn't it?" I agree, enthusiasm returning. "If there's anything I can teach you in this world, it's desserts. Real ones, not that healthy junk on your farm. Just sweet sweet refined sugar."

"Yay!" She claps her hands, bouncing on her toes.

"C'mon, let's go in back."

Jane is equally pumped to see the cake decorating spread and instantly jumps up on a stool to get a better look. "Is this all for me?" she asks innocently.

"Of course!" I say. "You're the birthday girl!" I introduce

Ella, who initially approaches the little matchmaker with the caution of a woman scorned, but they take to each other pretty quickly, since Jane has no trouble diving into the magic before her. She grabs a strawberry cupcake and slathers it with green buttercream even before I've finished tying an apron around her neck, then moves on to creation number two, a vanilla base with extra, extra, extra M&M's on top. Not that I'm surprised. Extreme sweet tooth is a well-known matchmaker trait.

After her third cupcake is complete, Jane asks, "Can I eat them?"

I shove a double fudge cake in my mouth, choking out a "Duh!" through the crumbs for dramatic effect. She bursts into laughter, childlike squeals filling the kitchen before taking a bite of her own treat.

While Jane's busy chowing down, Rose pulls me aside. "Thanks for doing this," she says without a scowl. "Her spirits are already much higher than they were. She's really been missing Peter."

"Speaking of which," I start, sensing an opportunity. She can't totally blow me off on this subject when we're standing face-to-face, can she? "I meant it when I said he seems out of sorts. I don't know Peter that well, but when I saw him last night, he was like a different person."

Rose sighs, glancing up at the ceiling as if she'll find some serenity there. "Look, I don't want to seem like I don't care, but Peter has never been my favorite. His worldview is so simplistic, all rose-colored glasses and whatever. He always thinks everything will be fine."

"Okay . . . Isn't that just . . . optimism?"

"It's inaction," she grumbles, pierced eyebrows pinched in disapproval. "Yeah, things *will* work out, but *you* have to work them. You can't just sit around expecting that things will go your way. Peter's never been through a hardship, and if he is now, maybe that's a good thing." She shrugs with a little too much satisfaction. "Let him see what it's like to struggle. It'll make him stronger in the end."

There's a lot I could say to this, but getting in a heated argument when Jane is a few feet away doesn't seem like the best birthday gift. I can't expect to understand the Wisterias' entire family dynamic, but all this super-strict tough-love stuff doesn't sit well with me. "I'm not going to force you to get involved, but let me just tell you this: I tried to get Peter here today, so he could spend time with his sister. Isn't it concerning that he didn't show up?"

Rose considers this. "I mean, it's not great. But I stand by what I said."

This is pointless, and beyond frustrating. I shake my head, dropping the conversation to rejoin the birthday girl. Ella has willingly brought out her various piping bags and icing tips, showing Jane how to make intricate frosting flowers on top of her cupcakes. The kid's a natural, and I shower her with praise. We crank up the kitchen radio and start dancing as we decorate, spinning and twirling as sprinkles and edible glitter rain from our fingertips. It's so fun, I let out a crybaby whine along with Jane when Rose says it's time to go home.

"Sorry, kiddo, but I told your parents we'd only be gone a little while," the fairy says through a frown. "It was already a stretch for them to let me take you anywhere, so I don't want to disappoint them."

Jane pouts, sadly stepping off the stool.

"But don't worry," I say, trying to end on a high note. "You can take all these cupcakes home!"

"Really?!" Her face lights up again.

"Totally! You decorated them; you deserve to eat them."

Once we've boxed up the dozens of desserts and said our good-byes, Rose pulls a handful of fairy dust from her trench coat pocket, and my naïve little heart does a backflip. Maybe she wants to reward me with a wish as a thank-you for Jane's special day? I would forgive all her crabbiness and unwillingness to help in Operation Peter if that were true.

But upon seeing me eye the golden glitter like a drooling fiend, she shakes her head, sprinkling the dust over herself and Jane. "Fairy dust: it's the only way to travel." And with a wish, they're gone, causing Ella to yelp in surprise and fall backward into the cooler.

"Did they just . . . What in the . . ." she gasps, pinching a hand over her heart in shock. "Amber, you live in such a different world!"

Yes, yes, I do. Which is why I'm not going to give up on Peter, for Jane's sake. I've seen a lot of weird magical stuff, and I don't want him falling down the wrong rabbit hole. Something is up with him, and I'd rather stage a magical intervention before this Jekyll becomes a Hyde.

Twenty-Five

I NEVER UNDERSTOOD THE POINT OF VIDEO GAMES UNTIL I STARTED dating Charlie. They always seemed like a colossal waste of time. Why would you want to traipse around artificial worlds when there's so much magic in real life? But then he introduced me to an old-school version of *Mortal Kombat*, and I found knocking someone to the ground—even virtually—to be highly satisfying. It's not like I've never punched anyone (thanks, Ivy!), but this is a much safer, less punishment-inducing way to let off steam.

"Boom!" I shout, standing up for a victory lap after my Sonya Blade destroys Charlie's Johnny Cage. I run around his couch, punching the air in front of me.

"Boom? Really? That's your throw-down phrase?" Charlie complains, tossing his controller on the floor.

"That's right." I hover my nose an inch from his and whisper, "Boom."

"I never should have showed you this game."

"Too late now!" I raise the roof, do the running man, and every other lame move I can think of. His eyebrows jump above his glasses in an "Is that so?" expression. Then he ropes me back to the couch, smothering me with a pillow as I dissolve into laughter.

"When did you say Peter would be back?" I ask once I've settled my silliness. "We've been waiting for hours."

"He's not exactly forthcoming with his schedule," Charlie says. "He definitely comes and goes as he pleases."

"Have you guys, like, bonded since he's been staying here?" I ask.

"Do you mean, have we talked about sports and girls?"

I roll my eyes. "Yes, obviously that's what I'm asking."

"Well, then, in that case, no. I know he's been here a while, but Peter's not really a talker. At least not to me." My boyfriend shrugs.

"But do you agree he's different from when he first arrived?" I snuggle into a pillow.

"I can't judge the behavior of a person I don't know that well. But if you say he's losing it, I stand beside you and will echo that sentiment with confidence." He straightens his tie for emphasis.

It takes three more rounds of *Mortal Kombat*, two *Mario Kart* tournaments, and a weird segue into *Call of Duty* before Peter shows up. We hear a thud against the door—did he fall into it first?—before he stumbles in, looking like a wild animal. In a complete transformation from his appearance at the Black Phoenix, he's lost all his swagger: peachy hair disheveled, eyes bloodshot, clothes covered in dirt. He staggers around the living room, searching for something but not landing on anything, not even realizing we're there.

"Peter?" Charlie jumps into his line of sight, forcing him to focus. "Are you okay?"

Peter studies Charlie like he's a ghost, lashes blinking furiously at the strange apparition before him. "What are you doing here?"

"I live here," Charlie says gently. He glances over at me like "Okay, I get it now." "Amber is worried about you."

"Worried?" Peter laughs too forcefully. Irritated eyes shoot a glance my way. "Why? I've absolutely never been better!"

Well, that's a crazy statement coming from someone who smells like he just crawled out of a gutter.

"Peter, you don't look like yourself," I insist. Charlie keeps trying to grab any accessible part of him—his wrists, his jacket—but he's like a cyclone, spinning without direction. Every time he evades Charlie, he lets out a high-pitched laugh that filters all the way into my nervous system.

Peter runs his fingers through his hair, making it stick up in all directions. "Don't you think I look dashing? Debonair?" He strikes an awkward pose, completely oblivious as to how uncomfortable he's making us. "I think I've finally come into my own. No more naïve farm boy!"

"I liked that Peter," I say quietly. But this comment rubs him the wrong way.

"No, you didn't!" he snarls. "I was stupid and passive, a total jerk. But now things can be better." Peter grabs me by the back of my arms, hard. I let out a small cry, and Charlie rushes to my side.

"Hey, bud, let's take a step back," he insists.

Peter flinches, insulted. "I'm not going to hurt her."

"I didn't say you were. I just want you to relax." Charlie is all softness, trying to defuse a bomb, but the fuse is burning brighter.

"You know what would help me relax?" Peter snarls, still clutching me. "If you could give me some money."

His totally random request catches both of us off guard, but most of all Charlie. "What?"

"C'mon, I know you have plenty," Peter continues, digging himself a very strange grave. "I mean, look at this place!" He releases me—finally—to gesture wildly to the panoramic city view. "You're loaded."

The two face each other from across the room, the start to an Old Western duel, complete with a damsel in distress. I half expect a tumbleweed to roll by.

Sheriff Blitzman pushes his glasses up on his nose, defenses rising. "What do you need money for?"

"What does it matter? Clearly you can spare it. You probably wouldn't even know it was gone," Cowboy Peter spits.

Oh boy. Things are getting weird. Charlie is not one to Hulk out—in fact, he keeps his cool way more frequently than me—but if there's one thing he hates, it's being used for his wealth. He always hated the way people treated him in school, like he was a prize to be won just because of his dad's celebrity. This led to Charlie shutting almost everyone out, doing his best not to bring attention to himself. Which is a shame, because obviously Charlie is awesome because of who he is, not what he's worth, and all those high school losers seriously missed out. The Blitzmans *are* more well-off than most, but they also never hesitate to help those in need, which is exactly why Peter has a room to stay in, thank you very much. But no one likes being taken advantage of, and it's definitely Charlie's biggest trigger.

"Okay, um, let's take an intermission here, shall we?" I assert myself in the center of the rumble. But Charlie's still in this showdown, ignoring my comment completely.

"It matters because you are having some sort of issue, and I'm not funding anything that would inadvertently hurt Amber," he says firmly, fists clenched. I know now's not the appropriate time, but damn, my heart is pounding for this boy.

"I know you have money stashed around here." Peter starts casing the joint. "You probably have gold bars in your under-wear drawer." With only that misguided visual to lead him, he takes off, running toward the bedrooms.

"Hey!" Charlie shouts, sprinting after him. I take a beat to massage my tricep, before heading to the back of the penthouse, where Peter has already ransacked John's bedroom, clothes strewn from closets and drawers. He's about to pocket a pair of very sparkly cuff links when Charlie tackles him, and both guys crash to the floor. I can't look away; I've never seen Charlie fight someone before. They roll around for a couple seconds, both grunting and gritting their teeth as they tumble, and while Peter may be much taller than Charlie, he's barely in control of his limbs, hopefully giving my boyfriend an advantage.

"Give those back!" Charlie yells, right before Peter swings and manages to hit him on the bridge of his nose, breaking his glasses. Without a second thought, I fling myself next to Charlie, just as Peter makes a dash for the door. My brain knows I should try to stop the thieving fairy, but my feet must be controlled by my heart, because they take me to my love, who is curled into a ball.

"Charlie?" I gasp, rubbing his back. He's so tightly huddled, I can't see his face. The stillness of his shape is making my nerves explode. "Charlie, say something, please." As gently as possible, I roll him over, revealing a small trail of blood running down his face, his nose crooked and red. "Oh my Gods! Um, um, don't move, okay? Oh, you're already not moving, so um, keep doing that!"

I carefully slide a pillow under his head, then go to the

bathroom and grab a wet washcloth. Sweaty and swollen, he reaches for me as I wipe blood from his mouth.

"I'm here, it's okay." I push damp hair off his forehead. "I love you; you were very brave."

"Did we win?" he asks before closing his eyes and passing out.

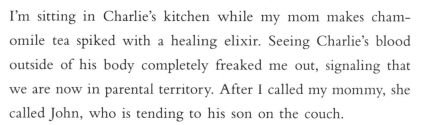

I'm sitting in Charlie's kitchen while my mom makes chamomile tea spiked with a healing elixir. Seeing Charlie's blood outside of his body completely freaked me out, signaling that we are now in parental territory. After I called my mommy, she called John, who is tending to his son on the couch.

"My boy, taking a punch like a man," John boasts to no one in particular.

Charlie winces, both from pain and the random comment. "Dad, maybe cool it with the alpha male stuff?"

"What? Do you know how many hits I took in my day?"

"This isn't football."

"I know, but—"

"Anyway!" I interrupt, since we're veering into unnecessary territory. With a hot mug of magic tea, I take a spot next to the Blitzmans. "So, I'm gonna go out on a limb and say Peter is having an adverse reaction to magic. What do we think?"

"It sounds like it, yes," Mom agrees, joining the group.

"We didn't give him anything potent, but everyone reacts differently."

I stare at her blankly. "Like an allergy?"

"Kind of." Mom's face pinches in thought. "But I guess I'd compare it more to a sugar rush or coffee buzz. If you're not used to consuming those substances, you get all riled up, and once they're in your system, you want them even more."

Well, I can definitely relate to that. I get pretty stabby without a regular stream of cookies. "But where is he getting all this magic? Even if he downed all that stuff he bought, it wouldn't be enough to make him act all wild like this for this long," I reason. "He hasn't been back to Windy City Magic, so who's he been going to?"

Yet even as the words cross my lips, I know the answer. We Sands know when to turn away someone who's abusing limits, but on the black market, the limit does not exist. Maybe he's visited my pal Roscoe, or maybe someplace else, but either way, those waters are too deep for a newbie like Peter to navigate.

John rubs the back of his neck with his giant hand. "Maybe we should call his parents."

"What? No!" I cry. "This is exactly what they feared would happen! They will never trust anyone magical ever if they find out!"

"Not to be lame, but I don't really want him here," Charlie says from under his ice pack. "I'm probably biased, though, since he punched me in the face."

"It's not the worst idea to get the parents involved," Mom says hesitantly. I give her a look, but she doesn't flinch. "We'd have to find him first, though."

I can't believe this. I CANNOT. Peter has been acting like a total ass, but calling the Wisterias seems like a horrible idea. Not only will they have major "I told you so" face, but I doubt their methods or rehabilitation would be beneficial. If they had just taught their kids how to include magic in their lives safely, none of this would be happening. Instead, they filled their heads with stories about how evil magic is, and now their son is on the receiving end of the nightmare. It's beyond frustrating; there has to be a better way to help him.

"Will you use a locator spell?" John asks.

Mom nods. "It shouldn't be too hard. But before we do that, I want an idea of what kind of magic he's been playing around with. If we know what he's been exposed to, it will make it easier once we find him. I don't want us walking into a situation we aren't prepared for."

She and John get up and talk quietly in a corner, in that hushed tone that parents use when life gets serious. I want to say something more about how calling the parents is the absolute worst idea, but it seems I'm in the minority here. So I stroke the side of Charlie's arm, letting him relax as the healing powers of Mom's elixir swirl inside him. I can't believe these gentle spells are having such an adverse effect on Peter. I almost want him to be involved in more insidious magic, because I can't imagine anything my mom brewed would turn someone into the worst version of himself. Delving into the darker sides of witchcraft is not an interest of mine, but I guess it's time for another installment. GREAT.

Twenty-Six

YEARS AGO, I REMEMBER A VAMPIRE COMING INTO WINDY CITY Magic in need of help. He'd been in some kind of major brawl, almost staked through the heart, but his attacker missed. There were wood splinters scattered inside his chest, and he couldn't dig them out on his own because his vamp healing powers had already closed up the external wound. We had to find a way to remove the wooden shards without puncturing his heart. Mom scoured her grimoires, and finally came across a gemstone that, when combined with the right spell, could open any barrier—flesh included—creating a pseudo portal to wherever you needed to go. Well, since portals aren't something you see popping up all over the city, you can imagine how rare this gemstone was. Time was running out, and Mom went through some dark channels to save this guy (luckily, I was not present for the whole chest-cavity game of Operation). Mom is well connected, and Dawning Day does what it can too, but occasionally we've all had to work outside comfort zones to get the magic we need. In extreme emergencies, we have to go underground. Literally.

There's a stretch of road in downtown Chicago called Lower Wacker, an underground tunnel that follows the course of its sunlit sister, Upper Wacker. This subterranean avenue was designed as an expressway to help people travel through the Loop faster, bypassing the bumper-to-bumper traffic stopping at every single light, and has evolved into a dark, lawless roadway where cars race through at extreme speeds, with no regard for safety or courtesy. Lit only by sporadic yellow bulbs, the underpass takes on a sickly hue, and the farther you go, the more it feels like you won't come out the other side alive. Strangely enough, this sunken hellscape exits right near the entrance to Navy Pier, which is like one nightmare opening up to the next.

Even though we make our way to Lower Wacker in the middle of the day, the tunnel blocks out all sunlight—and happiness—in a matter of seconds. It melts my brain how one minute we can be surrounded by carnival lights and the next plunged into oblivion.

"So, um, which shop are we visiting again?" I yell against the roar of cars speeding by. Lower Wacker was not created with pedestrians in mind, and the one walkway that runs along its treacherous course is so narrow, it makes you want to clutch the cement walls, except not really, since the walls are cold, dirty, and covered in much more than cobwebs.

"Nico's place," Mom calls over her shoulder.

"Is that the name, or is it just a place owned by a dude named Nico?"

"The latter, I think." Hard to be sure, I guess, since it's not like underground lairs print up business cards. When Mom suggested we visit a former "associate" for more information on Peter's extracurricular activities, my heart skipped a beat thinking it could be Roscoe. He did seem to know her after all, and while visiting his Instagrammable shop would have been more comfortable than trekking through this underground tunnel, it would have been hella awkward for me, since I didn't exactly share the details of our dark pact with Mom. So I'm weirdly relieved to be making this journey instead, even though my insides are crawling with fear.

Bob is grunting behind me, struggling to squeeze his frame into this terribly narrow space. We brought Bob along for the intimidation factor, although he wouldn't hurt a fly (figuratively speaking—one time I did see him tear the wings off a fly, an act that was both impressive and shocking).

"Amber, are we there yet?" he whines.

"How should I know? This isn't my regular hangout." I don't mean to be so harsh with him, but my anxiety is through the roof. I feel like any minute now the Batmobile is going to race by in a shootout with the Joker, and while that would be insanely cool to witness, I'm also not looking to be caught in cross fire today (or any day, for that matter).

Mom finally stops in front of a gray metal door that is almost the same color as the surrounding concrete, effectively camouflaging its existence. Its only distinguishing characteristic is a small, rectangular peephole looking out. Mom knocks three times, and a panel opens, revealing two orange eyes staring us down. I can only assume this to be Nico, and fully expect him to ask for a secret password, but instead he slams the panel shut, opening the rust-covered door a crack, its metal bottom screeching against the pavement. It's somehow even darker inside his place, yet we all foolishly proceed. I can practically hear Bob rubbing his lucky rabbit's foot behind me.

It takes a few seconds for my eyes to adjust, but when they do, I realize I'm standing in what I bet Peter thought a magic shop would look like. Illuminated only by candlelight, the room has no ventilation, leaving a thick layer of smoke. And the smell, well . . . I wonder if they make bleach to clean nasal passages. Exposed pipes crisscross the ceiling, along with countless animal carcasses, each in different stages of decay. Besides a very real human skeleton with several missing bones standing in the corner, there isn't much inventory on the floor, though our proprietor has strategically positioned himself in front of a large closet where his supplies must be stored.

"What brings you here today, Lucille?" Nico asks with a

sneer. He's giving off very strong troll vibes, and those dudes really like to rub it in when higher magical creatures ask for help. Since almost any mystically inclined person ranks higher than trolls (well, except me, of course), he must get that sense of superiority from every single customer. But he's wearing a cape, so how cool can he really be? (Answer: not at all.) "Care for a goat brain? They're fresh."

He holds one out to her, throbbing coils oozing on his meaty hand. A creepy smile reveals teeth in all shades of yellow.

"I'm not looking for merchandise today," Mom says, keeping her cool despite the pulsating organ inches from her face. "I'm wondering if you've seen someone here."

Nico sticks a pinkie finger in his ear, pulling out a giant blob of wax, which he flings to the floor. "I don't trade in information."

Mom rolls her eyes. "That's not true and you know it. Remember the nymph turf wars several years ago?" She raises an accusatory eyebrow.

The troll swirls his cape up around his shoulders. "Oh, who even cares about nymphs anyway?"

"Nymphs probably do," I mutter under my breath, putting me on the receiving end of orange stink eye. I quickly stare at the nearest candle to avoid his gaze.

"Bob, do you have the drawing?" Mom asks. Bob fumbles through his satchel, nervously pulling out a piece of parchment. I worked with him to do a sketch of Peter, detailing him somewhere between his normal self and magically insane state. "We're looking for this person." She holds out the drawing to Nico. "Have you seen him?"

Nico steps closer (visibility is truly awful in here), squinting for a second before a flash of recognition crosses his face. "Ah yes, a fairy, right?"

"Yes. Have you seen him?"

"Maybe. But it will cost you."

Mom is not in the mood to play games. She whispers some inaudible Latin, and red sparks leap from her fingers. It's nothing more than a parlor trick—something fun to do on the Fourth of July—but Nico doesn't know that. He stumbles back, pulling his cape up higher as a shield.

"Tell me," Mom demands.

"Yes, okay, yes!" he whimpers. "He was here but not for long."

"Why?" she asks. "Did he find what he was looking for?"

"No, there wasn't time." Nico presses himself up against his closet.

"What does that mean? Why not?"

We hear a scraping noise from behind him, and though it's hard to see, it's clear he's trying to make an escape. Mom and Bob flank him. Nico drops to his knees as she shoots off more sparks. Nico emits a strange, strangled cry. For a troll who must see bad guys on the regular, this dude is not very brave, but it works to our advantage since he starts spilling the beans.

"A minute after he walked in here, I knew he was a fairy. I mean, it's pretty obvious when those guys are around. Do you have any idea what a fairy would go for in this market? Even just a pinch of dust would let me retire early. So I tried to catch him, but he flew away. I can't even believe he came in here in the first place, asking for a silly invigoration tonic." Nico shakes his head. "Reckless."

It's an element of danger I didn't even think of but should have. His parents warned us about this, how fairies have to be careful everywhere they go, always watching the wings on their backs. I knew places like this were bad and dealt in dangerous products, but I didn't realize they would buy and sell actual living creatures. Now not only do we have to worry about what Peter is doing to himself but also what others could potentially be doing to him.

Mom gives Nico her best "You should be ashamed of yourself" stare-down, though considering where we are, I don't think her disapproval will have the same soul-crushing effect as it does on me. She nods at us to head out, and as we do, she magically extinguishes all the candles while simultaneously sending another round of red flames into the air. A badass exit, if there ever was one.

"Holy crap. What are we going to do?" I yell once we're back in the echo chambers of Lower Wacker.

"We need to do a locator spell. Now." Mom's face pinches in worry.

"Here? In this tunnel?" Bob asks, hoping for a no. The walkway is too tiny for us to set up supplies, plus the rush of cars would make it impossible for the Fates to hear us, let alone grant our request for help.

Mom curses under her breath. "Let's head back to the shop, but quickly."

"Do you think Peter could have been kidnapped?"

"It's possible," she sighs. "From what you described, it doesn't sound like he was acting with a clear mind. He may have stepped into a trap."

Only we have our own trap to worry about, because when we get back to Windy City Magic, the parents Wisteria are waiting for us.

Twenty-Seven

CREDIT WHERE CREDIT'S DUE: MR. AND MRS. WISTERIA HAVE completely mastered the withering stare. It's a look I know all too well, one that I save for my worst enemies and people who stand too close to me in checkout lines. Neither of Peter's parents clear five feet tall, but their faces are so stony and menacing, I want to melt off the sidewalk into Lake Michigan. Bob, who is triple their size, takes one look at them and walks in the other direction. Kim stands in the back with a "So sorry" grimace. All in all, it's a wonderful welcome home.

"We demand to see our son," Papa Wisteria booms, skipping over all introductions and pleasantries. But Mom is the queen of manners, so she extends a hand, even if they refuse to touch her.

"Mr. and Mrs. Wisteria, I'm Lucille Sand, Amber's mom.

Amber told me all about your beautiful farm." I try to make eye contact with Mom, but she seems to be tracking an invisible butterfly, looking every which way but mine. Did she call the Wisterias? I get why, as I'm sure adults have some kind of unspoken parent code, but dammit, I really wish she hadn't. The Wisterias will not enjoy learning that their sweet baby boy is a manic mess, in love with a siren and possibly being sold on the black market. And since they're allergic to magic, I don't see how they'd contribute to a rescue mission in any significant way, except for making it a billion times more stressful.

Mom continues. "I know you're worried; I would be too. I don't want to frighten you further, but we don't know where Peter is at the moment."

"WHAT?!" they collectively scream, so loud that a woman passing by drops her snow cone.

"Please, let's go inside, where we can talk in private," Mom insists, ushering them into the shop. The Wisterias are practically performing backbends to avoid contact with her, as if they're worried they might contract cooties. As soon as we're inside, Mom does a sweep for any lingering customers (there are none), then pulls down our silver security gate, effectively closing up shop. Papa shakes his head, icy-blue hair flopping back and forth, while Mama whispers some kind of prayer to herself over and over. Both of them drop the shawls they were wearing, wings fluttering to full attention, almost doubling their height. "We're safe in here," Mom says.

"What have you done to Peter?" Mama cries. "You said on the phone he's been dabbling in magic?" She says "magic" like it's *murder*.

But Mom stays calm against the accusations. "It's true. Peter came to us injured, and we offered him help. We had no way of knowing what would happ—"

"But *we* knew!" Papa yells, wings snapping forcefully behind him. "We told you what fairies have been through! We told you what we believed! And still, you gave him access to the one thing that's destroyed us!"

"He was already destroyed," I jump in. "He was hurt. We did what we could to help."

"You should've sent him home," Mama sobs.

"You're the ones who sent him away!" I throw my hands up.

"Stop!" Mom sends a yellow flare into the air, effectively silencing all the yelling. "I called you here because Peter's in trouble, not to incite a war. We're not going to help him by screaming at each other."

I retract my claws, even though I know I'm in the right. Papa makes an actual harrumph sound, which I didn't think existed outside of cartoons.

"We were just about to perform a locator spell," Mom continues. "You are more than welcome to participate.

Mama clucks her tongue. "We most certainly will not."

"Be reasonable!" I groan. I really don't like these people,

and I know the feeling is mutual. "Peter may be in danger. This will help us find him faster."

But Mama Wisteria shakes her head, resolute. I'm not really sure what wonderful plan they have to find their son—flying around the city with flashlights, calling his name?

"It doesn't matter. We can do it without their help." Mom turns to me. "Amber, Bob—please get the supplies." We scurry around the shop gathering the necessary components: a sage stick to purify the air, candles for guiding light, a crystal ball for visions. Outside of matchmaking, locator spells are our most popular service. Mom usually performs them behind her red curtain. There are two kinds of locator spells, actually. The first involves the crystal ball, bringing the missing person's location into focus; the second conjures tiny, firefly-like lights that lead you directly where you need to go. Most go with the crystal ball, since you never know if the fireflies will lead you to a strange scenario. Peter's situation seems destined for danger, so I'm relieved when Mom places the ball in the center of the room. Mama and Papa stare at it like she just set a naked statue out for display.

Mom takes several deep breaths, clearing her aura, then sits cross-legged, and rests her hands palms up on her knees. I light the candles, and she begins her spell.

"We call upon you, all-knowing Fates, to guide us toward a friend who's lost his way. Where we are blind, share your sight. We are humble before your omniscient greatness." (Ugh, seriously, the Fates are such narcissistic turds. Who makes some-one praise them before agreeing to offer help? The worst.) Mom continues her controlled breaths, keeping her soul open to other-wordly messages, as the clear orb begins to cloud, its watercolors swirling into focus. At first, they are an inky blue-black, making me think Peter must be somewhere nefarious, but then they brighten, like sun-piercing rainclouds, revealing a neon light in the shape of a goat. But before anyone can jump to conclusions about animal sacrifices, I blurt out, "The Girl and the Goat!"

"Excuse me?" Papa frowns, thoroughly unimpressed by the scene he just witnessed. "A girl and a goat have captured our son?"

"No, nothing like that," I say. "It's an über-bougie restau-rant. Crazy-weird entrees like escargot ravioli, but it's amazing. Charlie took me there once."

"Why would Peter be at a five-star restaurant?" Kim asks. I think she's been too afraid to speak up until now, but she's not wrong: it wouldn't make any sense for him to be there. The last time we saw him he clearly had zero cash, and you can't get an artisan roll at that place for less than twenty bucks.

Wait a minute. A twinge of fear worms its way into my heart, curling tighter as a few puzzle pieces begin to snap into place. The Girl and the Goat is in the West Loop, and while I'm not super familiar with that neighborhood as a whole, I do know one resident who is highly interested in magical creatures. . . . Oh no. OH NO.

"Can the crystal ball zoom out?" I ask, prompting a strange stare from Mom. "Like to get a better view of the surroundings?"

"Amber, you know it doesn't work like that." She frowns. "But why do you ask?"

Well, there's no real way around this one. I can't suggest that Peter is probably trapped at Roscoe's Runes without revealing how I know about his shop in the first place, and my involvement with a dark warlock is not going to endear me to anyone in this audience. Still, I can't keep this secret when he could very well be in a glass box wedged between a vat of stomach acid and a case of werewolf fangs at this very moment.

"Funny story . . ." I nervously chuckle and launch into a high-level overview of my fancy little contract and Roscoe's wheelings and dealings. By the time I'm done, Mama and Papa are sharpening their pitchforks, and Mom is not too far behind.

She steps closer to me, not immediately exploding since we're in the presence of strangers, but breath hot with fury as she says, "We will talk about this later." Gulp. But luckily for me, there's a fairy to save, so my punishment is temporarily put on hold.

Despite the methods used to find Peter, the Parents Wisteria are gung ho about moving forward, tucking their wings into their shawls and getting ready to head out the door. I feel compelled to loop Ivy into this mess. If the tables were turned and Charlie were missing, I'd appreciate the heads-up.

Peter's in danger, but we think we know where he is, I text her. A reply buzzes almost instantly.

Omg, I've been trying to get ahold of him for hours.

Text me the address. I'll meet you there.

A second later, she adds: I'm so worried.

I am too.

Twenty-Eight

IT'S DECIDED THAT SINCE I'M CURRENTLY IN A MAGICAL BUSINESS arrangement with Roscoe that I should take lead here. It won't seem like a reconnaissance mission if I stop by to check on how my matchmaking remedy is going, especially since Kasia has been MIA, and once I determine if Peter's there and how he's doing, the more powerful people—Mom and the fairies—can save the day. Even though I know I will pay for this later, this quest does allow me to find out what—if anything—has progressed with my contract, since I've waited long enough for answers. Summer is almost over, and I am more than ready to have all of this over with.

Ivy meets us on the sidewalk outside of Roscoe's Runes, ready to kick ass and take names in a leather jacket and low-cut tank top.

As she stomps up the street to meet us, blond curls flying behind her in a fury, Peter's parents turn to me with looks of horror.

"What is she doing here?" Papa asks as Mama grips his arm.

"She's Peter's girlfriend, remember? I figure she has the right to be here too."

"But a siren?" he continues, cheeks reddening. "They are even worse than witches. All they do is abuse magic." Mom stares off into the street, crossing her arms in disdain. He didn't even have the courtesy to throw in a "No offense." (Although I've always loved how people toss "No offense" over clearly objectionable comments as if that makes it acceptable.) "How could a fairy be matched with a siren?"

I lean my head back, sighing at the stars. We don't have time for this right now. "I don't know, okay? But you'd better get used to it, seeing as how she could be your daughter-in-law someday." This makes Mama blubber into her husband's shirt, but I ignore them, filling Ivy in on our plan.

"Great, let's go," she says, cracking her knuckles and not giving a single crap about the massive amount of shade she's being thrown. It's pretty awesome.

Charlie demanded to come along once I looped him in. He reaches for my hand, squeezing my silver ring into my palm. "Hey, um, I know you're a strong, ferocious woman and can handle yourself in any and all situations, but be careful with this guy, okay? Any person who steals dragon eggs away from a dragon mama is not a good dude."

I smile, leaning in for a quick kiss. "You are very right. And I promise to stay safe."

The door to Roscoe's Runes now has a lock and intercom system, a new addition since the last time I was here. I guess they don't like people barging in without an appointment (ha!) or maybe since acquiring special items such as fairy dust, the shop now requires an extra level of protection. Either way, we need to get inside without busting down the door, which Ivy looks inclined to do. I don't think she can siren anyone via intercom, but stranger things have happened. As a glossy thumbnail presses the buzzer, a camera lens I didn't even notice lights up, zooming in on her face. She strikes a menacing pose, ready to rumble with whoever is on the receiving end of the transmission.

"Name?" asks a disembodied female voice. I recognize Kasia's purr and picture her licking her paws on the other side of the screen.

"Ivy Chamberlain," the siren states, stealing my thunder.

"Reason for visit?"

Without flinching, she boldly replies, "Let me in now."

There's a pause as the camera surveys the ragtag posse behind her. "You can't bring that many people up at one time. Choose one from your party." Ivy immediately grabs my wrist, holding up my arm like a trophy. Kasia must recognize me and buzzes us through, but just before the door slams behind us, my mom calls out, "Amber, don't be a hero! Get the info you need and leave!"

Pshh, as if I've ever concerned myself with being a hero. I

am like one notch above "total wuss," and most of the dangerous situations I've found myself in were definitely not my idea.
I'm not looking to save the day, but I do think I deserve some
answers.

As we start ascending the metal staircase to Roscoe's shop,
I'm treated to a clear view of Ivy's behind, tightly wrapped in
black leather.

"So this Roscoe guy," she says, "you've dealt with him
before?"

"Yeah, well, not in like a hand-to-hand combat kind of way.
He's supposed to be helping me fix my matchmaking magic."

"And he's not?"

"Unconfirmed. He's definitely taking his sweet-ass time."

Ivy shakes her head. "Typical man. They are mostly useless."

"Aww, but what about Peter?"

"I mean, he's good. I care about him a lot—obviously, or I
wouldn't be here. But dang, being in a relationship is a lot harder
than I thought it would be. It takes so much . . . effort. Especially when you have to put other people's needs first. Yuck."
She climbs a few more steps before asking, "Do you ever feel
that way about Charlie?"

"We've had our challenges, sure." My relationship with
Charlie is pretty unique. We aren't perfect, but our problems
have been skewed toward the supernatural side. How many
couples argue about seeing another person in the other's eyes?
Not a common argument, I'm guessing. It is a lot of effort, but

after everything we've been through, we've come out on the other side so much stronger. I hope Ivy will see that everything she's doing is worth it someday. "What's important is that you're happy."

"I'll be a lot happier when all this magical crap is over," she huffs once we've reached the top of the stairs.

"That makes two of us."

Even though I've been here multiple times, it doesn't make the disjointed combination of creeptastic items in an urban-chic setting any less strange. Ivy's blue eyes grow wide as she takes it all in, nose turned up at an artfully arranged crate of cat skulls.

"What is this place?" she whispers under her breath, and I give her a knowing "Yup, it's the worst" nod just as Roscoe enters the room, grinning like a used-car salesman.

"Amber!" he cheers, holding his arms out for an embrace I choose not to engage in. "Kasia just told me you're here! Did we have an appointment?"

"No, no," I say, backing away from a python curling around a driftwood display table. "I was in the neighborhood, just thought I'd stop by and see how it's going. . . . It's been a while since I've heard from you."

Eyebrows pinching under his fedora, he frowns. "Your case is very challenging, young matchmaker. We need to be patient."

Patient? I need to be patient?! "I'm not really sure how much more patient I can be, Roscoe. I gave you fairy dust, and what have you even done? Anything?"

"I can assure you—"

"So assure me, already!" I yelp, my frustration pushing Peter's plight aside for a bit. "What have you accomplished, what progress have you made? Every day my magic fades more and more. I cannot keep waiting!"

"Amber," Ivy interrupts my meltdown. "Aren't you going to introduce me to your handsome friend?" Upon hearing a compliment come out of a pretty girl's mouth, Roscoe perks up, and I remember our mission.

"Oh right, silly me." I pantomime bonking myself on the head. "Roscoe, this is my friend Ivy. I told her all about your shop, and she just had to come and see it for herself."

"Charmed," he says, lightly kissing the top of her outstretched hand.

"This is quite the place you have here," Ivy breathes, dialing up her charm to the max. "So much power in this room." She traces her tank top's low-cut neckline with her finger, easily baiting her prey.

"Thank you." He smirks, proud of what he's created. "What can I help you find? I just got in the freshest batch of baby skin if you're interested."

I throw up in my mouth as Ivy shimmies up to him, doing her best to mesmerize. From the way he hungrily eyes the contents of her tight skirt, I can tell it's working. "We're looking for something extremely rare," she coos, and I have to give it to her; the girl knows how to navigate an uncomfortable situation.

I can barely think of anything to say other than "Why haven't you found my cure already, you fraud?!"

Roscoe grins like a viper. "Well, I recently acquired the most interesting of pieces. Not for sale yet, but I'd be willing to let you sneak a peek."

"Show me."

"You won't believe this," Roscoe teases, guiding us to the back of the room, where several cases are draped in velvet. One is so tall it almost touches the ceiling, and as our proprietor pulls off the fabric, I almost fall to the floor.

It's Peter, curled into a ball, forehead on knees, wings draped around him like a blanket. Trapped inside the glass case he looks tired and broken, like he's lost all hope in the world. He doesn't even flinch at the sudden influx of light, eyes unfocused. Dirty and defeated, he's stepped into the worst of possible traps. It takes everything in me to not start screaming; I have to keep up appearances. *Remember, don't be a hero.*

"A fairy—can you believe it?" Roscoe laughs, so incredibly pleased with himself. "I've been trying to catch one for years, but they're notoriously tricky to find."

Ivy takes a sharp breath, her whole body clenched tight. She quickly blinks back a few tears, touching her chest to distract the warlock from the emotion on her face. She places a palm upon the glass as her beau slowly looks up, movements like molasses, but his wings flutter ever so slightly upon seeing his lady. With a huge effort, he manages to meet her hand on the other side.

"How . . . how did you do this?" Ivy asks Roscoe through gritted teeth.

Roscoe leans against the case, mistaking her coolness for approval. "There were rumors about a fairy working his way through the black market. I didn't believe them, of course, because how could a fairy be so foolish? But I guess he didn't expect my shop to be run by an actual wizard and not some dumb troll."

"And what are your plans? For him." Ivy's eyes never leave Peter's.

"Well, isn't it obvious?" He shrugs. "To get fairy dust. Not for me, personally"—he gives me a wink—"but to sell. He didn't have any on him, unfortunately, but I figure . . . after a few days in the box, he'll be ready to oblige." Roscoe smiles greedily at his prisoner, dollar signs in his eyes.

Ivy cocks her head to one side, contemplating how she can destroy this horrible man. "I want you to give him to me."

He laughs, shocked. "And why would I do that?"

"Because I'm asking you to," she says matter-of-factly.

His whimsy fades, cocky grin replaced by a cold sneer. "Don't think I don't know what you're playing at, siren." Roscoe reaches out, curling a strand of her golden hair around his tattooed fingers. From his cage, Peter struggles to get to his knees, helplessly watching the scene. "Your magic has no effect on me."

Ivy steps even closer to him, pressing her chest up against

his. Like a stupid boy, he can't help but quickly look down her top. "Oh really?" she whispers, and I don't know how she can stand to let any part of her body touch him.

Taking advantage of his distraction, she suddenly grabs his head, digging her nails into his temples. He screams as an invisible current seems to jolt through him, his limbs convulsing. Ivy probes deeper, breathing heavy, like she's using every ounce of her siren abilities to overpower his warlock status and make him bend to her will. I've never seen anything like it. Every time I've witnessed Ivy siren someone, it's been completely covert, so subtle that no one, not even her victim, realizes it's happening. But this is different. This is not magic fueled by a petty desire. This is raw, mystical fury funneled into a passionate plea. It's awesome, but also frightening, to see this kind of power at play. Magical creatures usually can't be sirened, but that's not stopping her now. Teeth gritted, arms clenched, Ivy gives it everything she's got. Roscoe tries to fight back, flailing to release himself from her grip, but she's stronger than he guessed, so focused that even his attempts at shouting spells in Latin don't break through.

"Go . . . to . . . sleep!" Ivy screams, and the intense influx of magic coming from two very powerful creatures makes all the surrounding cases shake. Roscoe and Ivy collapse just as all the glass in the room shatters. The sound is ear-piercing, and I take cover, burying my face as tiny shards prick my skin all over. It feels like the spray of glass goes on for ages, and when I finally look up, the floor is completely covered in broken, glittering pieces, along with the contents of the glass cages, some of which start to slither and crawl.

Ivy struggles to a standing position, Roscoe temporarily crumpled at her feet. This defeat won't last long. We have to hurry.

"You okay?" I hobble over to her. I have a few small cuts on my arms, but those are nothing compared to the battle scars covering Ivy and Peter. She's sweating, breathing like she just ran a marathon, skin bright red. She nods, but there's no way she's fine. "C'mon." I grab her hand and pull her over to Peter, who has noticeable gashes in his wings. My barely existent strength is not enough to pull two exhausted bodies to safety, but adrenaline takes over, helping me at least get them both upright. Ivy and Peter reach for each other, neither able to vocalize the fear of the moment, but looking stronger now that they're together, limbs entwined. We stand in the wreckage, tons of terrible magic effectively destroyed. Call me crazy, but I'm pretty sure my chances of Roscoe fulfilling my contract are finished.

"You . . . saved me," Peter croaks, in a voice so tired he sounds like a mummy recently awoken from his tomb.

Ivy smiles weakly. "Of course, dummy. We'll talk about how you can make it up to me later."

We start heading down the stairs, but a few steps in, Ivy crumbles, knees buckling as she grabs for the handrail. That magic took a lot out of her, and she's struggling to catch her breath.

"Let us help you," I say, removing her heels. I expect her to resist, but she nods thankfully, bottom lip trembling. I pull one of her arms over my shoulders, and Peter, barely able to walk himself, takes the other. Together we half drag, half carry the depleted siren to the ground floor. Upon opening the door out onto the sidewalk, the rest of our group turns in shock, rushing to our aid.

"What happened?" Papa cries at the sight of his injured son. Ice-blue eyes flit between Peter and the girl he's carrying.

"Ivy saved Peter," I say, voice trembling, to the shock of the Wisterias. Both Mama and Papa make an O shape with their mouths, for once not ready with a magical insult. They reach for their boy, worried fingers examining his tattered wings, but in a surprising twist, they don't entirely discount Ivy, cautiously viewing the siren with fresh, curious eyes. There isn't time to share the harrowing tale right here, right now. Any second, Roscoe will come back to his senses, ready for revenge. We need to get out of the West Loop as quickly as possible.

Charlie runs to me, breathless, cradling my face in his hands. We make quite the pair right now, what with him and his busted nose and me covered in scrapes, but he kisses my forehead, a fat tear rolling down his cheek.

"You look terrible," he tries to say, but chokes on his joke, swallowing a sob. I want to return the sarcastic remark, yet feeling the safety of his touch makes the danger we just survived all the more real, and I can't think of anything else except how grateful I am to have him next to me.

I'm just about to sink into Charlie's open arms when a light so bright it's blinding makes everything disappear.

Twenty-Nine

I'M UPSIDE DOWN, HANGING—OR I GUESS SUSPENDED IS MORE accurate—within some kind of invisible bubble a few feet above the ground. The only thing I can move is my eyeballs, and as I strain to get my bearings, I see Ivy floating next to me on my right, Peter on my left. Both of their bodies are contorted in unnatural positions, their faces frozen in silent screams. I can't feel my fingers or toes, so I can only assume my face is making a similarly strange expression. From what I can tell, we're in some kind of vacant warehouse. A sliver of windows traces the ceiling's edge, but it's so dark, I can't make out any discernible landmarks outside. That, and the fact that so much blood is rushing to my brain, it's making it hard to think.

I want to scream, to run, but I'm trapped in my thoughts,

unable to communicate with my fellow captives. How did we get here? Why are we upside down? What is going on?! I can only assume that someone or something associated with Roscoe is behind this; only a truly powerful witch or wizard could have pulled off the spell that transported us here without memory. It happened so fast. One second Charlie was kissing me, the next, the world was blanketed in oblivion. Did he and the others get away? Is my mom here too? I can't see past Ivy and Peter, but it's possible the whole crew got kidnapped to this magical prison. This is usually the time when I'd start to panic, but I guess the advantage of being mystically paralyzed is that your breathing remains steady. We hover in silence for the longest stretch of time of my entire life, when I hear a door open behind us, voices echoing throughout the cavernous room.

". . . and that's the advantage of using live specimens over freeze-dried: the freshness really enhances the spell," says a male voice I don't recognize. Two other voices laugh in agreement, their footsteps getting closer and closer.

"Now we have to deal with this," a female voice says in disgust. I can't be sure, but I think it's Roscoe's assistant, Kasia. "Please tell me we can use *them* as live specimens?"

"No, no," says a third. "They're much too valuable to use as ingredients. Well, except the matchmaker. She's worthless." The longer he talks, the more I'm certain it's Roscoe, and a few seconds later, his smug face is peering into mine, albeit upside down. "Hello there, did you hear what I said?" He smiles, perfectly white caps in an ugly expression. "Worthless. That's what you are. I'm not even sure how someone like you would get mixed up with actual impressive creatures like a siren and a fairy."

"But matchmakers are cool now, Roscoe," Kasia purrs. "Don't you watch that YouTube show? What is it called? *The Magic of Matchmaking,* or something?"

He turns in her direction, annoyed. "Does it look like I spend my time watching useless Internet drivel? You know I've been working on my *Artisanal Wizardry* podcast."

"Oh right. Really loved your last episode on the magic of avocado toast."

"Thanks. I've been trying to hit that sweet spot of trendy yet authentic, you know? Keeping it real."

Oh my Gods, can they just kill me already?

Roscoe returns his attention to me. "We don't have any use for you tonight, matchmaker. Although I should thank you for your contribution. You've inspired all of this!" He waves his arms around as if I'm able to turn my head and look. No matter. I'm convinced whatever he's cooked up is completely terrible. "When you came to me with your box of dust, I initially thought, who could ever be so foolish as to give this away? But, being the entrepreneur that I am, I decided fairy dust is too valuable to waste on a wish. Why not sell it to someone with deep pockets?"

What? He's not even going to use it? I thought it would be

too tempting for him to pass up, and now he's going to make a profit? I feel sick, and not just because my stomach is hanging about my heart.

"And why stop at the dust?" he continues, much to my disgust. "I have a whole collection of items that are purely priceless, and I intend to get the best price. I'm setting up a pop-up shop tonight, and your magical friends will be the pièce de résistance. Can you imagine how much someone would pay for a lifetime of wishes and a personal siren pulling strings? Because I can." I want to look away from his twisted smile, but I can't turn my head.

He never intended to help me at all. How could I be so stupid? I should've known—I did know, deep down—but I was so desperate to see clearly, I couldn't detect what was right in front of me. Now we're all in danger, for while Roscoe is despicable, I'm sure anyone he associates with is just as bad, or worse. And it's all my fault.

"In the meantime, you can go," he says. "I have a lot to do, and you're taking up space." His palms fill my range of vision; then I'm falling, landing with a hard thunk. Instantly my head throbs, but I don't want to show fear, so I pop to my feet, ready to let this guy have it.

"You are disgusting!" I shout, anger burning my throat. "A disgrace to the magical community!"

Roscoe rolls his eyes. "Yes, I'm sure that will haunt me as I roll around in my piles of cash on my private beach." He chuckles, sighing at his own fantasy. "Sorry about your match-making, though I guess if you weren't broken, I'd try to profit from you too." He motions to Ivy and Peter, still trapped in their concealed cells, and I look up at them, their pained eyes trained on me. I reach for Ivy, but the invisible barrier that contains her shocks me, propelling me backward a few feet. On the floor again, voiceless and powerless, I mouth an "I'm sorry" to which they only blink.

There's nothing I can do here. I can't perform any helpful spells, but if I'm fast enough, I can get to the people who can, so I take off running, fighting back tears, as Ivy's and Peter's lives literally hang in the balance.

"Feel free to tell anyone you want about our pop-up shop, especially your mom!" Roscoe calls as I reach the door. Cocky bastard. Even if he didn't use the dust, it's clearly gone to his head. He must truly think he's untouchable if he doesn't think inviting my mom is a terrible idea. "The more the merrier! The fun starts at midnight!" I step onto the sidewalk as laughter spills out behind me. I slam the warehouse door behind me, wiping my cheeks free of the few tears that managed to escape.

Deep breaths, I tell myself. *You can cry later. First, figure out where you are.* The neighborhood is dark and poorly lit, nondescript commercial buildings crowding every corner. The lack of light and human presence makes the area feel abandoned, but a rumbling behind me gives me hope. I jog two blocks over to find elevated "L" tracks, the Green Line swaying toward downtown.

Any Chicagoan can find her way once the skyline is in sight, and I determine I'm still in the West Loop, but on one of the less populated blocks. A stab of fear plunges through me. I need to make my way north, but how? I gave Charlie my phone to hold, and I have nothing on me: no money, no ID, nothing. GAH! What am I supposed to do? No CTA employee will just let me on the bus or train for free, and even if they did, that will take forever to get up north at this time of night. Although I made peace with the fact that I am not a witch long ago, I really, really, deeply and truly wish I was a witch in this moment so I could just beam my way out of here.

Instead of wandering alone under the "L" tracks like a person screaming, "Please come murder me without witnesses!" I head a few blocks south to a more populated area. I don't know what time of night it is, but the foodies are still out in full force, spending top dollar at all the trendy eateries. Though I don't fit in with this crowd, I definitely feel comforted to have people around as I try to come up with a plan.

It doesn't seem like Roscoe is going to hurt Ivy and Peter. He's clearly the world's creepiest, most disgusting profiteer, meaning he won't damage his merchandise. But if somebody does end up purchasing them (gross, this potential transaction is making my skin crawl), who knows what they'll do to their fancy prizes? How does one "own" a fairy or siren, anyway? I can't imagine that mindset. *Oh, I'll just force my siren to help me take over the world! Everything's fine. Tra la la!* No. A pop-up shop like this is going to attract the worst possible people, so we need Team "Not Jerks" to intervene. And though I can't vouch for every single creature who walks through the door, at this time of night, the Black Phoenix is probably my best bet to assemble a collection of magical superheroes willing to save the day. There has to be more good than evil in this world, and if we can harness the light, we can stomp out the darkness.

After a few failed attempts, I manage to hail a lonely cab in a sea of Ubers. We fly through the city streets, whizzing past the bright lights of downtown, until we reach the quiet block disguising the supernatural hotspot. The cabbie gives me a confused look in the rearview mirror as he pulls to a stop, since apparently I'm not dressed like I live in this neighborhood, and the Black Phoenix entrance is hidden.

"One moment, please," I say as the cabbie brings up my total. I dash out the back of the cab, running into the Black Phoenix as the driver yells in my wake. As I burst through the door, my eyes scan the room for Vincent, who is at his usual perch behind the golden bar.

"Vincent!" I yell, causing him to drop the glass he was wiping.

"Amber? Are you okay?" he asks, searching my person for signs of injury. His vamp senses detect the blood screaming through my veins, and he does his best to comfort me.

"Yes, I mean, no . . . I mean . . . I don't know!" Too much is happening for me to even comprehend my state of being. "But could you pay for my cab?"

Vincent sends one of the busboys outside with some cash as Amani rushes in from the back.

"Amber?" Her jaw drops in relief. "Amber! Oh my Gods! Charlie called me. Everyone is freaking out! Are you okay?"

I shake my head again and give a quick recap of what happened, including how we need to recruit a gang of do-gooders to save Ivy and Peter. Like now. By the end, Vincent and Amani are both nodding along with my plan.

"I hate those black-market-magic guys," Vincent says, licking his fangs. "Always causing needless drama."

"Do you think anyone here would be willing to help?" Amani asks, nodding toward the packed house.

"They better be if they ever want to drink here again." He kisses the top of his lady's head. "You two light a fire under the customers. I'll go round up the kitchen staff."

Amani grabs a spare barstool, holding it steady as I climb on top. Only a head or two even notices the random girl towering above them, so my bestie whistles loudly, a goddess commanding the attention of the room. Dozens of pairs of eyes—various shapes, sizes, and colors—gaze up at me.

"Hi, everyone, sorry to disrupt your evening, but, um, we need your help." I swallow, trying to find the right words as everyone falls silent. "Don't you hate it when people abuse magic? I do. When they take something so beautiful and twist it into dark, self-serving spells that not only bring harm to others, but the entire community as well?" A few heads nod;

some raise their drinks in agreement. "I think we've each encountered a bad apple or two over the years, someone who thought they could take a gift and mutate it into something ugly. In fact, many of you may have met someone like that here, someone who ruined your evening with their black heart." There's a couple of "yeah"s and more emphatic nodding. "These beings give supernaturals a bad reputation, and I know most of you would rather see their villainous ways put to rest so you could just enjoy your life."

Clapping, more hollers. They are getting fired up! Now, for the big ask.

"A few of our own have been caught in a trap by a warlock who profits on misery. Some of you may know them—Peter the fairy and Ivy the siren. They've been here together and are one of those perfectly matched couples that make us all believe in that wacky thing we call love."

I see some of the beings gasp and exchange concerned glances. Peter definitely has some fans around here after his antics the other night. It's a good thing they saw him on an up day.

"We don't have much time, but if you're willing, we can stop the warlock and save Peter and Ivy tonight. Who's with me?"

Chairs scrape back as dozens of the patrons stand, raising fists and claws in the air.

"Let's do this!"

I jump down, wrapping my BFF in a hug, adrenaline coursing through me. Maybe we can pull this off. Maybe I can help right my mistake.

"Wow," Amani says. "That was pretty impressive, my antisocial friend."

I grin. "Thanks. I gotta call my mom, Charlie—everyone," I say.

"Of course. Don't worry; we got this." She nods as a pack of fired-up goblins, witches, vampires, and more start to gather around to make a plan.

You wanted a full house, Roscoe? Here they come.

Thirty

THE BLACK PHOENIX IS BUZZING WITH ANTICIPATION. FOR A GROUP that likes to stay under the radar, they sure seem psyched to suddenly jump into mayhem. All the vamps, witches, and whatnot have abandoned their cocktails and appetizers to swap war stories and discuss dueling strategies. It's not every day you get to be part of magical battles, so there's tangible excitement in the air. Amani, Vincent, and I race around, making phone calls and prepping our action squad with our quickly formulated plan.

I climb up on a barstool again, giving the final instructions. "Okay, everyone! You all should have the address by now. Has everyone phoned a friend to meet you there?" Heads bob in agreement. "Good. The more magic we can have on our side, the better. We want to fill that warehouse with friends! Remember, pretend to be psyched for the pop-up shop, not morally disgusted. Everyone here will bid on Ivy and Peter so we can win and get them to safety. Only then will we show this Roscoe guy what's up. Sound like a plan?" Whoops of encouragement flood the room, and Amani claps along with the crowd. "All right! Let's start filtering out! Not all at once. We don't want to show up like an angry mob."

Seeing this disparate crew band together and take up the call to fight is truly inspiring. Everyone's unifying to stop an injustice that affects our community as a whole, and it's awesome. Power to the people.

Marcus comes out from the kitchen, his team of chefs behind him. It's not a full moon, so it's not like he'll have his werewolf strength, but seeing him join in warms my heart.

Amani jumps to his side in full organizer mode. "Hey! Are you sure you want to come, even though you aren't wolfed out?" she asks him.

He shrugs with a mischievous smile. "Yeah. I'm always happy to help." Marcus gives me a wink and turns back to his kitchen staff. The next thing I know, a pair of arms comes up from behind and squeezes all the air from my lungs.

"You're okay, you're okay," Charlie breathes into the back of my neck. I squirm to meet his face, but his hold is too tight. "Do you know how scary that was? To see you disappear into thin air?" Before I answer, he continues. "It was terrifying. Zero out of ten would recommend. Please don't ever vanish from my life again."

He hugs me tighter, and I lay my arms on top of his, pretzeling our limbs together. After having my life hang in the balance, unsure of where I was or what would happen next, it feels so good to stand still and have him next to me. Solid. Secure. Exactly where I need to be. For once, I'm unable to add some quippy remark, my mouth always ready to fill the air with sarcasm and sass, but as I sway safely in his arms, I realize that doesn't have to be my go-to. Letting the moment speak for itself has a place too, and it's actually kind of nice to just be.

"I'm not going to let you out of my sight," he insists as our fingers entwine. "No arguments, young lady." He mockingly points a finger in my face. But instead of rolling my eyes (my signature move), I kiss his fingertip, smiling in agreement before burying my nose into his chest. His hand runs up through the back of my hair, and we both sigh deeply as the army assembles around us.

Mom shows up a few minutes later, and we share a round of hugs, her tired arms holding me extra tight. Dark shadows hang under her eyes, and I feel terrible for putting her through this. It had to be so completely scary to watch us vanish due to Roscoe's spell.

Mysteriously, the Wisterias are nowhere to be seen. It would be straight-up insane for them to miss their son's rescue.

"Where are Peter's parents?" I ask, to which my mom sighs.

"Of course we were all extremely freaked when you three disappeared," she starts, "but the Wisterias were on a different level. They started whispering about 'last resorts' and 'final straws.' Then they just took off." Her face turns hard. "It's difficult for me to believe they'd bail when a rescue mission is under way, but maybe they have their own plan." I can tell there's more she wants to say, but out of respect for fellow parents, she holds back.

I pull her in for another hug, thankful to have my mom by my side. Through it all, she's never abandoned me, and that's not something to take for granted. I think of sweet little Jane and her complicated relationship with her family. I hope, for her sake, we can pull this off. Not just the rescue but salvaging some semblance of her family. Jane deserves to have people in her life who care about her and support her, no matter what. I'm happy to assume that post, but I haven't given up hope that Team Wisteria will rally.

It's getting late, and most of the Black Phoenix Fight Club has already left. Our core group decided to hang back as long as possible, giving us the chance to sneak into the warehouse once it's already full. But that isn't the only precaution Mom has in mind.

"Amber, what I can't understand is why Roscoe let you go," she wonders. "Why release you when he'd have to know you'd only send in reinforcements?"

"I got the sense that he pretty much wanted me to spread the word." I shrug. "Maybe he thinks his merchandise is so good, it will blacken even the purest of hearts."

"Hmm." Mom nods slightly, as if that logic isn't entirely far off. I guess she would know. Windy City Magic doesn't carry certain merchandise for a reason. "Whatever his intent, I don't want you to be spotted, so you'll need a disguise."

I'm more than willing to don a trench coat and fake mustache, but unfortunately Mom's stealth mode is a lot different than mine. I groan as she pulls a smudge stick from her bag, because I automatically know it's not your standard bundle of Wiccan purification. Nope, when this particular tied-up cluster of enchanted herbs is lit, it temporarily distorts or "smudges" a person's features, making them morph just enough to make an ex-boyfriend or parole officer second-guess your identity. I've seen Mom do this a couple times at the shop and it always freaks me out. It's like watching a painting melt. Mom waves the crackling stick under my nose, filling it with a super-intense sage and cedar scent. Everything from my lips to eyebrows starts tingling, and I watch as my best friend's jaw drops.

"Well, you look . . . um . . . hmm." She squints, gritting her teeth. "No one will recognize you, that's for sure."

"It's only temporary, Amani," Mom reassures us. "Her swollen features will go back to normal in about an hour, two tops."

I touch my misshapen face, visualizing an elephant trunk sticking out from the middle, but Charlie kisses my forehead and says, "You still look great." I give him a shove, since he's clearly lying, but I love him for it anyway.

When we get to the warehouse, there's a line outside the door. A centaur bouncer hands us each a bidding paddle, and as we walk inside, it's clear our supernatural phone tree achieved our desired effect. The room is absolutely packed with every kind of mystilogical creature you could imagine. Elves, banshees, change-lings, and more mingle and sample passed hors d'oeuvres, sipping champagne like we're at an art gallery opening. I spot a few Black Phoenix regulars and several members of Mom's coven, Dawning Day, but I guess one flaw in our bring-a-friend plan was that now I have no clue who's on our side or not. Any one of these strangers could be actually interested in acquiring a fairy or siren, meaning we have to be ready for anything and everything.

Roscoe wasn't lying about having a whole mess of magical stuff to sell at this pop-up shop. Everywhere I look, there's another glass case filled with some kind of novelty. Enchanted talismans, a cauldron that promises perfect spells, lots of very rare ingredients hailing from far-flung corners of the earth. We split up, Amani and Vincent circling the left side of the warehouse while Charlie and I take the right. It's hard to see everything with so many bodies crowding around the items, though one in particular seems to be drawing extra attention. I push my way through the crowd, weaving in between horns and tails alike, to see if it's Ivy and Peter attracting all those eyeballs. But they're not.

It's a unicorn.

A real, honest-to-goodness unicorn, positioned right before me in all its glory. Frozen in the same transparent orb as I was earlier, this beautiful, majestic creature stands proud, silver swirled horn pointing to the sky as a rainbow mane falls down its back. Star-shaped freckles dust its flank, and its existence is so completely astonishing, I stumble back into Charlie, who barely manages to catch me, he himself lost in wonder.

"Holy . . ." He trails off, dark green eyes wide behind his frames. "Is that a . . . ?"

"It's so . . ." I start, but there doesn't seem to be an adjective worthy enough to describe the all-encompassing glory of this enchanting animal. I want to reach out, to touch this miraculous being I always hoped was real, but remember how Roscoe's spell zapped me before. Suddenly, a terrible feeling squeezes my chest. If we'd made this discovery anywhere else, it'd be a blessing, a gift to celebrate, but given the circumstances, having a unicorn present is anything but good luck. While I would spend my life serving this magical horse, giving it everything it could ever want, someone purchasing this creature could have the worst of intentions. Cutting off its horn as a trophy, drinking its blood for eternal youth . . . oh Gods, my head spins with endlessly evil possibilities.

I spin around, grabbing on to Charlie's tie. "If someone here is intending to hurt a unicorn, I WILL END THEM!" I shout in his face. Fire burns from my belly to my brain, and if I wasn't already set to destroy Roscoe and everything he stands for (I was), I am definitely beyond ready now.

"I know, shhh," my boyfriend soothes, wiping my rage spit from his glasses. He pulls me into his chest, gripping my back with the same fear that pulses in my veins. "I don't like this any more than you, but we have to stay chill, okay? You aren't going to save a unicorn by screaming."

"But—"

"We're here to put an end to this, right? So let's do it."

I nod into his button-down, feeling a mix of awe and terror that's wearing me thin, and we haven't even spotted Ivy and Peter yet. Charlie pulls me away from the unicorn, and we continue to make the rounds. I catch a few repulsive conversation fragments about what people would do with fairy dust or how having a siren servant would make life that much easier. Gods. We meet back up with Amani and Vincent just as we find Peter and Ivy, still hovering in their invisible prisons. Only now Roscoe has positioned their bodies in more presentable, less jagged poses. Ivy stands with her hands on her hips like Wonder Woman, while Peter's wings are spread wide, his full span shining against the transparent orb that holds him. I guess you have to stage your merchandise for premium sales, but still, moving them upright hasn't erased the fear from their eyes.

"Oh my Gods," Amani gasps as we approach our confined friends. Vincent turns her away, holding her face in his palms.

"Best not to look, okay?" he says gently, wiping her cheek with his thumb. "We'll put a stop to this, don't worry."

She nods, but of course she's worried; we all are. I can barely endure any more, but luckily the fluorescent lights start to dim, signaling the start of this terrible event. We find a spot on the edge of the crowd, keeping ourselves out of sight. Mom and Vincent instruct us to stay together before disappearing to different corners. Charlie's hand still has not left mine.

A hush falls over the room as Roscoe makes his way through the crowd, ceremoniously taking his place on a shipping pallet in between Ivy and Peter. Dressed in some kind of getup probably worn by an old-timey railroad tycoon, he holds his palms up to quiet the audience.

"Welcome, friends," he starts, such a casual address for such a disgusting event. "How encouraging it is to see so many curious faces tonight. Whether you've come to bid or simply to observe in wonder the extraordinary boundaries magic can break, the strength in these numbers is noted." He beams, making my stomach crawl, then looks back over his shoulder, signaling a line of witches and wizards to inch forward, each looking scarier than the next. "It should be stated that if anyone came here tonight looking for trouble, I have taken the necessary precautions to protect my investments."

The kick line of wizards links arms, simultaneously sending

a current of lightning into the air. The room collectively gasps, eyes wide at the man-made force of nature, but I am not easily dazzled by tricks like this. Instead I search for Mom, finding her in the corner across from us, unperturbed by the display. I examine the surrounding faces, most of which are at least semi-impressed, when I spot a head of icy-blue hair poking out from behind a towering troll. It's Papa Wisteria, cloaked in a black shawl, with Mama's cotton-candy curls right beside him. In fact, that entire section of the room is about two feet shorter than the rest. Did the Wisterias recruit their own fairy army? It's a bold move to bring fairies into a room where a fairy hangs in danger, yet there they are, faces locked in battle mode. Whoa.

"Now that we understand each other," Roscoe continues, lips curled into a snarl, "let's get down to business, shall we? While I have many treasures here tonight, two very magical acquisitions have quickly become my favorites. They both exhibit unbelievable strength and abilities." He turns to Ivy, greedy eyes crawling all over her body in a way that's beyond creepy. "I do believe this is one of the first—if not *the* first—time a siren has been available for service. Luckily for you, I've devised a spell that will keep her doing *your* bidding and not her own. Imagine the possibilities!" Ivy closes her eyes, her only possible act of defiance. "The stories you've heard are true! Sirens can make anyone do anything at any time, and for the right price, that power will be yours." A chorus of "aahhh"s echo throughout the warehouse as Roscoe shifts toward his next victim.

"And I doubt my next item needs much introduction. We all know the potential of fairy dust, and under coercion, this fairy admitted to me that his family harvests the dust themselves! If that isn't worth its weight in gold, well . . . I don't know what is." He's met with enthusiastic applause from everywhere but the fairy corner, where Mama and Papa look like they could kill him with looks alone. Their accompanying crew is equally agitated. A male fairy in the very back shifts ever so slightly, and a twinkle of dust from under his shawl catches my eye. Oh my Gods . . . are they going to attack using fairy dust? I can't even imagine what will happen if they let that loose in this room. The dust could exact any number of punishments, and coming directly from the fairies' wishes, there's basically no limit to what they could do. I squeeze Charlie's hand in shock, and he looks over at me with an equal amount of fear.

"Let's start with the siren, shall we?" Roscoe grins. "Opening bid of a hundred thousand dollars." How he came up with this number I don't know, since clearly Ivy is worth much more than a luxury sports car. But the number quickly swells as bidders raise their paddles higher and higher until they're in the multimillions. Vincent has very deep pockets (being immortal really helps for amassing a giant fortune) and agreed to bankroll any Black Phoenix guest able to help. I can sense Charlie itching to get in the game, to use his wealth for good, but I pull his paddle down, shaking my head. Even with my ballooned features from the smudge stick, we're too recognizable. It's better for us to stay hidden.

"This is just . . . I can't," he moans. "I've seen a lot of messed-up things since I met you, but this is by far the most wretched." There's nothing I can say, because he's completely right.

"This is a nightmare," Amani adds. "Vincent is going to rip this guy apart."

"Really?" I ask. "You think he'll kill Roscoe?" Though I know he's a creature of the night, I've never seen him truly vamp out. I'm not sure I really want to. She shrugs.

Turning back to the scene, a werewolf woman I recognize from the Black Phoenix has just "won" Ivy for a quarter of a billion dollars. Roscoe slowly lowers the siren to the ground, catching her in his arms before gently placing her on her feet. Ivy's fingers rush to her temples, woozy and disoriented, but when she gets her first real head-on view of Peter, still trapped in his prison, it lights a fire in her, venom seething from her skin. Fists clenched, eyes shooting daggers, Ivy looks ready for war, but before she strikes, the werewolf whispers something in her ear, pulling her aside. Ivy's head whips around, searching for evidence of what she was told, and somehow her stare finds mine, sending a visible wave of reassurance through her. Taking a deep breath, she nods in assent, as the bidding begins on her beau.

The promise of fairy dust ignites the crowd, and Peter's

price rises even faster and higher than Ivy's, much to Roscoe's delight. With all this money, he can go start an organic fedora farm or whatever it is people like him dream about. He's practically levitating as he answers bids, completely unbothered by the truth about what he's selling. The Wisterias are primed to pounce. Mom, Vincent, and our crew are at full alert. It's about to get crazy up in here.

Finally, Peter has been claimed, and a pang of fear runs through me when I don't recognize the buyer. It could be a Phone-a-Friend, but based on the hungry grin on the mystery goblin's face, I don't think so. I shake both Charlie and Amani in alarm, trying to also catch Mom's eye from across the room, because everything inside me is screaming *THIS IS NOT GOOD!*

Roscoe, almost floating with glee, claps his hands together to regain attention. "Well, this is exciting, isn't it?" He giggles. "And we have even more magic to auction! If you'll turn your attention to—" A loud boom ricochets through the room, sending Roscoe flying back, landing on the concrete. I don't know who sent the first fire, but then all hell breaks loose.

Thirty-One

MOST MAGIC IS SUBTLE, A SUPERNATURAL TWIST ON THE DAY-TO-DAY that goes unnoticed by the naked eye. Matchmaking, sirening, even most witchcraft takes place without spectacle, quietly bending the natural world into something special and new. But this is different. When magic is used in anger, the energy shifts, crackling the air and alerting all to its presence. It burns, it ravages, it doesn't care who gets caught in the cross fire.

"Look out!" White-hot comets and firecracker flames whiz past our heads as the warehouse becomes an explosion of pure mystilogical force, with people using every magical wrist, claw, or tail flick imaginable. Charlie, Amani, and I have to duck as a troll punches a beastly fist into a warlock, who retaliates with a surge of something piercing cold. We crawl into a vacant corner to take cover, but quickly realize this vantage point does us no favors. Not only can we not see anything except the duel immediately in front of us, but we'll probably get trampled any second. I spot stairs leading up to a hanging iron catwalk, so I lead the way, forcing us to travel through a cloud of something green and stinky on the way up. We flatten ourselves on the walkway to try and stay out of sight, and though we now have a much better view of the mayhem below, between the physical and magical blows, it's almost impossible to gauge who's winning or even who is who. Mom and Vincent are completely lost in the crowd, and even Peter and Ivy seem to have disappeared into the fray.

"Wait, there's Vincent!" Amani exclaims, pointing down to where her boyfriend is kicking ass and taking names. Fully vamped out, fangs bared, he grabs a goblin by the throat, then casually tosses him aside like an empty pop can. "Thank Gods he's okay."

"Damn, he's on fire!" Charlie replies. He touches his still swollen nose, remembering his own mini battle. "Get it, Vincent!"

After a few frantic minutes, I manage to find my mom, who has luckily gotten ahold of Ivy and placed a protective barrier around her that ripples with a pale blue shimmer. Members of Dawning Day surround her like a shield, hands entwined in solidarity. Any time a baddie comes near, the witches chant, *"Prohibere,"* and the perp falls to the ground, temporarily crippled by their unified spell. All this safety allows Ivy time to recharge. She stands with Mom, palms pressed together, as Mom infuses the siren with healing strength. I watch as Ivy breathes deep, letting Mom's magic sink into her soul.

Meanwhile, Roscoe and his group of gross are not backing down, fighting off enemies with impressive force. Kasia has her claws out, while Roscoe's go-to move seems to be a reflective spell, allowing him to absorb his enemy's attack and flip it right back to them. A Black Phoenix friend attempts to immobilize the warlock, but his spell is caught in time as Roscoe seemingly grabs the magic with his bare hand and throws it away, turning his attacker into a statue. His cronies aren't faring as well, though. As the fight rages on, it's clear our team had better manpower and talent, and as a last resort, Roscoe angrily charges toward the goblin guarding Peter, grabbing the fairy by his wings and dragging him toward the center of the room. This profiteer isn't leaving empty-handed, and with Peter too weak to defend himself, he is at the warlock's mercy.

Ivy breaks free from her protective cocoon, running toward Peter at full force, blond hair blazing behind her. She jumps onto Roscoe's back, and he releases his hold on Peter in surprise, pulling the warlock to his knees. He whips around, ready to exact revenge, not on Ivy, but Peter, an angry fist glowing with a destructive spell. But before it unleashes, Ivy hurls herself on top of Peter, taking the hit for her love. She shudders in pain, crying out in agony, yet curls tighter, doubling down as a protective shield.

"No!" I cry, clutching the metal edge of our hanging hiding spot. At that same moment, the parents Wisteria emerge from the shadows, dropping the shawls hiding their wings and soaring into the air. One after another, more and more fairies join until I can't count their number, shimmering wings of every pearlescent shade filling the formerly gray space. They hover in unison, tiny frames no more as they form an airborne army ready to strike. Papa leads the way, eyes as icy as his frosty-blue hair, holding glittering palms toward the ceiling. Heaps of fairy dust in hand, he nods as his commune comrades mirror his stance, each grasping enough dust to do some serious damage. It is unbelievable seeing all these fairies fly out in the open, and all the sparring below stops as the fighters take in the spectacle. I can't tell if the people down below can see the dust, but from our catwalk, we're shocked into silence, mouths agape, with no clue what will happen next.

Roscoe also can't help but stare at the wonder above, but just as the fairies are about to release their mountains of dust, he reaches into his blazer pocket, pulling out his own secret weapon: the cookie box. The fairies halt their descent, pausing their attack as Roscoe rips open the top and pours a handful of sparkling specks into his bare palm. He holds out his treasure, waving his fistful of power in their faces, cackling with glee. A few glittering granules fall through his fingers as he cries, "That's right, fairies! You stay put! You think you can defeat me? You'll have to catch me first!" He tosses up the fairy dust directly above him as he yells, "I wish to be anywhere but here!"

Tilting back his head like he's taking in a warm summer rain, he becomes completely drenched in glitter, sparkles covering his upper half. The whole room holds its breath to see what will happen next, and seconds later, a bloodcurdling scream echoes through the warehouse as the dust somehow pulls him to the ground, like microscopic magnets exerting their force. At first, I think my eyes must be playing tricks on me because it looks like this villain's frame is shrinking, but when Amani gasps too, I realize what is happening. The dust is corroding his body, eating away at flesh and bone like rabid termites on a log. Roscoe tries to fight it off, but soon his arms dissolve underneath the golden cover, his outline imploding and disintegrating into nothing but a fedora and a pile of glitter.

Anywhere but here? How about the afterlife, buddy? Wish granted.

Once the remaining evildoers see that, they hightail it out of there, running for the door like the room is on fire, leaving all potential prizes behind.

"Holy crap!" I yell. "Did you guys see that?"

"Of course we saw it, are you insane?" Amani jumps to her feet, and we follow her down the stairs. She runs straight to Vincent, who sweeps her up in his arms, while we make our way to the pile that is Ivy and Peter, where the fairies have landed and are getting to work. They gently roll the couple onto their backs right next to each other, taking extra care to spread Peter's tattered wings on the concrete. Mama and Papa Wisteria look over them both, sad eyes examining their wounds. Peter is badly battered and bruised, while Ivy's injuries are more internal. She weakly clutches her stomach in pain.

Mom and her coven join the scene, but Papa waves them off with a stately hand. Face serene, he nods to Mama, and together they reach into pouches overflowing with dust, glitter spilling from their fingers. Slowly, they sprinkle sparkles over not only Peter, but in a surprise turn of events, Ivy too, working their way over their beaten bodies, ensuring every injury is adequately covered. Lightly falling specks cling to Peter's wings, Ivy's abdomen—all over—spreading a warm glow that emanates throughout the surroundings.

"We wish for you to heal," the fairies say in unison, and right before our eyes, the dust goes to work, closing the gashes in Peter's delicate wings and easing the pain on Ivy's wincing face. Just like when we were on the farm, the fairy dust revives them, but this time it's even more remarkable, considering what we just witnessed. Mama and Papa stand back as their wish takes hold, and Ivy and Peter carefully rise to their feet, looking at each other with exhausted eyes.

Immediately Peter starts crying, reaching for Ivy, who tiredly collapses into his arms. "I'm sorry," he sobs, unable to contain himself. His freshly healed wings wrap around them both. "This is all my fault."

He's not wrong, and yet his father steps forward to disagree. "Peter, no," he says in an uncharacteristically gentle tone. "I believe the blame lies here."

Wet, confused eyes stare back. "What do you mean?"

Papa clears his throat, reaching for Mama's hand. "We almost lost you tonight. Parents are supposed to keep their children safe, but in trying to protect you, we failed." He swallows hard, voice cracking as he struggles to find the words. "We . . . regret sending you away, and turning you and Jane against magic." Papa winces while Mama wipes her cheeks with a handkerchief. "What we saw here today was eye-opening. We rallied the fairies to save Peter, but in the end, we didn't need to." He turns to Ivy, bottom lip trembling. "You sacrificed yourself for him. It was . . . so unexpected. We've always believed magic to be so self-serving, but you . . . all of you"—he motions to the entire room—"showed us something different."

Mama sniffles, blowing her nose loudly as her pink curls bounce. "You've given us a lot to think about." Her voice shakes. "But we hope you'll come home, Peter."

He takes a beat. "I . . . I think I need time too," Peter agrees, fair skin splotchy from crying. "I have a lot to learn about this world, and . . . I want to do that here, with Ivy." She rubs his arm, and his wings flutter at her touch. Something tells me that siren wouldn't let him go anyway. She's pretty good at getting what she wants.

The Wisterias nod in disappointed acceptance, holding on to

one another. They hug their son good-bye before gathering up their winged gang, all covering their backs before they disappear into the night. Many of the Black Phoenix fighters start going through the forgotten auction items, congratulating each other on a job well done and laughing about how they'll never top tonight's plans. Summer is almost over, after all, so now's the time to sneak in last-minute adventures.

I walk over to what I guess is Roscoe's grave, a pile of glitter on the floor. I run over it with my shoe, wondering if it will feel like crushed bones, but it's soft like sand, already blowing away. I grind an extra bit of it into the concrete, just in case.

"What should we do with this?" someone calls from the other side of the room. I turn to see the unicorn, free and proud, shaking its rainbow tail against its white body. Without thinking, I run over, nearly collapsing at its golden hooves in praise.

"Can I keep it?" I beg to no one in particular. "Please? I will take the best care of it ever! I'll bake it cupcakes, take it on walks, and—"

"I think it's pretty clear you have no idea how to take care of a horse," Amani laughs, coming up behind me.

"But I'll learn! I will!"

"And where would we keep this unicorn, Amber?" Mom adds to the Total Downer Parade. Why is everybody hating on this amazing idea of mine?

"I don't know! It can have my room! I'll sleep in the

kitchen! I WILL LITERALLY DO ANYTHING!" My voice has reached an upper register that probably only dogs can hear at this point.

Mom shakes her head, squeezing my shoulder to let me down gently. "Something as precious as this deserves to be protected, and while we can't keep it, how about you brush its mane, feed it an apple? Help it feel cared for after such an ordeal?"

My heart explodes into a million pieces. Dreams do come true, my friends.

Thirty-Two

WHEN YOU'VE DEFEATED EVIL WARLOCKS, PAVED THE WAY FOR FAIRY harmony, and oh, MET A FREAKING UNICORN, what's left? Why, shopping for shower caddies and dorm room essentials, of course!

I'm pushing a blue cart through Bed Bath & Beyond with Amani, who is slowly finishing up her giant college checklist. This shopping spree is taking forever, and I don't see how she'll be able to fit any more items into her tiny dorm room.

"Amani, be real: Do you actually need a set of bed risers?" I ask, holding up the box she just casually tossed into the cart.

"Um, yeah, how else am I supposed to feel like I'm sleeping in the clouds?" she jokes.

"I doubt five inches of plastic will help you achieve that."

"Maybe not, but they will help me cram more stuff under the bed."

"Fair enough." I shrug. "What's next on the list?"

She scans her list. "Mmmm . . . Extra-long bedsheets. I guess the ones I'd already bought were not long enough."

"Extra-long? Who has extra-long beds?"

"That's what it says."

"You know what else I don't understand? What is the 'beyond' part of Bed Bath and Beyond, anyway? Like, we're not currently traveling to a separate realm . . . are we?"

"It's possible," Amani deadpans. "I saw a device that makes little pancake balls back there."

"Whoa."

We make our way to the bedding section, perusing all the patterns and colors. Since I'll be living at home when school starts next week, I don't need to buy this mountainous pile of junk, a savings I should probably bring up to my mom to see if she'll let me get some new copper baking sheets instead. Amani picks sheets that are pink and flowery (shocker), and we've finally made it to the end. We load up all her gear and head back to her house, but walking into her room is like a punch in the gut: it's practically empty, all packed up and ready to go. It's not like I didn't logically know—her school starts earlier than mine and she's leaving super early tomorrow morning—but something about seeing her space free of fluffy pillows and ruffled everything makes it all real. Posters off the walls, books off the shelves: mementos of my best friend stripped away. This is why I tagged along on this errand in the first place . . . this will be the last time I see her until Thanksgiving. I have to grip the doorframe to keep from falling over.

Amani, sensing my mood swing, wraps her arms around her waist. "I know. It's weird. It's like I don't live here now, but I don't live there either, so . . . where am I?"

"Limbo," I whisper, a sudden wave of emotion crashing over me. I told myself I was okay with this, but how can I say good-bye to this beautiful creature who has been there for so much? She is more than a best friend; she's a force of nature, a pillar of strength who's made me a better version of myself. Amani's friendship saved me when I was drowning; her hand kept me from being completely lost at sea. How am I supposed to go out into the world without her guidance, her humor, her all-encompassing Amani-ness? I would be a melting puddle of nothing without her, kind of like how my brain is now.

"But we're gonna be okay, right?" she asks, worry creasing her brow. "College will be awesome, the future is bright, blah, blah, blah?"

I don't even know what to say. I feel like I'm going to barf up my heart. "You tell me; you're the precog," I choke out.

She closes her eyes, though I know she can't make herself have visions on demand. Long lashes flutter open, and she forces a smile. "Okay. I just fast-forwarded through a montage of both our lives, and they both turn out great."

"Will we still be best friends when we're old and gray?" I ask.

"Duh. We'll be the most awesome old ladies ever, bragging about the days we hunted leprechauns and swam with mermaids."

We both laugh, and I help her pack up a few more things, extremely conscious of the countdown clock. We pretend not to notice the setting sun, ignoring that the Sharmas have reservations for family dinner tonight, choosing instead to talk and joke like always. But she's slipping away even as we're here together, and there's nothing I can do but savor each second.

I stuff a stray cardigan into a suitcase, noticing a glimmer of gold peeking out under the clothes piles. I reach out to find a framed photo of the two of us from middle school, both rocking braces and smiles too big for our faces. We were such an unlikely pair—Amani in a sundress, me grunged out in flannel—but thinking back to when we met, when I was a friendless nobody wandering the halls alone, is the final blow to my fragile heart. I can't blink back the tears any longer.

"Hey, um." I turn to her, sniffling up snot. "Can I tell you something?" Her mouth opens at seeing my blubbering face, but I shake my head vigorously, forbidding her to talk. "You know how we've been through everything together?" I sniffle as the crying intensifies. "You are the best person I know. You have made my life, and I'd be so lost without you. I love you, Amani." And it's so true. I think of little Jane, just learning how to exist in this crazy, mixed-up magical world, and where I would've ended up had I not found a friend who stood by my side no matter what stupid choices I made or trouble I got into. I wouldn't be the person I am today, I know that for sure. Love that accepts you inside and out is true magic.

As I completely dissolve into tears, she rushes toward me, crushing my rib cage with her long arms. "Same," she cries in my ear. "Same, same, same. I love you too, Amber." We cry until there's no more tears, laughing when we're empty. Amani wipes away trails of mascara while I clean my face with a tissue. I guess this is it.

She walks me to the door, and we hug one last time. I make her promise to text me every five minutes. Amani makes me promise to mail her samples of all my latest culinary creations— a challenge I gladly accept.

And just like that, I'm out on the street, on the other side of good-bye.

Even though my apartment is only a short walk away, I don't feel like being alone right now, especially since I know my fridge is empty and unable to soothe my soul. I find my way to the nearest bus stop, and take a long, lonely ride to Navy Pier, where at least the lingering August heat and hordes of bodies will keep me distracted from what's going on in my head. As soon as I get there, though, I know it's a mistake; watching friends share snow cones and good times makes my ache worse, and I resolve to just stop at a 7-Eleven and load up on cookie dough for the trip home. Before I go, I decide to swing by Windy City Magic real quick to see if Mom wants anything, when I spot a familiar lavender fauxhawk heading toward the shop, an unseasonably warm leather jacket hiding wings I can't see but know are there.

"Rose?" I call out, prompting the fairy to turn.

"Amber! Hey!" She pauses by a frozen lemonade stand.

"What are you doing here?" I ask.

"Some sightseeing." She smirks.

"Liar."

She snorts out a laugh. "No, I just wanted to say thanks, for helping my messed-up family. I didn't realize how crazy it would get when we first met, but it was really cool of you to see everything through. Things back home have lightened up a bit, and while there's still a lot of progress to be made, they are headed in a better direction."

"I'm glad," I admit, and I truly am. Even if my relationship with Rose has been a little confusing, I'm happy Jane's home life is improving. I wish them all nothing but the best.

"Did you ever get your problem worked out?" Rose asks, raising a pierced eyebrow. "Whatever it is you were going to wish for?"

"No," I say, sinking lower into my dark mental place. Despite all my efforts, I still don't know what's wrong with me, and at this point, maybe I never will. Maybe my visions will continue to distort, eventually fading into a magic that's only a memory. Maybe happily-ever-after is only meant for fairy tales.

"That sucks," Rose says callously before adding, "Oh, I have something for you." She reaches into her jacket and pulls out an envelope with my name written in messy, childlike handwriting. "It's from Jane."

Opening the seal, I pull out a card with a drawing of me and Jane standing under a rainbow. I have my peacock hair and everything. What a cutie. I start to read:

DEAR AMBER,

THANK YOU FOR EVERYTHING YOU'VE DONE. YOU ARE AN INSPIRATION TO ME AND I HOPE WE CAN STAY FRIENDS. I WANTED TO TELL YOU YOUR MATCH, BUT I THOUGHT IT WOULD BE MORE FUN FOR YOU TO SEE IT WITH YOUR OWN EYES.

LOVE, JANE

With my own eyes? What in the—

But before I can think about it more, Rose is sprinkling golden sparkles all over me, blowing dust free from her hands until my face is covered. It's pleasant, like little drops of sunshine kissing my cheeks. Is this really happening? I've been so close before only to have my hopes squashed, but Rose touches my chin with her fingertips, raising my gaze to hers. For a second, I see her match—it's spotty, like watching a movie through the holes of a colander—but I can barely focus on that.

I hold my breath as she whispers, "Amber, I wish for your matchmaking powers to be restored. Forever."

Warmth runs through me, swirling 'round from head to toe, bringing a lightness to my body I've never felt and doubt I ever will again. Pure love rises from within, and I feel like I could cry, though I'm not sure if it's from the magic or just total happiness.

Eyes watering uncontrollably, I look back up at Rose, who gives me a lopsided grin. Her match floods my system again, but this time it's clear, a perfect montage of her and her future beau. I let it play in full, watching her go skydiving and take cooking classes with her husband, and find myself crying by the end.

I'm fixed. My magic is whole. For the rest of my life, I'll be filled with love stories, and I'm so unbelievably thankful, I wrap Rose in a tight hug. She recoils at the affection.

"Yeah, that wish was from Jane, by the way." She cringes, gently trying to pry my hands off. "And me too, I guess." Once she's successfully retracted my claws, she brushes off her jacket, erasing any lingering dust.

"Thank you," I sob, eyes still overflowing.

"Don't mention it," she says, brushing me off. "Like really, don't. I have a reputation to uphold. Don't wanna come off all soft." Rose winks and turns on her combat-boot heel, giving me a short wave as she disappears into the masses. For a moment, I'm frozen, stopping to stare into the eyes of anyone and everyone who passes me by, filling my sight with countless happy endings. They're beautiful, all of them, and I didn't truly realize how much I missed my magic until it was almost gone. All this love, it's a sight to behold. I feel so lucky I'll get to see it forever.

Forever. Something about the word lights a fire in me, the weight of it buzzing in the space between my ears. I can finally see; maybe now I can finally know. I start running, weaving through the Navy Pier crowds, not stopping until I get to the cab corral, launching myself into a yellow car and yelling an address much louder than necessary.

I barely register the passing buildings and streetlights as we drive into the city, my heart throbbing at what I'm about to do. There's no turning back. Once I look, it could change everything forever, spinning my path in a new direction, turning all that I know upside down. Do I want to take that chance? Will it even make a difference? I know what's in my heart; I know what I want. No matter what happens or who is by my side, I know I'm destined for greatness, and my life will be the stuff of magic.

I spill out of the cab, waving to the doorman as I mash the elevator button, holding my breath all the way up to the penthouse. I pound on the door, praying he's home, because I can't take it any longer.

Charlie opens the door, instantly confused at the manic girl standing before him, but he smiles anyway as I topple into him, knocking him over as we fall to the ground. Before he can say a word, I stare deeply into his dark green eyes, waiting to see what kind of destiny will unfold before me.

My heart stops, tears rushing down my face as the vision plays, illustrating a future I thought was only meant for dreams.

There's no more need to wonder. The match is clear.

I see myself.

THE END

♥

ACKNOWLEDGMENTS

I want to first thank you, the lovely person holding this book. Stories need readers to thrive, and thanks to your support, Amber found her happy ending in a truly magical way. Writing this series has been one of the most fulfilling experiences of my life, and while it is bittersweet to let this snarky little match- maker go, I'm so glad she found her way into your heart like she did mine. Thank you for your love, your enthusiasm, and your ongoing readership.

To Kieran, for guiding me through this series with wisdom and kindness. Working with you makes me want to be a better writer, and I am forever in debt to your insight and collaborative spirit. Thanks for not thinking I was crazy for adding a unicorn to this story.

To the entire Hyperion team, for seeing this series through to the end. Your belief in me has helped me live out my childhood dreams, and I am in awe of this team's talents and creative skills.

To Jess, for your helpfulness and friendship. You always go to bat for me, and I don't know what I'd do without your strength and smarts.

To Todd, for keeping me calm when I'm trapped in a hamster wheel. You always listen to my crazy and tell me everything will be okay, helping me reach my goals. Sorry I couldn't get you a writing credit on this one, but I appreciate everything you do.

To Molly, for sharing your endless creativity and unique sense of humor. There's nothing I love more than watching your inner artist come to life.

To Autumn, for inspiring me with your love of reading. It's so fun to share your passion for books.

To Quigley, for protecting the house and being our friendliness ambassador.

And to all my friends and family, for cheering me on and coloring my world with your beautiful hearts. I am so lucky to have people in my life who I can lean on, learn from, and laugh with. I could not embark on this journey without this community of weird, wonderful people. Thank you.